The Butler

DANIELLE STEEL

The Butler

A Novel

RANDOM HOUSE
LARGE PRINT

Copyright © 2021 by Danielle Steel

All rights reserved.
Published in the United States of America by
Random House Large Print in association with
Delacorte Press, an imprint of Random House,
a division of Penguin Random House LLC, New York.

Cover design: Derek Walls
Cover images: © pink_cotton_candy/Getty Images
(man's head), © Jacobs Stock Photography Ltd/Getty
Images (man's body), © Maggie Brodie/Arcangel (estate)

The Library of Congress has established a
Cataloging-in-Publication record for this title.

ISBN: 978-0-593-50382-9

www.penguinrandomhouse.com/large-print-format-books

FIRST LARGE PRINT EDITION

Printed in the United States of America

10 9 8 7 6 5 4 3 2 1

This Large Print edition published in accord with
the standards of the N.A.V.H.

To my darling children,
Beatie, Trevor, Todd, Nick,
Samantha, Victoria, Vanessa,
Maxx, and Zara,

In a book about courage,
to face the hard times,
the hard blows, the losses,
I wish you above all
the courage to love
and be loved
by someone who treasures you
and treats you well,
and may you find the right person
to love and be loved by,

With all my love
forever and beyond,

   Mom/d.s.

The Butler

Chapter 1

The moment the plane touched down at Ministro Pistarini de Ezeiza airport in Buenos Aires, Joachim von Hartmann knew in every fiber of his being that he was home. It was almost as if his heart and soul, and even his body, knew it. He had left as a boy of seventeen, twenty-five years before, when he'd moved to France with his mother and new French stepfather. Eight years later, he went to England on a lark, which turned into a worthy career for the past seventeen years. His roots were now firmly planted in Europe, but Joachim realized as he breathed the air of Buenos Aires that his heart had remained here. He had never fully cut the cord that bound him to Argentina. There was a magic to it that was still in his blood.

This was a long-awaited pilgrimage to the place where he had been born. All his boyhood memories were here, and what he had been too young to remember, his mother had told him again and again as he grew up. He felt as though he had never left as he came off the plane, like an old childhood friendship, or a great love.

Both his name and his tall, thin, aristocratic looks, with blond hair and blue eyes, were familiar in Argentina. With the influx of Irish, English, and German immigrants over the years, Argentines with German and Anglo-Saxon surnames and looks were not unusual. On his mother's side, all of Joachim's ancestors were German, originally from Bavaria and later from Berlin. His father, whom he never knew, had been from a distinguished banking family in Argentina. He had died when Joachim was less than a year old, and the rest of his father's family had died within a few years, so Joachim never knew them either. The mainstays of Joachim's life growing up had been his mother, Liese, and his identical twin brother, Javier. Joachim had a special relationship with his brother because they were twins. He felt at times as though they were two halves of the same person.

Joachim's German maternal grandfather, Gunther von Hartmann, had been widowed when his wife was killed in the Allied bombings of Germany. Like others who could still afford to leave, he hadn't wanted to stay in Germany and live through the disarray and reconstruction of the country. He was accustomed to a genteel world that no longer existed after the war. As soon as possible after the war, he had taken his five-year-old daughter, Liese, and what was left of his once-vast family fortune, and moved to Buenos Aires, rather than be treated as a defeated enemy in Germany. He had enough left to live extremely well in Argentina, which wouldn't have been the case in Europe. Argentina was a country that welcomed the Germans who had chosen to settle there, as they had been doing for generations.

Joachim had never lived in Germany, and knew very little about it, or his mother's life there, except that she had experienced great wealth and luxury as a young girl, first in Germany and then in Argentina. But his mother had often told him about the beautiful house where she grew up with her father in Buenos Aires. It was filled with antiques, and the fine works of art her father had been able to bring with him. He had a passion for the beauty of art in all its forms and had passed it on to his daughter. She had told Joachim too of the pretty finca they had outside of the city, where they spent weekends, and the many servants her father employed. They had never gone back to Germany, even for a visit. They had no one left there. Gunther von Hartmann had only his daughter in the years after the war. He had nothing left in Germany, and he had forged a new life in Argentina. They spent their holidays in Uruguay, Colombia, Brazil, and other parts of Argentina. Gunther had no desire to see Germany or Europe again, and Liese no longer remembered it. He became an Argentine citizen, and Liese grew up feeling entirely Argentinian. Her father never remarried. She went to the best schools in Buenos Aires, and she eventually married Alejandro Canal, the son of one of the city's finest banking families. She lived in what seemed to her a perfect world, as she remembered it and described it to Joachim. Her only sorrow, once married, was their inability to have children. She and her husband, Alejandro, had been married for ten very happy, fairly glamorous years, and had given up hope of having children, when by some miracle she conceived and gave birth to Joachim and his identical twin brother, Javier. She was thirty-nine when they were born. She told her sons that their birth was the happiest time of her life, but it all ended in tragedy a year later.

Her father, whom she adored, died suddenly at seventy-three, four months after the twins were born. Her husband, Alejandro, was killed in a riding accident three months later, as she told her sons when they were older. She rapidly discovered after her father's death that his money had been poorly invested and he died leaving her nothing. Her husband's family lost everything they had in the political upheavals that shook the country and left many of the previously wealthy penniless. By the time Joachim and Javier were a year old, Liese was living in a small apartment. Her in-laws' bank was bankrupt and they were unable to help her. She explained that her father-in-law had mishandled the bank's funds in desperation, and to spare her sons embarrassment later, she took back her maiden name, von Hartmann, and gave it to her sons as well.

Unlike his mother in her privileged youth, Joachim had grown up in modest circumstances. He had never known anything different, and neither he nor his twin, Javier, was unhappy. They lived in a poor neighborhood where there were always other children to play with, and their small apartment was a loving, warm home, thanks to their mother. They had food on the table, decent clothes, the basic necessities of life, and a mother who loved them. It had always seemed like more than enough to Joachim, who didn't hunger for more. Javier had a less contented nature as he got older, and in his early teens he argued with everyone and reproached their mother for what they didn't have. He had begun to notice the inequities between the rich and the poor in Argentina and was angry about the injustice of it. Joachim was content and satisfied with what they had. And it began to cause dissent between the two brothers, although Joachim loved his twin unconditionally.

Their mother had studied art history at the university before she got married, and had also been carefully schooled by her father, who knew a great deal about art, particularly the Impressionists. When the bottom fell out of her world, after her husband's and father's deaths, Liese was able to get a job she loved as a curator of French art at the National Museum of Fine Arts of Argentina. The job was poorly paid, but she was respected for her expertise and extensive knowledge of art. She tried to share her passion for art with her sons, but neither of them was particularly interested. They preferred playing soccer and other sports with their friends in the street.

They were fifteen when Liese met Francois Legrand, an art expert from the Louvre in Paris, who came to Buenos Aires to verify the authenticity of several paintings that the museum had recently acquired. Although she had always led a retiring life, and spent all her free time with her boys, she and Francois fell madly in love. After his visit, they maintained a constant correspondence, and he came back to Buenos Aires several times to see her. She was fifty-four when she met him. As with the birth of the twins, meeting Francois Legrand seemed like a miracle to her. There had been no man in her life for years, and it had never occurred to either of her sons that that could change. They were the center of her universe before, and even after, she met Francois. The correspondence with Francois Legrand and his occasional visits had gone on for two years. He was sixty-four, ten years older than Liese, and had been widowed for many years as well, with no children of his own. He wanted to marry Liese and bring her and her sons to Paris. He had even found a job for her at the Louvre. He was by no means a rich man, but had lived carefully, and could support her and the boys comfortably, and provide them a security they didn't have living on their mother's meager salary. Francois was genuinely fond of the boys and loved Liese deeply.

His relationship with Joachim was easy. He was a happy-go-lucky boy who didn't require more from life than what he had. He was planning to go to university in Buenos Aires but hadn't found his direction yet. He wanted nothing more than his happy, easy life, among his friends in Buenos Aires.

Javier, by contrast, was always the voice of discontent. He became angry as a teenager, at not having a father, at the money his family had lost before he was born, at what they didn't have, at being the youngest twin by eleven minutes. He resented his brother for that. He was hard on Joachim, who forgave him all, because they were twins. Joachim was unfailingly loyal to him. Javier resented their mother as well. He hated her stories of her golden youth, thanks to a grandfather he never knew, and who had managed to lose his entire fortune at his death. Javier was angry at his paternal grandparents too, for the fortune they had lost, which made him feel doubly deprived. Javier had a hunger in his belly that nothing could satisfy or cure, and he blamed his mother for not providing them with a better life than the one they had growing up. Joachim was grateful for all she'd done for them. Javier wanted more than a life of poverty, and his mother's and brother's love wasn't enough for him.

Unlike his mother, Javier didn't think Francois Legrand was the answer to their prayers, or his at least. He wanted much more than the comfortable, secure middle-class life Francois could provide. He didn't want to move to Paris if she married him. He had no interest even in his own ancestral roots in Europe. Javier was an Argentine to the core. Whereas the blue blood that ran in his German mother's veins, and even in his twin brother Joachim's, was always evident in subtle ways, good manners, and a natural compassion and generosity toward others, Javier related better to the common man in the streets of Buenos Aires. He acted like them and had a rough edge. He was always out of step, picking fights in school, and on the streets when he grew older. There was a violent side of him, despite his mother's efforts to quell it. Joachim tried to reason with him to no avail in their late teens. They were turning into very different men.

Joachim had a thirst for life, for new discoveries and the knowledge he acquired. He loved his studies. To him everything new he encountered was an adventure, and he was intrigued by the idea of attending the Sorbonne in Paris. He had learned French and English in school as a boy, and his mother had taught him German. He managed all four languages well. Javier had had the same education and had benefited from none of it. He was a poor student and felt most at ease among the lowest element on the streets. Joachim didn't like the new friends his brother sought out as they got older, although they'd had the same friends as young boys. He thought his twin's pals were "cowards and little jerks." By their late teens, and even before that, the two brothers couldn't have been more different. Despite that, Joachim loved Javier deeply and had an older brother's protective instincts toward him, and felt sure he'd outgrow his rebellious nature. He frequently reassured his mother about it, and she hoped Joachim was right.

It had taken considerable convincing and re-assurance, but Francois had finally overcome Liese's reservations about remarrying. After two years of correspondence and courtship, they were married in a small ceremony in Buenos Aires with only her two sons present. After a brief honeymoon in Punta del Este, Francois went back to Paris to ready his home to receive them. Joachim had been accepted at a lycée near Francois's home in Paris, where he would spend a year, pass his baccalauréat exam, then hopefully get into the Sorbonne, to pursue his education. He was planning to major in literature and art.

Much to Joachim's chagrin, Javier flatly refused to join them. At seventeen, he wanted to live with a friend's family for a year in Buenos Aires after his mother and brother left, and then go to work after that, without bothering with university. He grudgingly agreed to come to Paris in a year when he finished school, if his mother would allow him to spend the year in Buenos Aires. He didn't want to graduate in another country, without his friends. His new, wild friends meant more to him than his education or his family. Liese didn't like the family that Javier wanted to stay with, nor their son, and Joachim was upset at the thought of being separated from his brother for a year. He had never lived away from his twin, and even though they were very different and didn't always agree, he still felt that Javier was a part of him, like a limb, or his heart, a vital organ he couldn't imagine losing. He didn't want to be away from him for a year, but Javier fought like a cat to be left behind.

Joachim was always more protective of their mother, and it didn't seem fair to him to let her go to her new life alone, without her sons, even though Francois was a kind man and would take good care of her. Joachim got along with him particularly well, and Francois enjoyed having a son for the first time. Javier treated him as an unwelcome stranger, an interloper, but Francois warmly invited him to live with them in Paris nonetheless. He knew how important her sons were to his new wife. She had made countless sacrifices for them while they grew up.

Eventually, after struggling with the decision, Liese gave in to Javier's constant pleas and arguments that went on day and night until she conceded. She agreed to let him stay with the family she didn't like. She thought they were coarse, and their children badly behaved, but they weren't evil people. And Javier solemnly promised to come to Paris in a year when he graduated. It was a major victory for him, which he celebrated with his friends for weeks, which made his mother even more uneasy. She wasn't fully confident that his best friend's family would supervise Javier as closely as she had, and he was hard to control. He was far more eager to fly free than Joachim was, and do what he wanted. Joachim still enjoyed family life, and never chafed over his mother's parental control. He liked the idea of Francois as the father figure he'd never had. He'd been hungry for a father all his life. And Francois was kind to both boys.

Liese felt their departure from Buenos Aires like a force tearing her in half, leaving one of her sons behind. They had packed up everything she wanted to keep, and sent it by ship to France. Her father's books, his letters to her, and all the souvenirs of the boys' childhood and youth. She kept only what was of sentimental value to her, and owned nothing of great worth. But she felt as though she was abandoning her whole life since she was five. She had strong ties to Argentina, despite all the material things she had lost long before.

Joachim felt as if he had left half of himself behind, the beating heart or the lungs with which he breathed. He believed that the bond between twins was a sacred one, more than that of ordinary brothers. He had a deep psychological bond to Javier, despite their differences. At seventeen, the tears had poured down his cheeks when he said goodbye to his twin brother. He could not imagine a single day of his life without his brother in it, no matter how different they were becoming. The next year was going to be hard for him, in a new country and new school without his twin. Just knowing Javier was in his daily life was a comfort to him. In contrast, Javier could barely conceal how excited he was to be left on his own, living with his friend, without his mother and brother, and their supervision. And right up until the last minute, Liese was tempted to tell Javier she had changed her mind, but Francois convinced her that it might be better to let Javier do as he wished for a year, rather than bring an angry, sulking, rebellious teenage boy to Paris, which could only lead to trouble. He had already threatened not to go to school in France at all, if they forced him to leave with them, and he had promised to continue his schooling in Buenos Aires.

Liese had a thousand admonitions and instructions for him when she left. She and Joachim sat together on the plane, crying and holding hands. It was hard to feel happy about their move to France, while leaving someone so important to them in Buenos Aires. But Francois had done so many things to prepare for their arrival, and welcome them— a freshly painted, newly furnished room for Joachim, new curtains he'd had made for Liese, a new couch, and new china and utensils in the kitchen. He also bought a new television for the living room, so they could all watch sports together, and a stereo system for Joachim's room, so he could listen to his music. Francois was so overjoyed to see them when they arrived that he looked like he was going to explode. He had tried to think of everything to please them. And within days, Joachim could see his mother start to relax. It was the first time in seventeen years that his mother had a man to lean on and take care of her, since her husband's and father's deaths when he and Javier were only a few months old.

Francois wanted to do everything he could to make up for the hard years she'd had before she'd met him, the struggles and the poverty. She was happy with him, and the only sadness in her life was her constant worry about Javier. Joachim missed him too and knew that his mother would not fully feel at ease until his "younger" brother joined them, and she could keep an eye on him herself. Javier was a child who needed supervision and guidance, and no one watched him as carefully as she did.

Joachim adjusted rapidly to his school in Paris, made friends with his classmates, and played sports after school. His French became even more fluent. Francois had arranged for dual citizenship for him and Liese and planned to do the same for Javier when he arrived. Joachim didn't feel French, but he felt at home there. And Liese loved her husband and her new job. She was deeply grateful for his kindness to her and Joachim.

Francois had secured a job for her at the Louvre. He was one of the experts who certified the authenticity of all paintings acquired by the Louvre. Liese soon discovered an organization that traced paintings stolen by the Nazis and returned them to their rightful owners whenever possible. She was offered a position by them and accepted immediately. They worked closely with the Louvre and other museums around Europe, and occasionally South America, tracking down works of art that had disappeared during the war, identifying where they had wound up, and then attempting to find their original owners and return the paintings if the owners were still alive. Many weren't, and had died in German concentration camps, if they were Jewish, but sometimes a family member had survived and was grateful for the return of their family's lost artwork and possessions. It was slow, meticulous, painstaking work tracking down both the work of art and the original owner, but she loved it. Francois called her an art detective and admired her dedication to her job. She was tireless in her efforts.

They were a happy couple, and Liese felt surprisingly at home in France. She spoke French, German, English, and Spanish, which made it easier for her to do the research, in many countries, to trace works of art that had been missing for fifty years.

Many of the world's masterpieces had disappeared during and after the war. A great number, particularly from France, had fallen into Nazi hands, and the works had then gone underground, hidden by those who had taken them, or sold privately by disreputable, dishonest dealers. Some had been honorably or anonymously returned to museums, but very few. It became Liese's passion to ferret out the provenance of each work. It was heartbreaking to try to locate the original owners. Most of the heirs were astounded to suddenly find themselves with extremely valuable art. Liese did the work with passion and unrelenting perseverance. She loved telling Francois and Joachim at dinner about the particular painting she was currently pursuing.

Fresh battles erupted with Javier when he begged for another year in Buenos Aires after he graduated. He wanted to do a year of university there, instead of at the Sorbonne in Paris, like Joachim. Liese didn't want to agree to it and let Javier stay, but in the end she had no choice. He was eighteen and refused to come to Paris for another year, whether she agreed to it or not. Francois thought it best not to cause a long-term break with him and let him have his way again. They discovered months later, through friends and some of his old teachers, that he had not enrolled in the university, and was working instead. He had taken a job with a man who owned a freight company that shipped goods throughout South America. Javier was driving a truck for him, doing deliveries. Francois didn't like the sound of it but didn't want to worry Liese more than she already was. Once again, Javier promised to come to Paris in a year, after he'd saved some money, so he wouldn't be dependent on his step-father when he arrived.

Liese's job was poorly paid, and a labor of love. Francois paid all her expenses and Joachim's, so she could afford to do it. He was as generous as his own salary and savings allowed, and they had everything they needed. She wasn't an extravagant woman, de-spite the comforts with which she'd grown up, and Joachim made few demands on them. He spent very little money as a student. He was a serious boy and never any trouble, unlike his brother.

Joachim felt it as a physical blow when Javier re-fused to come to Paris after their year's separation. Joachim felt his absence acutely. Javier's refusal to leave Buenos Aires threw Joachim off balance for his first year at the Sorbonne. He couldn't concen-trate on his studies, worrying about his twin. He wrote to him, and called him from time to time, begging him to come, but Javier sounded different now. He was no longer a boy, but a man living on his own in a small studio apartment near the freight company's warehouse.

He had moved out of his friend's home when he had graduated. He alluded to some kind of falling-out with him, and disagreements with his friend's parents, without explaining in detail. He was driving a truck now most of the time. To Joachim, it didn't sound worth staying in Buenos Aires for that, but Javier had no interest in coming to France for the time being. He always promised that he would eventually when he had saved enough money. Paris held no lure for him, even to see his twin or their mother. He said he felt Argentinian to the core and didn't want to live in France. He liked earning his own money, and his job, which didn't sound good to Joachim.

The second year of their separation was harder for Joachim than the first, because his brother's promises to come to Paris no longer sounded convincing, and Joachim was beginning to fear Javier would never come. Joachim wanted to visit Javier during the summer, to convince him in person, but Francois got Joachim a summer job, working for one of his friends at an auction house, carrying artwork on and off the stage during the auctions. It was hard work, and only manual labor, but it paid well, and Joachim didn't want to let his stepfather down and back out of the job. Javier said he was gone all the time anyway, driving the truck, so he would have seen little of him. He did all he could to discourage Joachim from coming, and the chasm between them seemed wider than ever. Joachim felt it like a loss, and feared they would be separated forever. He mourned their boyhood closeness, which had been the happiest days of his life, having his identical twin always near him, and now it was all over.

Joachim started his second year at the Sorbonne, studying literature and art history, at his mother's suggestion. They hadn't heard from Javier for two months by then. The home number they had for him had been disconnected, and the main office of the freight company said simply that he was "probably on the road" and they would give him a message. Two months later, his family still hadn't heard from him. To put Liese's mind at rest, Francois hired a detective firm with an office in Argentina to track him down. They heard back from the agency a few weeks later. He confirmed that Javier was still working for the same freight company, driving between Argentina, Colombia, Uruguay, and Brazil, as he had said, but he was based now in Colombia and living in Bogotá. Discreet inquiries with the friend he had lived with revealed that they had had a falling-out and lost touch. The friend said that Javier had been too hard to live with and had caused problems with his parents. The parents had told their contact in Buenos Aires that Javier was disrespectful, followed no rules, and had fallen in with what seemed to them like bad company. He accepted no supervision or control whatsoever. Further inquiries supported the theory that he was hanging out with a bad group, and it was possible that drugs were involved, but there was no proof of it. At no time had the detective in Buenos Aires been able to lay eyes on Javier or connect with him. He had successfully slipped through his family's fingers. Liese wanted to go to Bogotá to try and find him herself, and Joachim volunteered to go with her, but the detective thought they would not be any more successful. Javier was on the road or in

Colombia most of the time now. None of his old school friends had heard from him. He was leading a very different adult life from his peers or past connections. The detective's suspicion was that he might be transporting drugs, had fallen in with disreputable people, and would hardly welcome a visit from his mother and brother if that was the case.

The mood in the house was heavy after that. By Christmas, they hadn't heard from him for six months. He called Joachim late one night. He sounded high or drunk, and tried to pick an argument with him. There was no longer any question of him promising to come to Paris. He accused Joachim of still being a child, tied to their mother's apron strings, and bragged that he was a man now. He said he was earning a decent wage, better than what he could earn in Paris, but he was vague when Joachim asked him what he was transporting. All he was willing to say was that he was well paid for it and sounded like he was bragging.

Joachim was haunted by their conversation and reported it to his mother. Francois engaged the detective service again. They were able to find out very little, except that Javier was alive, spending more time in Colombia, and only occasionally in Buenos Aires. The detective still suspected that he might be working for a drug dealer. Their contact with Javier was sporadic from then on. He would disappear for months, surface, and then vanish again. He called home very rarely.

Once on Christmas, he called his mother and started a heated argument with her when she complained about how elusive he was. It ruined the holiday for all of them. He called her on her birthday, and she cried for weeks afterward. Everything in her life was going well, except for the son she could no longer see or touch. He was lost to them, which was how Javier wanted it. He had ranted about politics to Joachim during one of their phone calls. He sounded revolutionary in his ideas and hostile about the middle and upper classes and the Establishment and referred to Francois and his mother as "bourgeois." He was a changed person, and no longer the boy Joachim had come into the world with and grown up with and had loved so fiercely. And eventually, Javier stopped calling entirely and they had no way to reach him. It was agony for Joachim and his mother, a wound that never healed, always hoping to hear from him.

When Joachim's flight landed in Buenos Aires during the Argentine summer, it had been twenty-five years since he had seen his twin brother, and more than twenty years since he had spoken to him. Their mother no longer had any contact with him either. Francois had hired the detective a few more times, but they finally all agreed that it was a waste of money. Javier had disappeared into another world, another life, and until he wanted contact with them, it was unlikely that they would find him. He had slipped into a dark underworld where it was easy to hide and disappear. Liese wasn't even sure that she would know if he died, since no one he knew would know how to find her. They checked prison records, but he hadn't been in prison so far, and with the kind of people he worked for, if they wanted to get rid of him, or he betrayed them, or let them down, they would have him killed, and his family in Paris wouldn't know that either. Joachim had lived with Javier's silence for almost twenty-three years, and his mother for just as long. It was a bond between Joachim and his mother, the agonizing loss they both lived with, of brother and son.

For a long time, it felt like a death to Joachim, to have lost his identical twin, like losing a part of himself. He could no longer contact his brother, hear his voice, or see him. He had no idea where he was, or if he was alive on any particular day. And given the rough people he was involved with, it was never a certainty that he was still alive, or for how long that would last. It disrupted Joachim's life in countless ways. He couldn't concentrate on his studies at the Sorbonne, which seemed meaningless to him. He didn't care about art history or literature and had only taken those classes to please his mother. He didn't know what he wanted to do for a career. He often wondered if his brother was right, and he was being a "baby," still close to their mother. And finally, with failing grades, he dropped out of the Sorbonne, feeling lost and aimless, and unsure which way to turn.

Francois got him minor temporary jobs, as an art handler at the Louvre, then working in one of the restaurants there. Joachim went back to the auction house for a while but was nothing more than a furniture mover. He took a job running the Ferris wheel at a carnival one summer. Liese told Francois that was the bottom of the barrel. Joachim was intelligent, and capable of much more than that, but he seemed lost without Javier. But they all had to live with it. It was Javier who had distanced himself from them, severed all connection, and wanted it that way.

Joachim was nineteen the last time he heard from his twin, and spent five years after that doing odd jobs, going nowhere. He rented a tiny studio apartment in a dilapidated area of Paris. The building smelled bad, and the apartment was barely bigger than his bed, with a small battered fridge and a hot plate and sink, a toilet, and tiny shower. Liese hated to see him live that way, but he didn't want to take advantage of his stepfather. He felt that he should be independent by then, and living on his own, although Francois would have been happy to house him. He enjoyed having him around, and it made his mother happy.

Liese worried about both her sons constantly, for different reasons. Javier was destroying any chance he had for a good life, and he was affecting

Joachim's life from a distance, with the grief of having lost his twin. Joachim doubted he would ever see Javier again and, at the same time, always hoped he would, and Javier would magically reappear, which never happened.

Liese had to make her own peace with having a son she might never see again. She prayed every day that he was still alive. Some sixth sense gave her the feeling that he was, and Joachim had the same intuition that somewhere out in the world, his brother was still living, but they had no way to verify it. The detective had found no trace of him during his last mission for them. Javier had vanished.

Liese had had her share of grief in her lifetime, the loss of her father and then her husband only months later, and then Javier's determined disappearance. Then eight years after she came to Paris, Francois died quietly in his sleep, lying beside her. A massive stroke was the cause of death. He was only seventy-four years old, but mercifully, he had died peacefully, hadn't fallen ill, and hadn't suffered. And Liese was a widow again at sixty-four. She was still passionately engaged in her work for the organization that located lost and stolen artwork in order to return it and had no desire to retire. She was healthy and strong, and loved going to work every day. Francois had still been working as an expert at the Louvre, but he had been tired lately, and thinking of retiring, and now he was gone.

He left almost everything he had to Liese, since

he had no children or relatives. He had a very decent insurance policy he had taken out when he'd married her. And he had left a nice amount of money to Joachim, not enough to go crazy with, but he wouldn't have anyway. Francois knew that about him. It was enough for Joachim to buy himself a small apartment, nicer than the ugly one he rented, or study somewhere abroad, if he wished to. Francois gave him a little start in life. He had hoped that Joachim would go back to school, to learn a trade or pursue a career of some kind, but he hadn't. The loss of his twin had been a huge blow and took him years to adjust to. There were girls in his life, but they never lasted long. And he never got deeply attached to any of them. Having lost Javier, he seemed to have a hard time getting close to anyone, for fear of losing them too. At twenty-five, he had no particular direction and hadn't found a career that inspired him, only the temporary jobs he took as filler. He was just passing time. Liese and Francois had talked about it a great deal, and Francois had been as concerned as any father would have been. Joachim had been lucky that his mother had married a man with a big heart who had wanted to take him under his wing, although Javier had thrown them all off balance. Liese always wondered if Joachim was just waiting for Javier to return.

Liese continued working after Francois died, with no intention of retiring. More than ever, she needed her job now. It gave her some purpose in life, a place to go every day, and contact with people. She was doing some good, or trying to, tracking down art and returning it to people who had been so severely wronged. She felt as though she was part of some form of justice, compensating in some small degree for all that had been lost or taken from them, most of it so enormous that no one could ever really make it up to them. But what she was able to return to them gave them something, and in some cases, with important works of art, it gave them an object of great monetary value. She was only a child when most of the art had been taken from them, or their relatives, during the war, but at least as an adult, she could be part of the restitution. It was very meaningful work for her, and she was proud of what she was doing. And Francois had been proud of her.

Joachim was shocked that Francois had left him anything at all and was deeply touched by it. Two months after he died, with his new inheritance, Joachim was having Sunday lunch with his mother at her apartment and saw an ad in the newspaper that intrigued him. He folded the paper and handed it to his mother, who looked at the page blankly. She couldn't see why he had shown it to her. She didn't see anything of interest.

"What am I supposed to look at?" she asked. They were both still shocked to have lost Francois, and Joachim had been checking on her a lot, to make sure she was all right. They were both doing the best they could to get used to it. He had been a benevolent force in both their lives, a truly kind and loving man. And Joachim knew how lonely she was without him.

Joachim pointed to the newspaper. It was a fairly large ad for a butler school in England.

"That?" She looked surprised and he nodded. "Butler school? Why would you want to do that?" It sounded like another dead end to her, like all the jobs he had had since he'd dropped out of the Sorbonne.

"I don't know. I'm not sure I do. But it sounds like fun, at least for a while anyway. Like a part in a movie." He was twenty-five years old, and wanted a job that was fun, and so far none had been. He had no passions, like his mother's love of art, or Francois's. All he had was a bright mind, the strength of youth, and the fact that he spoke four languages, which wasn't unusual in Europe. Many people did.

"You don't need a part in a movie," she said, frowning. "You need a real job, a career, something you'll want to do at forty or fifty. Why would you want to be a butler? What gave you that idea?"

"The ad makes it sound interesting. You learn to run a fine home, have a supervisory position over other staff, how to take care of silver, fine porcelain, and antiques, and impeccable service, how to serve at table. It sounds like a very varied and responsible job."

"Those days are gone," she reminded him. "Everyone had formal staff, in full uniform, in Argentina when I was a girl. I'm sure no one there does now. And I don't think anyone has a butler here either."

"They have them in England. That's where the school is. The course lasts six months, it might be fun."

"Would you want to work in England?" She was surprised. He was so Latin by nature. He'd been in France for eight years by then and was at home there.

"I don't know where I want to work, or what I want to do. But I've got time to spare. I'm only twenty-five, Mom. I can afford to waste six months of my life, especially now, thanks to Francois." He was frustrated by his own lack of direction, but nothing interested him and there was nothing he wanted to do.

"I don't think he intended the money for you to study for a job you'll never want."

"Maybe I will want it. Maybe being the head man in a grand house would be interesting."

"You need to do more in life than learn how to set a table," she said sternly.

"I don't think I'd mind a life of service. I kind of like the idea of keeping people's lives in good order. I wouldn't mind that at all, especially if the house is impressive. I have nothing else to do at the moment, and shoving furniture around at the auction house has no future either. It's a laborer's job. I don't like leaving you, though. I could come home on weekends, while I'm taking the course."

"Don't worry about me, I'm fine," she said bravely. She wasn't fine, but she thought that eventually she would be. And she didn't want to stand in his way or be a burden to him. She just thought that being a butler sounded like a crazy idea with no future.

"I'll call them and see what they have to say," he said, and didn't mention it again for the rest of lunch. They went for a walk together that afternoon, as she used to do with Francois on a Sunday afternoon, strolling in the park. She didn't say it to Joachim, but now she had to adjust to one more person she loved missing from her life. It had happened to her much too often. Joachim thought the same thing, as he tucked her hand into his arm, and they walked along in silence, each of them lost in their own thoughts. She was thinking of Francois, and Joachim was silently mourning his stepfather and his brother and musing about butler school again. It sounded like a crazy idea to him too, but he had nothing else to do, and a lifetime ahead of him, with no set career plan. It might be amusing for six months. And nothing else appealed to him at the moment. Growing older was just no fun without his twin brother and hadn't been for eight years. He had always thought that Javier would settle down once he got out of his teens, and they would be close again. And instead, he had disappeared.

Chapter 2

When Joachim went to London to visit the butler school two weeks later, he was surprised by how seriously they took themselves. He had asked a friend in Paris who was a desk clerk at the Crillon to check out the school for him. The friend had reported that people in the catering department had heard of it, although they'd never hired anyone who'd trained there. They said the school was respected, but mostly trained people who wanted to work in fancy homes for fancy people, usually in England. So at least it was known and reputable. The question for Joachim was whether that was what he wanted to do when he grew up. And his mother had a point. Did he want to work in England? The weather there was even more miserable than in Paris, nothing like Argentina. He still missed the warm weather and atmosphere in Buenos Aires. South America had a style and energy to it and an innate joie de vivre, a kind of lively, sexy undertone that he had encountered nowhere in Europe. Maybe a little bit in Spain and Italy, but he still preferred Argentina, even though he didn't plan to go back there. He lived in France now. He didn't want to leave the only relative he had, his mother, to go back to live in a country with a brother he hadn't seen in eight years, and probably never would again. Now that Francois was gone, Joachim didn't want to abandon his mother, and leave her alone at her age. But the chilly formality of England didn't seem too appealing either.

He went to the school and met with the admissions director. She was a thin-lipped, formal, uptight woman, who had him fill out a long questionnaire about his life experience so far, and why he thought he wanted to be a butler. She told him the school itself occupied two floors of a small house in Knightsbridge. There were proper classrooms, and a conference room set up with an enormously long dining table, where they practiced formal table settings and formal service. The students were all men, they wore white tie and tails in class, and were impeccable. Personal grooming was part of the course. Joachim thought it was funny, like a costume party. But no one else thought it was amusing. He was the only foreigner in the class. The other students were all English.

There was another room set up with every kind of silver serving piece imaginable, which students had to learn to identify infallibly. There was a class on the selection of proper wines, with regular tastings. There were seminars on running staff, and the proper hierarchy in a large formal house. There were still enough of them in England to make the school viable. And there was a class dedicated to running weekend house parties. In spite of wanting to laugh and make fun of it, Joachim was impressed after his visit. This was clearly a life choice, and a career, not simply something one did as a filler between odd jobs. It took concentration, skill, intelligence, and dedication.

The head of students Joachim met with was a tall, dignified, fierce-looking man, who had served in two of the great homes in England for thirty years, and had come to teach at the school when he retired. He explained that in the old days, young men started as hall boys in their teens and worked their way up to footman, then first footman in charge of the others, under-butler, and eventually butler. And by the time they reached the top, they knew their job inside and out. Nowadays, staffs were smaller, there were fewer opportunities to train, and they could learn in the school in six months of intense, diligent study what might have taken them ten years to learn in the past. After that, they needed experience on the job to practice what they'd learned.

The school also offered a placement service for their graduates, much the way the Norland College for nannies placed their trained nannies, in their case, after a three-year course, with classroom and hospital training. The course for butlers was much shorter, but no less intense. They didn't need the medical skills or hospital training that formal nannies did, but there was much to learn to become a butler. In the current world, butlers were expected to know more than they had previously, since they were often expected to take on additional duties as well, and the entire house staff might come under their supervision. It sounded daunting, but intriguing. Joachim submitted his application, and spent two more days in London, staying at a small hotel. He went to museums, visited the Tower of London and Madame Tussauds, ate fish and chips, and the hottest curry he'd ever tasted in his life. London seemed like fun. He'd been there before, but never on his own. He had visited the city with Francois and his mother when he was younger. The weather was bitter cold the whole time he was there to visit the school, but Joachim didn't mind. London seemed much more exciting than Paris, busier, and more alive.

He thought about it when he got back to Paris. It was a relief to get back to a familiar city, even to his tiny studio apartment, but it was his home. He called his mother that night and told her about the trip to London and his visit to the school.

"They take it **very** seriously," he said, still surprised by it. "I kept wanting to laugh at some of the things they told me. They probably won't accept me. Most

of the students are older than I am, have previously
been in domestic service, and were very intense
about it." But she could hear that part of him had
liked what he saw. It was a career she wouldn't have
thought of for him, and she wished he wanted to
go back to university, maybe for a teaching degree,
but she knew he didn't want to. "There's a whole
class on how silver should be polished." She smiled,
remembering her father's house when she was a girl.
They had had a very snobbish German butler and
many servants. It was quite formal too. And then,
from one day to the next, it was all over, and everything was gone.

Much to Joachim's surprise, he was accepted at the
butler school. Then he had to make a decision. After
a week of debating, he decided to meet the challenge, and try it. He accepted the place they offered
him. The money Francois had left him made it easily affordable. For others, it was a financial stretch,
and they had saved in order to pay for it.

He was sent a list of the clothes he had to bring,
including formal livery, which he could purchase
in London. There was an advanced class for anyone who wished to work in a royal household. That
sounded interesting to Joachim, but he considered
it an unlikely possibility for him. He wasn't even
sure if he'd finish the six-month class. He accepted
the place offered him anyway, sent in his tuition,

and showed up at the school on the appointed day. He had to go to London a few days early to find lodgings. He got a room in the home of a woman who took in boarders. It was actually nicer than his studio in Paris, and close to the school. He arrived at the school the first day in white tie and tails, with several notebooks in his briefcase. It was much more straightlaced than the Sorbonne had been. Every move he made was closely observed and corrected the moment before another student made a mistake.

There were times during the six months that Joachim wasn't sure he would last. Sometimes the whole curriculum seemed utterly absurd in the modern world. It felt like an anachronism. There were a few times when he was bored, but not many. For the most part, his classes were interesting and a challenge. He enjoyed learning about fine wines, the best cigars, and proper table service. Table settings he had to measure with a ruler were the hardest part. He always left out one thing, and absolute flawless perfection was vital. The hierarchy of guests was stressed and had to be learned, along with titles, as well as the hierarchy of the servants, who outranked whom and who had to be seated where, even in the servants' dining hall. There were a million rules to learn and follow. There were no exceptions, and the attitude of the instructors was rigid and unforgiving, but Joachim was surprised that he genuinely enjoyed it, and when he did something right, it felt like a real accomplishment. At the end of the six months, he graduated with excellent recommendations from his teachers. There was satisfaction in it, because it hadn't been easy. His mother was fascinated by everything he told her, and how much he was obviously happy there. She couldn't understand why he would want to be a servant, but he had definitely been prepared for the very highest caliber of the job, and he took pride in what he'd learned.

The school placed him in his first job with an earl who had a house in London, an estate in Norfolk, and a castle in Scotland. He was hired as an under-butler, with a large, somewhat disorganized staff. But he found them fun to work with. The earl was massively in debt and put all three properties on the market within a year, and Joachim was out of a job. But he had excellent references from the head butler and his employer.

Joachim went to a high-end London domestic employment agency after that, and with his training at the school and a year's experience working for the earl, he landed a job as under-butler in the London home of the Marquess of Cheshire. The family had an estate in Sussex as well, with a butler there too. Their homes were beautifully maintained. They were distant cousins of the queen and the most elite members of the aristocracy came to the parties they frequently gave. Joachim learned a great deal while he was there. He honed his skills, and when the head butler retired four years later, Joachim became the head butler in the London house at thirty-one. He ran the staff with an iron hand by then and could spot a flaw in the table settings from a mile away. His understanding of the social hierarchy and etiquette was flawless. He was a perfectionist, and took pride in how well he did his job. And his discretion was legendary as to whatever he saw at house parties, among family or guests.

Joachim was equally discreet about his own life. The family he worked for was always his priority and his job. His personal life came last. There were brief affairs, when he had time, with domestics in other homes. He never dallied with the staff that worked for him, told no secrets, and although he liked pretty young women, he never made long-term promises or became too deeply involved. He felt he needed to remain a bachelor to do justice to his job. And he had little time for friends. It was a solitary life, which he accepted as part of his chosen career.

The Cheshires were quite old by the time Joachim was in charge. And the marquess needed considerable care when he fell ill. Joachim had a deep affection for him and frequently assisted him himself, although there were nurses to do it. The marquess was particularly fond of Joachim and trusted him. Joachim had been in the job for seven years when the marquess died. His children asked Joachim to stay on, continue to run the London house, and oversee the care of their mother, who had dementia by then. Joachim felt great concern for her and stayed for nine more years. He had been with them for sixteen years in all. The marchioness had finally died three months before. The children decided to sell the London house and the Sussex estate. Neither home suited their lifestyles, and they didn't want to employ the huge staff that houses of that size and age required to maintain them. Their parents' lifestyle didn't suit them, and they didn't want the burden or expense of great houses. They preferred to live more simply, and the family fortune was getting thin by then.

Joachim had helped them close both houses, sent the pieces they wanted to their homes, and helped arrange a massive auction at Sotheby's for the rest. He had just finished and left for Paris before his trip to Argentina. He was staying with his mother in Paris, for a breather before returning to London to look for a new job. After sixteen years with the Cheshires, he felt he had earned a break, and it seemed the perfect time to go to Buenos Aires, after having dreamed of it for years.

There had been no news of Javier for many, many years. Another foray with a detective had confirmed all their worst fears. There was no doubt now. Javier was deeply embedded with men who ran a drug cartel, had been in and out of jail a few times, and was beyond their reach. They had no access to him, but Joachim still wanted to go back, see his own friends if he could find them. If he learned anything more about his twin, he could at least tell his mother. Joachim had no hope of seeing Javier, but they were always hungry for news of him after nearly twenty-three years of silence, interrupted only by upsetting rumors from old friends every few years.

Quite remarkably, Liese was still working, still hunting down major works of art, and returning them to their original owners or their heirs whenever possible. She was eighty-one now. She was physically a little slower, and looked frail, but her mind was as sharp as ever. She had been a widow for seventeen years, as long as Joachim had been working in England.

She was surprised when he told her he was going to Argentina for a visit. He was forty-two now, and they had left when he was seventeen. She no longer wanted to go back herself. She was content to stay in France. Paris was her home now, not Buenos Aires.

"Who do you even know there by now?" she asked him.

"The boys I went to school with. I still get Christmas cards from some of them. It might be nice to see them, one more time."

"Are you looking for Javier?" she asked, narrowing her eyes at him, and he hesitated.

"Maybe. I always have fantasies that our paths will cross again one day. We were so close as boys. And even when he started to change as a teenager, he was still my brother. He still is."

"I was always afraid he would take a bad turn and head in the wrong direction. I should have made him come to Paris with us," she said sadly. It was one of her few regrets. She didn't have many and had led a good life. She was proud of Joachim. He was a decent, upstanding man, hardworking and honorable, and a good son. She was sorry he hadn't married and had children of his own, but he always said that marriage and a family were not compatible with a life of service, if you did it right and were truly dedicated to your employers. He had certainly put his heart and soul into his work for the past seventeen years. It had in fact turned into a satisfying career for him, and he was supremely capable. He didn't seem to be unhappy about being single and without children. Liese worried sometimes that the trauma of losing his brother had made him unable to attach to anyone. He never discussed his personal life with his mother when he came to Paris to see her, which he did as often as he could, sometimes even if he could only come for a day. But with her work, she was busy too.

"Javier would never have come with us, even if you had tried to force him," Joachim reminded her. "You forget how obstinate he was then. And I think he already had some bad plans by the time we left, which would have shocked us if we'd known about them. He started hanging around the wrong people as a teenager." It was hard for either of them to imagine who he was now. He had strayed so far

from anything familiar or acceptable to them that
Joachim suspected they were better off not knowing. As sad as it was, especially for his mother, the
silence was perhaps less upsetting than the truth.
But he was hoping to hear some echoes about Javier
anyway when he went to Buenos Aires. It was hard
to let go of the fact that he had a twin brother somewhere in the world.

"What are you going to do when you get there?"
Liese asked.

"See friends, enjoy the city. Visit my old favorite
places. It's sort of a pilgrimage. I haven't had time
for a trip like that. Now I do, before I take another
job, and get caught up in service again."

"When are you going to do that?"

"I'm in no hurry." The marquess had left him some
money, as had Francois. Joachim had been careful
and invested what he had. He had enough to be
comfortable for quite some time without a job. He
didn't want to make a mistake and take the wrong
one. He had enjoyed his first job briefly, and his
second one had been deeply rewarding. He wanted
to take his time and find the right job and employer
for the next round, although there were fewer and
fewer great houses and grand estates anywhere anymore, even in England. Few people wanted a large
formal staff, which was Joachim's forte to run. His
skills were outstanding. He had listed himself with
the best agency for butlers in London and had told
them he was in no rush. He could have his pick of

the best jobs, with his experience. He doubted he would find a new one he liked as much that used all his skills.

Seeing his mother made him think that he should stay in Paris for a while, to spend time with her and make sure she was in good health. She was remarkably energetic for a woman her age, but she lived alone, and at eighty-one, he was concerned that she might fall ill, or injure herself. But she'd had no problems so far. It was nice staying in the apartment with her. He'd been so busy preparing the Cheshire homes to be sold that he hadn't been to see her in three months and felt guilty about it. He was planning to spend a month with her after he got back from Buenos Aires. He had a flat in London, which he rarely had time to use, but it would give him a comfortable place to stay when he went back to look for a new position. He used it on his days off, sometimes to meet women, but he was always available to the family and staff, if needed. He was feared, and admired, by the employees he managed, and held in great respect by his employers. He was well liked but kept to himself. He saw his life as a butler more as a vocation than a career.

When he got to Buenos Aires, the city was as beautiful as Joachim remembered, and he still felt at home there, even after so long. He easily found the small, shabby apartment building where they had lived.

He was shocked by how dreary it looked to him now. The neighborhood had gotten worse than he remembered. His mother had often pointed to the house she had grown up in. Other people had lived there for more than forty years now. It had been sold when her father died, right after the twins were born. It had changed hands several times with reversals in the lives of the owners, which had become run of the mill in Argentina. Many fortunes had been lost, and once very wealthy people had almost nothing now. Their exquisite homes had been sold, their French antiques filled the antique shops, and there were wonderful purchases to be had, which wealthy Americans and Europeans had known for a long time. Liese had only once pointed out the pretty house where she had lived with Joachim's father before he died. She said it was too painful for her to talk about, so he knew very little of his father's history, except that he had died in a riding accident, and his family had lost everything, and had all died shortly after he was born. Liese didn't like to talk about the sad times in her life. She was private about them and was vague whenever he asked.

He walked all over Buenos Aires in the first few days he was there, soaking up the sounds and smells and familiar sights. Having lived in France for so long after he left, he realized now how French the architecture of Buenos Aires was. The wide boulevards, impressive buildings, small lovely parks, and famous plazas all looked similar to the landmarks of Paris he knew so well now. The Avenida de Mayo looked distinctly like Paris, and the Plaza de Mayo, with historic monuments. The Congreso de la Nación resembled the grandeur of the Paris opera house. He remembered the Plaza del Congreso from his youth, and the Casa Rosada, the pink palace of the presidential offices.

He sat in small parks, wandered through the barrios, and remembered his childhood on the streets where he and Javier had played. It was a trip back in time for him, full of sights he remembered, smells which jogged his memory, and familiar music. It was different now, seeing it as an adult, and a tourist. And everything he saw brought back tender memories.

Joachim contacted all the old friends he'd planned to in Buenos Aires. He hadn't seen them since he'd left, and no one had heard from Javier in at least twenty years, or longer. Joachim and his twin had shared many of the same friends in their childhood, and it touched Joachim to see them again. But in his mid-teens, Javier had collected another group of friends, racier, tougher, from a different background. Joachim was told that his twin had gotten in trouble with them, once Joachim and their mother left. It was everyone's opinion, among the people he spoke to, that Javier had disappeared into a dark underworld. Some of their old friends were outspoken, saying how dangerous his friends and connections were, and that many of them were suspected of being involved in the drug cartels of Colombia, once they were adults. They were a bad lot, and they suspected Javier had become one of them. Joachim believed that too and wondered if his twin might be dead by then. But he had a gut feeling that he wasn't. Joachim knew no one in that world to contact.

An old friend of his who was high up in the police volunteered to do some investigating and told Joachim a few days later that a police contact he had called in Colombia said that they thought Javier was alive, and deeply embedded in a very dangerous network of drug dealers. It wasn't reassuring to hear that, and the friend told Joachim to stay well away from his brother, that he might regret it if he finally reached him. In that world, family ties and loyalties by blood didn't exist. Their only family was the group of highly dangerous men they worked with, and Joachim could be at risk, now that he was in Buenos Aires. Joachim had trouble believing that Javier would be a danger to him, but he had no way of reaching him anyway. The drug world was entirely removed from Joachim's life, he had no access or connection to it, nor did his friends, who had grown up to be wholesome men.

He left Buenos Aires with regret after a week there. It was still a beautiful city and held a warm place in his heart and memory, but it wasn't home anymore. He had ties to France because of his mother and had lived and worked in England for seventeen years. Buenos Aires was the home of his childhood, but he had left so long ago, he no longer had a strong bond there.

He had nothing concrete to tell his mother when he went back to Paris, except that somewhere, in a very dark underworld, Javier might still be alive, but he was no longer the same person, and lost to them forever, which they had suspected anyway. It didn't come as a surprise.

He was heading back to Paris to stay with his mother and figure out the next steps in his life. He closed a door behind him in Buenos Aires, and in the world he'd left behind was the twin he had loved so much, who was a stranger to him now. Too much time had passed, and Javier had drifted too far on the tides that had carried him away. It was almost as if Javier had died. Joachim felt a strange sense of freedom when he left Buenos Aires. He was glad he'd gone to say a final goodbye.

Chapter 3

Olivia White stood looking around her mother's apartment, not sure where to start. Everything about it seemed sad and faded to Olivia now. It was all tidy and in order, but the familiar surroundings thinly masked an unlived life. Olivia was a beautiful, vibrant woman, with dark hair and green eyes. Forty-three years old, she had focused on her career, and shied away from marriage and long-term relationships all her life. Her mother, Margaret, had been beautiful once too, a tall willowy blonde. Margaret had grown up in Boston in a genteel family that had slowly lost their money over several generations. She had dreamed of going to New York to become a book editor, and had headed there after graduating from Boston College, as a literature major, and gotten a job as an editorial assistant with a major book publisher. Her parents thought it was respectable. She could barely eke out a living on what she made, and had found a small walk-up apartment in a tenement on the Lower East Side, but was determined to become a senior editor one day. She did freelance editing on the side to supplement her income. She worked in a tiny office at a major publishing house and took manuscripts home at night. Her parents couldn't help her financially and were austere people who expected a great deal of their only child.

Two years into her fledgling career as a junior editor, she stepped off the elevator after lunch one day and collided with George Lawrence, the star bestselling author of the publishing house where she worked. He looked like he'd been hit by lightning when he saw her. She blushed and backed away. Margaret was twenty-four years old, and George was fifty, a handsome, dashing man with a powerful personality, a racy reputation, and an appetite for young women. His career was legendary, and his books at the top of the bestseller list every time he published a new one. He had a wife and four children, and his socialite wife was from an important New York family. They made a dazzling pair, and their image as a couple contributed to his charisma and success. They had a star quality about them and were often in the press.

It took George several days to track Margaret down. He showed up in her office one morning and filled the doorway of the tiny room with his presence. He took Margaret to lunch at the "21"

Club that day, and she was as impressed as he'd hoped she would be. Startled by him, excited, flattered, she had no idea how to decline his invitation and didn't want to. He pursued her relentlessly after that, roses, dinners, lunches, funny gifts that made her laugh, little essays and poems he wrote for her. She was breathless with his attentions, and then he showed up at her apartment one night. She was mortified when her doorbell on the fifth floor rang, she opened it and found him standing there. He must have followed someone else into the building.

"I couldn't stay away from you," he said with a tormented look. It took him less than a month to get her into bed, and after that they met at remote hotels, in houses or luxurious apartments he'd borrowed from friends. He hated her apartment, and said it pained him to see her living in such squalor. It was all she could afford. He didn't want to meet her there.

Their affair took off in a white heat. He was honest with her and told her he could never get divorced. His father-in-law would destroy him, his wife would take everything he had. He would lose his children, and his public image would be tarnished forever. He said his marriage was something they would have to work around, and somehow Margaret got swept away on the tidal wave of his attentions. She was fearful and meek, in love with him, and enthralled by who he was. Nothing in her life had prepared her for the sheer power of a man like him. He made her laugh, and feel beautiful and special, and almost forget that he was married. Almost. But not quite. He wanted her to forget and she hoped he would get divorced one day, but she never asked him to. She did whatever he wanted. She was unable to resist him.

A year later, as the affair continued, he moved her into a much nicer apartment on the East Side. It was still a walk-up, but the building was clean and nice. It was in a family neighborhood and George Lawrence paid the rent. On her meager budget, she turned it into a love nest for them. He loved it. They rarely went out after that. They had no reason to. They spent most of their time in bed. He told her that she invigorated him. Tragedy had struck him before they met. He had lost an eighteen-year-old son in a boating accident, and hadn't written a word since then. The first manuscript he had given Margaret to read had been written before his son died. And with her tender, gentle, loving ways, and nurturing, he began writing again, and claimed it was the best work he'd ever done. He insisted that they were soul mates and told her he couldn't survive or write without her. Her boundless love made it possible for him to tolerate his loveless marriage. Margaret actually made it possible for him to stay married.

Two years after they met, she became George's editor, at his insistence. She had talent, and helped him polish his books until they shone. There was a purity to them after she entered his life, and a strength that she didn't have as a person but was able to wield with the written word. He only worked with her from then on. And by tacit agreement, she entered into a life where she only lived and breathed for him. She waited for him night and day, he appeared for rapid lunches they spent in bed, late-night dinners they never ate. They made love in her office. She spent every weekend waiting for him when he could get away, and holidays alone, while he went to Palm Beach, Aspen, and skiing in Europe with his wife and children. Margaret was always there when he returned, faithful, loving, never complaining. In her own mind, she didn't exist except when she was with him. Her own personality faded into the mists, and she became a ghost for him, a mirror, a non-person, living in the shadows, always available to him. They managed to keep their affair secret for a while. Margaret demanded nothing of him, always impressed by who he was, thinking and acting as if he was some kind of god. She convinced herself that she was lucky to be with him and derive sustenance from the crumbs from his marital table. The center of his life was still at home.

She had been editing his books for a year and was twenty-seven years old when she realized she was pregnant. She was going to have an abortion, not knowing what else to do. George begged her not to. She was convinced that he loved her. And he wanted her to have his child, as a symbol of their love. He promised to support her and the baby, and she thought that with a baby of their own, he might get divorced and marry her after all. Somehow it all began to make sense, she thought George was her destiny, and went ahead with the pregnancy. When she was seven months pregnant, she told her parents. They accused her of gross immorality, told her she had disgraced them, nearly disowned her, and refused to see her and the baby until Olivia was five years old. She faced Olivia's first five years alone, with visits from George. He paid for the babysitters she used, so she could continue working as his editor.

Olivia was born when George was in Tuscany with his wife and children for the summer, and Margaret gave birth alone. Olivia was two months old when her father first saw her. Margaret had gone back to work editing his books by then. He was bowled over by how beautiful Olivia was, and she became the cement between them as soon as she was born, and the excuse for Margaret to never have a life again. She spent her spare time, when she wasn't working, waiting for him, when he could get away from his wife, for an hour here and there. Margaret and George agreed that it was too sensitive a subject to tell Olivia who her father was. They decided to tell her when she got older that her father had died in a car accident right before she was born. George was to be portrayed as a family friend who was loving and supportive and referred to as Uncle George.

He saw Olivia often, and gave her generous gifts. She truly believed he was just their friend, just as Margaret said. He improved their living situation as she got older with an apartment on York Avenue in the Seventies in a better building, close enough to where he lived to be convenient for him.

He set up a trust fund for Olivia, not comparable to those he was leaving his legitimate children, but it would be adequate to pay for her education and related expenses later on. He didn't want to create a situation that his wife and children would fight when he died and put Margaret in an untenable legal situation.

As Olivia got older, George was her champion. He helped her with math homework, gave her the gifts she wanted most, and wanted to get her a dog, which her mother wouldn't allow. He was the bestower of all bounty, and paid for private school for her, although Olivia didn't know he did. She often thought how lucky she was that they had an attentive, generous friend like him, when she had no father. They never told her the truth. Margaret continued to work for the publisher so she could edit his books at home, and wait for him in their apartment, long after his children were grown. He remained married to his wife, and they continued taking family vacations together. The subject of his marrying Margaret never came up anymore. She never mentioned it and accepted their situation as it was. She lived in suspended animation, waiting for George, and only came alive when he was with her, and faded away again when he left.

When Olivia turned twenty, her mother was forty-seven, and George was seventy-three. He was diagnosed with pancreatic cancer. It was their last chance to tell Olivia the truth before he died, so she could have an honest conversation with her father. But they didn't. They missed their chance. He felt ill and went home early one night. Within a short time, he was tended to by nurses and bed-bound at home. His wife had known about Margaret for years by then, and they had gone on pretending that it wasn't happening and his love child didn't exist. Margaret was forty-eight when George died at home, with his wife and children at his side. He hadn't seen Margaret in two months, or even been able to call her in the final weeks to say goodbye. Margaret had spent half her life with him by then. Olivia was twenty-one, a junior in college at Columbia, when her father died, and her mother explained to her about the trust fund he had left her.

"Why would he leave anything to me?" She was touched by his generosity as a friend, and much later, once she knew, Olivia wondered why she hadn't suspected before then. Her mother had been a convincing liar.

"He was our friend," Margaret said primly. Her own parents had died before that and had only seen Olivia a few times in her life, outraged by the fact that she was illegitimate, for which they blamed their only daughter. They remained at a distance from her, as though her immorality was contagious.

It took Olivia almost a year, till after she graduated from Columbia, to again ask her mother why George had left her a trust fund. It continued to puzzle her. Margaret finally told her the truth, that there had been no father who died in a car accident. George, the bestselling author and bestower of all gifts, was her father. Margaret had effectively robbed her daughter of the opportunity to speak to him, with the full knowledge that he was her father. It took Olivia a long time to forgive her mother. Margaret's life had begun when she met George Lawrence and ended when he died. He left her a modest bequest, which she could live on, though not lavishly. She stopped all editing and retired once she could no longer work on his books. She rarely left the house, and continued to hang around her apartment, as though she thought he still might show up. She slept much of the time, self-medicated with tranquilizers, and began drinking heavily after he died.

Olivia hated visiting her. Liver disease and dementia had taken over in Margaret's late fifties. She died at seventy, having given up on life twenty-two years before, when George died. She'd never really had a life. She had given up her soul, her dreams, and her youth to George Lawrence. Olivia had provided a nurse for her for the last few years, to make sure she didn't injure herself when she drank too much, added to her dementia. She often forgot that George was dead and thought that she was waiting for him to come.

Looking around her mother's apartment, Olivia felt anger rise in her like bile, thinking back to the years when her mother waited for George to show up, and all the holidays she and her mother had spent alone while he went on fabulous vacations with his wife and children. In the end, his wife out-lived both George and Margaret, and was in good health. Margaret had wasted her life waiting for him, thinking that one day things would be different. She had let it happen, had signed on willingly for a life where all of his needs were met, and none of hers.

Two editors from the publisher came to Margaret's funeral at Frank Campbell, her nurses, Olivia, and no one else. She had lived in hiding with no friends, always waiting for George, his willing slave.

Olivia started packing her mother's things the day after her funeral, which had been a bleak affair. Olivia went alone and held her mother's ashes in a wooden box at the brief service. She packed cartons full of clothes, to give away, and others with her books. Olivia wanted none of it, except for a few pieces of furniture she sent to storage. The lesson she had learned from watching her mother was not to fade away and die, but to live life fully, not give up, and be true to yourself. Margaret had rambled on sometimes when Olivia visited her, asking when George was coming, and if he'd arrived yet. She was a shadow person, a ghost, who had willingly surrendered herself to live with a man who never risked his marriage for her. His wife always had the priority, and Margaret spent half a lifetime waiting for him. He no longer seemed like a hero to Olivia, once she knew who he had been to her. He was a selfish man, willing to sacrifice the woman who had handed over her life to him. Olivia didn't know who she resented more, her mother for her lies and weakness, or her father for what he had done to Margaret in the name of love, because she allowed it. Nothing about it seemed loving to Olivia, and she wanted to erase all trace of them from the apartment. She had emptied it in two days and put it on the market to sell it.

And she found herself doing the same thing in her own office shortly after.

Olivia had worked hard for the last ten years on a decorating magazine she'd started. She had used some of her trust fund money to set it up and put her heart and soul into it. The magazine had failed at the same time as her mother's death. Olivia had to fold her business, let the employees go, and clear out her office, on the heels of her mother's funeral. All she seemed to do now was pack up painful memories. She put all the photographs of her mother and herself as a child in one box, to put them in a storage facility with the furniture. The rest of her mother's belongings she gave away, clothes, personal items. It all reeked of sadness. Her mother had a collection of all George's books. Olivia had read them before she knew he was her father. She thought his massive ego was evident on every page. She put them in a box to store them, since he was her father.

A month after she'd emptied her mother's apartment, put it on the market, and closed her business, she sat in her own small apartment, wondering what to do next. Her mother had left her some money. She'd been frugal, and hardly spent any after George died, since she didn't know how long it would last. As a result, there was plenty left, enough for Olivia to buy herself a new apartment eventually or go away for a long time. She could leave without having to worry about her mother dying while she was gone, or her business failing. It already had. The worst had happened now. She was free at last, with all the lessons her mother had taught her about how not to live a life. It was ironic that while trying not to get attached to the wrong person, and not following in her mother's footsteps, not surrendering herself to a married man, she had dedicated herself to her business as an alternative to marriage or a serious relationship. Like her mother, Olivia had few friends, and she was alone in the world now, and had lost her magazine after a decade of hard work. She didn't have to worry about the business anymore either. She didn't need to think about her mother. She could go where she wanted, do whatever she pleased. There was nothing holding her back, nobody to take care of, no business to grow, or think about. She had no parents, no husband, no children, no business, no job, and no boyfriend. And a small circle of friends she hardly saw anymore and hadn't seen socially in years. She was always too busy working. At forty-three, Olivia had nothing and she was alone. She could go anywhere in the world she wanted and had no idea where that would be. She had been to Paris a number of times and loved it. She knew no one there, and didn't speak French, but maybe it didn't matter. She had never felt so alone in her life, or so liberated and free.

She turned on her computer and looked on the Internet. She looked up prices of airline tickets. She could afford them, and to take some time off, with the money her mother had left her. Her pride was hurt by the collapse of her magazine, but she had free time now. She wanted to use it well.

Feeling bold and wanting to make a strong statement, she booked a first-class one-way ticket to Paris. She picked a website that showed short-term apartments to rent on the Left Bank. She took one for a month. It looked bright and airy, with a view of the Seine. She had no idea what she was going to do when she got there, but one thing was for sure, she had learned the most important lesson of all. Nothing and no one lasts forever, and the one thing she wasn't going to do was hide and let her life slip past her, like her mother had.

Whatever it took, and whatever it cost her, she was going to Paris. She would forget the magazine she had lost, and her mother's morbidly depressing life. She was going to **live**! If she didn't, she would have learned nothing from her mother, and Olivia's whole life would have been a waste, spent on a failed magazine, watching her mother fade away. She had even cheated Olivia of the chance to have a real conversation with the man who had been her father, and neither he nor her mother were ever brave or honest enough to admit it to her. They were weak, frightened, selfish people who thought of no one but themselves, without courage or integrity. Their lives were defined by selfishness and cowardice.

Whatever the future brought, Olivia wasn't going to waste it, or hide from it. She had only one mission now and that was to be fully alive and seize every minute that came her way. She had learned from her mother how **not** to be, and she was determined to use the lesson well, wherever it took her, whatever it taught her, even if it was frightening at times. She had a life to live, and nothing was going to stop her now.

Chapter 4

When Joachim's plane from Buenos Aires landed in Paris, he went straight to his mother's apartment. He had wanted her to get a better one for years, the neighborhood had become commercial, with shops and restaurants all around her, and the building was old and poorly maintained. But she said she liked where she was. It was where she had lived with Francois since she'd come to France twenty-five years before, and it was home for her. She had all her treasures and souvenirs there. It was orderly chaos, with clutter that she loved, although Joachim would have liked something better for her. He had offered to buy her an apartment from the savings he had invested well, and she always refused. She was happy where she was and had no desire for luxuries. She had learned how meaningless they were when her father lost everything he had.

She was still at work when Joachim got there, and he tried to tidy up some of the mess while he waited for her. He did her breakfast dishes and cleaned the kitchen. He had bought her a dishwasher, which she seldom used, and a washing machine she had grudgingly accepted, and conceded was practical. He vacuumed the living room when he finished in the kitchen, fluffed up the cushions on the couch, and made neat stacks of the art magazines she had everywhere. He was used to having other people do that kind of work in his job, but he liked doing it for his mother, and wished he could do more for her.

She arrived punctually at eight o'clock that night, after taking the metro home. She still worked a full day, from nine A.M. to seven-thirty in the evening, even at eighty-one. She didn't mind the long hours and loved her work, playing art detective as she tracked down paintings, as well as the people she hoped would receive them after the appropriate identification. The work still thrilled her after all these years. She had no intention of retiring, and didn't see why she should. She was blessed with good health and was agile and active for her age. Although her face was weathered, she still had a translucent beauty, and the same fair looks and piercing blue eyes as her father had had, and her sons.

She was startled to see Joachim sitting in her living room reading one of her art magazines when she got home. She knew he would be coming back from Buenos Aires soon, but wasn't sure what day.

"Oh, you're here," she said, smiling at him. He stood up to kiss her. She had a straight back and good posture for a woman her age. She was wearing a simple black dress, and her snowy white hair was pulled back in a tight bun. There was a severe simplicity and beauty to her, and always warmth in her vibrant blue eyes whenever she saw her son. "When did you get in?"

"This morning." She glanced around as he said it and smiled.

"I see you've been doing some housekeeping." Her apartment always looked better when he was there. Housecleaning bored her and she didn't mind a little friendly mess, as long as it was clean. She was immaculate, just messy.

"I was waiting for you to come home. You still keep such long hours, Mama," he reproached her gently.

"I have a lot to do. I'm hot on the trail of a family for a beautiful Monet. I'm trying to find the heirs. Two of them survived Auschwitz but would be very old now. I'm hoping they had children. I think they might be in London, or Geneva, if they're the right ones. They never came back to France." She knew all the stories, and the heartbreaks that had happened, the tragedies where entire families had been wiped out. Many of the paintings she was able to trace and lay hands on went to museums, mostly the Louvre, because of her efforts. She preferred the outcomes where family members, even distant ones, received the artwork in the end. She loved the human side of what she did, and it was a joy to locate the paintings too. Some had remained hidden in storerooms for nearly eighty years. A few were damaged almost beyond repair, but most had been well preserved. Some were still being found in Germany, and a great many had traveled to South America when members of the Nazi High Command had been able to escape and take their concealed spoils of war with them.

She took some pâté and sausages out of the refrigerator for their dinner. Joachim made a salad, and she heated some artichoke soup she had had for dinner the night before. It was an adequate meal and suited them both. She waited until they sat down to ask him about the trip.

"So how was it?" she asked Joachim with a tender look. Buenos Aires felt like another lifetime, and it was for her. It was still the home of her childhood and youth, where she had lived with her father and first husband, and where her sons had been born. She had a million memories that she rarely allowed herself to think of now. She had twenty-five years of memories in France to balance them, but knowing he had been in the city she had loved so much touched her heart, and she always hoped for some news of Javier.

"It was even more beautiful than I remembered,"

Joachim admitted. "I have such happy memories there as a boy. There's an undercurrent of sadness there now. The economy isn't good, and people are suffering because of it, but there's no place like it." He still felt Argentine in some ways, and had maintained his citizenship, although thanks to his stepfather he had a French passport too, and was a dual national, French and Argentine. He had only lived in Paris for his student years, and five aimless years after that, when he pined for his brother and felt lost without him. And he had lived in England now for almost half his life. He felt an allegiance to all three countries. But he had a particular nostalgia for Argentina, because of his boyhood there. It had been a time of innocence for him, and he remembered it as a happy, carefree time. Once he left Argentina, he had been separated from his twin, which had been painful for him for many years. He accepted that a part of his soul was linked to Javier forever, perhaps because they were twins, which was a special bond. Sometimes it was hard for him to know where he ended, and Javier began, they had been like one person for so long during the early part of their lives.

"I don't think I'll go back, but it was nice seeing old friends, and all our familiar haunts," Joachim continued, and he knew what his mother was thinking.

"Did you have any news of Javier?" she asked him

immediately. There was pain in her eyes the moment she spoke.

He sighed before he answered, not sure how much to tell her. But she was strong, and he felt he owed her the truth, as much of it as he knew. "Not much. Nothing we didn't know or haven't heard before. I contacted Felipe MacPherson," one of his old friends from school, with a Scottish father and Argentine mother. "He's high up with the police and has the right connections to find out. He said when last sighted, Javier was still in Colombia, working for some very bad people. I'm not sure how high Javier is in the organization, and Felipe said he moves around. We've heard it before, Mama. When he disappeared, he joined the dark forces that have poisoned life there. I think he's lost to us. But at least he's still alive."

"I've always felt he was," she said, her shoulders drooping as she said it. "I always knew he had this in him right from the beginning. He's not like you. He makes me think of Cain and Abel. I'm almost glad you did not see him or find him. I don't want him to hurt you." He thought his mother was dramatizing the situation, but admittedly, Javier was hanging out with, and presumably working for, the worst element of Argentine society, and the drug cartels in Colombia.

"Our life is here now," Joachim said. "There's nothing for us to go back to there. And even if we tried, we couldn't find him. If he is as deeply embedded in the drug business as Felipe says, he's probably in hiding. We'll never get to him, unless he wants to find us. And he won't come here."

"You're right not to go back," his mother confirmed. "I don't want you to. Leave it alone now. Francois said that too before he died. The people Javier is involved with are too dangerous. I was worried about your going this time, but I didn't think it fair to stop you. I know you've missed it."

"I needed to go back. I've wanted to for a long time. I've done it. I made my peace with it. It's in the past for both of us." She nodded agreement and had decided that for herself a long time before when she married Francois. She'd never gone back. The only remaining tie for her, like an unsevered umbilical cord, was the fact that her son was still there. But even that had slowly eroded with time, and was only a thin thread now, not strong enough to hold her fast. Her tie to Joachim was much stronger.

"So, what are you going to do now?" she asked him. "Go back to London?"

"Not yet. Don't be so eager to get rid of me." He smiled at her. "I'm in no hurry to go back. I've listed my details and qualifications with the best domestic agency there, and they say that there is very little demand for formal butlers now, very few houses that require one, or families that can afford them. I want to spend some time with you here." There was a kind look in his eyes, and she sat up a little straighter, with a slightly acerbic glance at her son.

"I don't need a babysitter, Joachim. I have a full life, and you must too. It's not good to remain idle for long."

"I could be your butler for a while." He laughed at the thought. "You need one. I enjoy spending time with you, Mama." His mother was reaching an age when he wanted to spend precious time with her. She had no health problems, but that could change in an instant, as he had seen with his long-term employers. He didn't want to miss an opportunity to be with her and regret it later. She was the only relative he had, other than his long-absent brother, and he was now her only child.

"I'm grateful that you want to be here. But you'll get bored hanging around while I'm at work, and I'm working on a big project right now." He knew that she sometimes stayed at the office even later than her co-workers and brought work home on weekends.

"I've been thinking that a temporary job in Paris might be fun, just for a few months. I've never worked in France, only in England." He had legal residence in England and the necessary work papers, and his French passport allowed him to work anywhere in the European Union, so he had many options.

"They don't have big houses that are fully staffed in France anymore, not like they do in England," she said. They were rapidly disappearing in England too, but he knew that she was right, and grand homes and large formal staffs had been gone in France for a long time, and with socialist governments and punitive taxes for the rich, no one liked to show wealth in France. A butler was a flashing red light to the tax authorities and shone a spotlight on a way of life that indicated big money.

"I thought I'd leave my name with an agency here, for qualified domestics, and see what turns up. It would only be temporary, until you get tired of me."

"You know I never will," she said gently, and patted his hand. He was a good son, and always had been. She had been lucky with him. Javier was her heartbreak.

After dinner that night, they talked about what he'd seen in Argentina. It brought back memories for her, both good and bad, and she thought about them late into the night as she lay in bed, and then drifted off to sleep peacefully. She didn't want to be a burden on her son, but she was glad that Joachim would be staying for a while. He was tucked away in her guest room sound asleep.

When Olivia got to Paris, she moved into the apartment she had rented for four weeks. It was on the top floor of a well-kept building on the quai Voltaire and was as modern and well decorated as the photographs had indicated. She had paid in advance. The guardian had the keys for her and showed her around. It had a big, spacious living room, sliding glass windows, a terrace, a single bedroom, bath, and modern kitchen. It was obviously owned as an investment to rent, so it lacked a warm personal touch. But it was wonderfully located, with a beautiful view of the river, with the barges and tourist boats drifting by, and a good view of the buildings on the Right Bank. It was perfectly adequate for a short-term rental, but she had a hunger to stay longer. The idea had been gnawing at her. She could even study French, not having the language might turn out to be a handicap, and she loved the idea of staying for six months or a year. She had no anchor anywhere now, no job, no family, no man in her life. Her relationships had never been long-term ones, or very successful. She had an aversion to getting too attached to anyone. For all of her adult life, and especially the last ten years, all her energy and passion had gone into her work, which hadn't saved her magazine in the end. For the first time in her life, she had no obligations and no reason to be anywhere, and thanks to what her mother had left her, she could afford to take a year off. Sooner or later, she would need another job, for her head as well as her bank account, but she was in no hurry, and had no acute need at the moment, as long as she was reasonable and somewhat careful about what she spent.

Once she was in Paris, Olivia knew she wanted to stay. She had no friends here but hoped to meet people. She was in touch with Claire Smith, her assistant from her defunct magazine, who had just taken a job in L.A., and encouraged her to try a change of scene too. They were unattached women who had put everything into their careers and were free to go anywhere they wanted now. It was both the upside and downside of having invested everything in their jobs and being unmarried and unattached at their ages. Claire had just turned forty, and had taken a job with **Architectural Digest** as their rep in L.A. Olivia was forty-three. It shocked her sometimes to realize that she was probably halfway through her life and still trying to figure things out, where she wanted to live, and what she wanted to do when she grew up. She was supposed to be grown up now, but didn't always feel that way, especially lately. She was starting over, and now she wanted to take a year off and sidetrack herself while she rethought her life and what her goals were. She didn't want to start another magazine, nor go to work for someone else, after having been her own boss for ten years, but she realized she'd probably have to. At least for now, there was no pressure on her to make any decisions. She could just enjoy Paris and adjust to all the recent changes in her life. She had no man she was involved with at the moment but had never wanted to base her life on any man, or to depend on one. She had seen what that had done to her mother, and the high price she had paid for it emotionally.

After Olivia unpacked, she flipped through a magazine, and saw an ad for Sotheby's real estate agency in Paris. She assumed they'd speak English and decided to call and see what kind of rentals they might have for six months or a year. She felt brave and adventuresome when she called them and spoke to a woman agent with a British accent. She promised to get back to Olivia after she checked her listings. She recommended the seventh, eighth, and sixteenth arrondissements when she heard where Olivia was staying. They were the three most elegant and desirable areas of Paris, as well as the first arrondissement, around the Place Vendôme. She asked if Olivia wanted a furnished or unfurnished apartment, and if a house would be acceptable. Olivia said she thought a house might be too big, and perhaps not as safe and protected as an apartment. She didn't care whether it was furnished or not. She thought it might be fun to furnish a place sparsely with special things she found and could ship back to New York when she left. Her apartment in New York was tired and dreary anyway, and some new pieces from Paris might improve it when she went back. It all sounded like fun to her now and was part of the adventure. What mattered to her was that she live her life fully, meet new people, do new things, breathe the air of Paris, and be completely alive, not buried in a job going nowhere, tied to a man who never came through for her, with her life on hold, waiting for a miracle that would never happen. Seeing how empty her mother's life had been right to the end had been a powerful wake-up call. It was everything she didn't want and was determined she wouldn't let happen to her. Her mother's life had seemed like a living death. She had sacrificed her whole life to George and what suited him, and in the end, he had died with his wife at his side, not Olivia's mother.

The Sotheby's agent promised to call Olivia as soon as she had something to show her. She said she was going to get right on it and do some research. Olivia was excited when she hung up. She went for a long walk along the quais of the Seine, with Notre-Dame behind her and the Eiffel Tower up ahead, underneath a gray Paris sky, filled with fluffy white clouds. She loved the Paris sky. She was happy just being there, and confident that it had been the right move, and good things were going to happen. She could feel it in the air.

The best domestic agency in Paris was surprisingly small, Joachim discovered when he went there for an appointment two days later. He had spent the days putting order in his mother's apartment. He had reorganized her closets, straightened the papers on her desk, which she had scolded him for, bought all the kitchen implements she was missing, sent drapes to the dry cleaners for her. He had been a whiz around her apartment, and she told him she was afraid to come home at night, for fear of what he might have done while she was at work. She tried to explain to him that she liked the friendly disorder in her apartment, it was her mess and it worked for her. She knew he meant well, but she told him he needed a job or activity of some kind to keep him busy. So he had called the agency to make an appointment, and look for something temporary.

The woman who ran it looked like a plump, friendly grandmother, or a schoolteacher. He filled out an application and handed it to her, and she frowned as she read it.

"Oh dear . . ." she said under her breath and glanced up at him. "You are **very** qualified, aren't you? I see you've never worked in France, only in England." But his French was perfect, and he had listed English, French, Spanish, and German for languages he was fluent in. His documents would allow him to work legally anywhere in Europe. "I'm not surprised you haven't worked here," she said kindly. "Unfortunately, there are no great homes here anymore. Most of the chateaux have been closed for years, or sold, most often to people from the Middle East, who bring staff from their own countries. Some are Americans, but they usually don't have a lot of help. And the French who still own their families' chateaux don't have the money to hire anyone and have ancient family retainers who are quietly letting the chateaux fall apart around them. There are no great homes left here as there are in England, or very, very few."

"I'd be quite satisfied working in a normal-sized house or an apartment," Joachim said, and the woman nodded thoughtfully, glancing at a list of her current requests, none of which really matched his qualifications, or even came close.

"I don't suppose you'd want just a driver's job. We have several of those."

"That doesn't really use the full range of my skills," he said, and she nodded again. It was true. There were so many things on the list of what had been his normal duties. He was an expert, highly trained, experienced butler, and knew how to do things that her clients hadn't requested in many, many years. And she had the best listings in Paris, for some very important families, and people with noble titles. But what he wanted and was qualified for was an extinct breed in Paris, a dinosaur that had disappeared.

"I'd actually prefer a temporary position here," he reminded the agent. "I probably will go back to England if the right job turns up there. But in the meantime, I'd like to have something to do, and I can be more flexible than I would be for a long-term job. Although I have to admit that just being a chauffeur doesn't sound too interesting."

"You're probably right. And all the chauffeuring jobs we have on the books right now are for very old people, and they don't go out much. Although it seems like you were used to that in your last job. Most younger people don't use chauffeurs anymore. Is there any particular reason why you want a temporary job here?" She wondered if he had a romance going and wanted to be in Paris for that reason. He was a very handsome, distinguished-looking man, and had worn a well-cut dark gray suit to come to see her, with a white shirt and dark navy tie. He looked better dressed and more respectable than most of her clients, but she didn't comment on it.

"I have an elderly mother here," he said, and then smiled guiltily, and she noticed that he had a cleft chin when he did. He was almost irresistible, he was so good-looking. He looked more like an actor or a banker than a butler. "She would kill me for calling her that, and she's very active. But I've spent so little time with her, living and working in England. Now that I have a break, I'd like to take advantage of it, and spend some time here, if I don't drive her crazy staying with her." The woman smiled. "I only want a live-out position here." In England, he would have to be live-in to run a house and staff properly, and particularly in the country. Head butler positions were always live-in, even today.

She asked him a few more questions, based on his application, and then stood up. "To be honest, I don't know if we'll find anything for you, but I'll certainly try. Any employer will be lucky to have you, even for a short time. I just don't know if I have the right prospective employer. You'll be over-qualified for any job, but it's a question of making the right marriage between your skills and their needs. You never know, something unusual might turn up. One of our Middle Eastern clients might want to hire someone local, but then they'd probably want you long-term. I don't suppose you want to stay here permanently?" she inquired. He looked hesitant and shook his head.

"I'm better trained for what I was doing in England, running two or three large homes at once. And I enjoy my mother's company, but I think she'll be ready for me to go back to England in a few months." They both laughed, shook hands, and he left a few minutes later. From what she said, he doubted that they would find him anything, and he didn't expect to hear from her again.

He went back to his mother's apartment and watched a movie on TV while he polished all her silver. She had a few pieces she loved that she and Francois had bought at auctions they enjoyed going to. Normally, in his jobs, he had the maids or footmen do it, but it was relaxing, and it all gleamed when his mother came home that night and she smiled when she saw it.

"I take it I have a butler now," she teased him. He bowed respectfully, and she laughed. He had made coq au vin for dinner. It had simmered on the stove while he polished the silver. He'd had a productive and relaxing afternoon. "I'm going to get awfully spoiled while you're staying with me," his mother said, "but I have to admit, I'm enjoying it, as long as you stay out of my closets and don't touch my desk again!" He laughed at the warning.

The coq au vin was delicious, and they finished it, while she told him all about the family she was searching for and the exquisite Monet waiting for them. It had been found in the basement of a chateau in Normandy that the Nazis had taken over during the war, and they had overlooked the Monet when they left, or it was too large for them to take easily. There were two other very important paintings found with it, which had belonged to another family. The retreating Nazis had abandoned the paintings in their haste when they left. It had happened in other places too. The Americans who had recently purchased the chateau in question had discovered them and very honorably contacted the Louvre to report them. They could have kept them and no one would have known, since the paintings had been missing for seventy years. The organization Liese worked for had been very grateful to receive the paintings so they could do their research on them, which as always had been fascinating. Joachim loved hearing her talk about it. It was always a detective story, and she took huge pleasure in it when it had a happy ending, which it didn't always, but sometimes it did.

"How did you ever get into this, Mama?" he asked her, as he poured her a small café filtre, and she looked up at him. "Did Francois get you interested in it, or did you find it on your own?" He knew she had worked at the Louvre briefly when she first arrived from Argentina. But she had been doing her artistic detective work for twenty-five years now, and he had never asked her how it started or how she'd found the organization she worked for. It was well known and respected in the art world, but little known to the public.

They worked in the utmost discretion, and worked with tragic family histories every day, mostly caused by the Germans in World War II, and involving the Jewish families they'd exterminated. Almost all of the French Jews had been deported. Their houses and apartments and their contents, vast fortunes, and incredible art and jewels had been taken and distributed among the German High Command, most of it never to be seen again. The stories about the deported children were even more terrible than those about the treasures that had disappeared. Non-Jewish French residents had turned in their neighbors in many instances, and trainloads filled with only children had been sent to the camps in Germany. It was the most ignoble time in French history, one that everyone wanted to forget. But Liese still lived with those stories every day. It was the stories about the children that pained her most. Pairing up living heirs with artwork was always a victory and a joy. The lost children could never be brought back, and few had survived.

Joachim had great respect for her for the work she did, but he had never asked her many questions about it.

Liese looked at him long and hard when he asked her the question he had never asked her before. A long time ago, when he was younger, she would have brushed him off, and responded in some way that the work was fascinating, or she loved working with lost art. There were many answers she could have given other than the true one. But he was older now, and it was different. She thought it was time to tell him the truth. She had always thought he should know one day. It was his history too.

"I always wondered if you'd ask me. You never have before," she said softly in her deep, smooth voice, like silk on a cheek.

"I guess I never wondered how you started. We get more interested in our parents as we get older, and they become real people to us, not just our parents." She nodded, knowing that was true. She had been curious about her own father too, and the mother who had died when she was two, whom she never knew. "And we have more time now, since I'm here with you, we're not in a hurry, and I'm not rushing back to England." They were both enjoying that, and it seemed like the right time to her to seize the opportunity.

"It's a long story," she said thoughtfully, wondering how much to tell him. But he was old enough now to hear the whole truth. He was a man, not a boy, and he deserved to know who his family was. She had been hiding it for years.

"We have time. I'm not going anywhere," Joachim said, and stretched out his long legs, as Liese looked at her son differently. And as he saw her eyes, he could see that something important was about to happen, and he sensed that neither of them might ever be the same again.

Chapter 5

"I have to go back to the beginning," Liese said to Joachim as they sat at her kitchen table at the end of dinner, their plates still in front of them. She looked into the distance as she thought about it, and her son watched her intently. He had never seen that look on her face before, of pain, of joy, of longing, and history remembered. "I was five years old when we came to Buenos Aires from Germany, at the end of the war. I remember that my papa, your grandfather, made it sound very exciting, and said we were going to a wonderful place. My mother had died in the bombing when I was two years old. I didn't remember her at all. I remember how frightened I was during the bombing of Berlin, and at the end. It seemed like a good place to get away from. My papa said there were no bombs where we were going, and it was very beautiful with nice people and lots of flowers.

"We moved into a big house, not a palace, but a very big house, and there were lots of people to help take care of me. They were all very good to me. My father was happy and it seemed like a perfect life for a long time.

"I remember how much he loved his art. He had brought some very fine paintings with him. He had them hung very proudly in our home. He always showed them to me, and explained them. He knew more about art than anyone I'd ever met. I suppose we had quite a lot of money, or maybe life wasn't expensive then. We had a country house too. He entertained a lot, and I had many pretty dresses. My father was a very handsome man, like you." She smiled at Joachim. "There were women in his life, but I think he loved his paintings more. Maybe even more than he loved me. He was always excited about new art he bought, and he had an important collection. Looking back on it, I'm not sure how he brought the ones that came with us from Germany. I suppose he smuggled them in. He never told me, and I never asked him when I was older. He was my hero and I thought he could do no wrong.

"I didn't know then, but he changed his name when we came to Argentina. Von Hartmann was my paternal grandmother's maiden name. He wanted no association with his own name, the one that he had used during the war. I only learned that later. He was from a noble family on both sides. His own

name, the one he grew up with, was von Walther."
A shadow crossed her eyes as she said the words and
went on.

"My father was at the center of society in Buenos
Aires, greatly respected and admired and very
popular. There were many Germans in Argentina
then, newly arrived ones, not just those who had
been there for generations. Many people went to
Argentina from Germany during and after the war.
There were questions one didn't ask. But how we
got there and why was never questioned, not by
me anyway. For much of it, I was a child. And then
I married Alejandro Canal, your father. He was
from one of the most social, important families in
Buenos Aires. They were related to Spanish royalty,
and very aristocratic.

"We were happy and went to every party we were
invited to. There had been five hundred people at
our wedding. He worked at his family's bank. We
had ten happy, carefree, easy years together. And it
took a long time for you and Javier to come along."
Her eyes filled with tears at the remembered joy.
"It was the happiest time of my life when you and
Javier were born, and your father was so proud
of both of you. We were doubly blessed, and you
completed our already seemingly perfect life." She
paused for a moment. "And then everything went
terribly wrong, all at once." Joachim knew that both
his grandfather and his own father had died within

months of each other, fortunes had been lost, and their lives had changed radically while he was still an infant.

"There was a famous hunter of war criminals who was very active then. He combed South America for important Nazis, with great success. It was roughly thirty-five years after the war by then, and they were still looking for Nazis from the High Command. Many were still in hiding. Some had covered their tracks well and were living out in the open. I had heard of it, but never paid any attention. It had nothing to do with my life or my father's. Until the hunter in question found my father.

"The man's skills were extraordinary. He had been looking for Papa for years but had had misleading information. Once he realized he had found my father, everything happened very quickly. My father didn't die suddenly, he was kidnapped, taken back to Germany, where he was charged with heinous war crimes, and stood trial. The testimony against him was horrendous. I read it all," she said, with tears still welling up in her eyes. It was hard to admit this to him now, but she thought he should know. "He was tried and found guilty. He was sentenced to hang, but they commuted the sentence to life imprisonment. He was seventy-three years old when they took him from Buenos Aires, and they took everything he owned. He had quite a lot of money, which the war crimes tribunal in Germany demanded as restitution to the victims. His art collection, our houses, everything he had, gone. It was the right thing to do, but it took away everything he had and that I would have inherited one day. I wouldn't have wanted it anyway, once I knew how he got it, but it changed everything for me.

"Once my father was convicted, your father's family demanded that he separate from me. We'd been married for ten years and had four-month-old twins. I begged him not to leave. It was an ugly time. He was a good person, but he was close to his family, and he saw me differently after what happened. I'm not sure he believed that I hadn't known about my father's past because we were so close, and apparently he thought I'd hidden it from him. I think he felt terrible about it, but he followed his family's wishes, and he left me very quickly. The governor and a judge they knew granted him a divorce almost immediately. They gave me a small amount of money to live on for a short time, until I could find a job, and for you. And according to his family's demands, your father renounced all rights to you and Javier. They wanted no connection to the bloodline of a criminal. He refused to see me or speak to me after he left, and he never saw you and Javier again." Joachim stopped her then, with a look of shock and horror on his face as he grabbed her arm.

"Wait, are you telling me that during all those years you told us our father was dead, he was alive?" The idea that their mother, whom they trusted implicitly, had lied to them about something so important was an additional shock.

She shook her head in answer to his question. "By the time you asked me about him, he was dead. He remarried almost immediately after the divorce, a very young, very beautiful socialite. He died in a polo accident three years later. They had ordered me to take back my maiden name of von Hartmann after the divorce. They denied you and Javier the use of their name too. They wanted nothing to do with any of us. So, I changed yours and your brother's as well. You were both three years old when he died. We never saw him again from the day he left. And I was ordered to leave our home within weeks, with both of you. They considered me the daughter of a monster, and a criminal myself by association. Your father and his family wanted nothing to do with any of us after that, no intermingling with their pure bloodline. I never heard from any of them again. Your father never saw you or Javier after he left us when you were four months old.

"I would have gone to see my father in Germany, but I never had the money. I wanted to see him at least once so he could explain everything to me himself. We wrote to each other several times. I moved from our big house to a tiny apartment. I got the job I had at the museum. They were aware of the scandal, but they knew that I was desperate and had two babies to support. And unlike my in-laws, they didn't blame me for my father's crimes. They were very kind to me. I was heartbroken over my father and what he had done. I never saw him again. He died in prison in Germany. And then, all those years later, fifteen to be exact, Francois and I met, and two years later, I married him and we came to Paris.

"Francois knew the whole story. I told him. I would never have kept it from him. He got me the job at the Louvre, and once I was there I discovered the organization I work for now. When I realized what they did I begged them to hire me, and they did. It is my way of paying penance for my father's sins. He took much more than paintings from the people he robbed and sent to their deaths. But with each painting I can find and restore to its rightful owners, I am doing some small thing to restore dignity to them, and justice, and often even money that they need. I can't bring their relatives back, but if I can find their art for them, that's something."

She had been doing it for twenty-five years and had returned an astonishing amount of art. She was driven to help them, and tireless. There were tears sliding down Joachim's face at the end of the story. He put his arms around his mother and sobbed, thinking of the blows she had survived, the heartaches she had endured, the loss of a father, a husband, dignity, protection, her home, and even the money she needed to survive and support her children. He had never known anyone so brave. And even now, when she told him, she didn't speak with bitterness.

He could only guess at the hardships she'd been through, how panicked she must have been when the father she adored was taken away and exposed as a criminal of heinous proportions, and how crushed she was when the husband she loved left her, abandoned her penniless with infant twins. And yet, she had survived. She had taken good care of them, been an admirable mother, and provided a good home for them. Now he realized what a savior Francois had been for her. She had spent twenty-five years atoning for her father's crimes, not her own. The losses in his mother's life had been monumental. Then on top of it, she had lost Javier. Yet, she was still standing, and strong, and compassionate. She was a living testimony to the endurance and resilience of the human spirit. Even now, she didn't condemn the husband who had left her. She had simply been resourceful and prevailed. She had had the hardest life of anyone Joachim had ever known, and he loved his mother more than ever after he heard her story.

"Why didn't you tell me sooner?" he asked in a hoarse voice.

"You were too young. And I was deeply ashamed of my father for a long time. And I saw no point in poisoning you against your own father. He wasn't a strong man. He did what his family wanted him to do. They saw me as a criminal, linked to my father. They treated me as if I was as guilty as he was, and Alejandro didn't have the courage to fight them. It was easier for him to let go of me, which is what he did, even if it meant giving you up too."

"He abandoned us. What if you couldn't support us? What if we had starved?" His voice shook as he said it and she smiled.

"I wouldn't have let that happen. And I didn't. We didn't have much, but we had what we needed, and we had each other. We always had food on the table and a roof over our heads." But the roof had been a thin one, and Joachim remembered now how she had washed their clothes every night, when they only had one set to wear, and she never bought anything for herself, and wore the same dress to work every day. He realized that she must have felt like a queen when she married Francois. He tried to spoil her in every way he could afford to. He wanted to make up for all the hardships she'd endured. And quite amazingly, she wasn't bitter about her father, or the husband who had left her. She had simply done whatever she had to, to survive and give her two boys the best life she could.

"I never felt the same way about my father again," she admitted, as Joachim looked at her.

"How could you? My father doesn't sound like much of a man either. How could he have left you alone to fend for yourself with your two babies?" She didn't tell him or his family, but the small amount they had given her had been enough to rent her tiny tenement apartment but had run out in a few months. They had never inquired how she was after that. She had sent a letter of condolence to his parents when their son died, and they had never responded. They were hard people and she had paid a high price for her father's sins. He had committed them when she was a small child, born during the war in 1940. It was an extraordinary life story, and Joachim felt numb with shock after she'd told him.

"How could you survive it, Mama?" Joachim asked her, profoundly shaken, and in awe of her.

"I had no other choice. I had to take care of you and Javier. He was always different, though. There was always something in him that worried me. You were identical physically, but there was something in him that was always very hard as he grew up, like your father's family." The rest of what had happened to her made Javier's abandonment and disappearance into the underworld seem even worse. Did she have to go through the pain of that too? It seemed so unfair. And Javier knew none of this.

Perhaps Javier was like their grandfather too. Javier had turned into a gangster and a hoodlum, and probably a drug dealer. Their grandfather was a war criminal of the highest order, destroying families and lives with the sanction and approval of the Nazi High Command. He was truly a monster. Javier was just a small-time operator, but a criminal nonetheless and would come to no good.

"Do you think your father regretted what he did after he was convicted?"

She thought about it for a minute. "I'm not sure. I asked him questions about it in my letters, but he never answered. He wrote about the books he was reading in prison, memories of his childhood, and mine. He said that a soldier's actions and recollection of them must stay in the confines and secrecy of the army he served, and at the time they existed. He said that war justifies all actions against enemy forces. But they weren't enemy forces," she said with tears streaming down her cheeks. "They were children deported in trains and sent to the gas chamber. And families, men and women. They stole everything from them. They robbed them of their homes, businesses, dignity, their lives, their futures. Their artwork is the least of it, and so little to give back to them. How do you make restitution for the children those people lost, the husbands and wives, their homes, everything they held dear? I can never make up for that."

"No one can. But you've done everything you could to make up with what you could restore. It's been your life's work, Mama." He had never loved or respected his mother more. "I wish I had known about all this sooner. I'm glad you told me now. Francois must have been so proud of you." She smiled through her tears as she nodded.

"He was. No one ever knew why I did it, except him. And now you. I'm glad I told you too. That's why I will never retire. This is my mission for as long as I live. And it feels so wonderful every time we make a match, and get a piece of art back to someone, even if only to a distant relative. It always matters to them, and to me too. It's a victory every time."

They talked for a long time that night and finally hugged each other and went to bed. She had given him much to think about, not only about who their father and grandfather had been, but their perfidy, and the heinous things they had done, to her and others. He had also learned about his mother, and the extraordinary woman she was. It was some small consolation, as he cried himself to sleep that night, knowing that her noble blood ran in his veins as well as hers.

Chapter 6

When the agent from Sotheby's called Olivia, she had three possible homes to show her. They were all available to rent for a year, sparsely furnished if she wanted them that way, or the furniture could be removed. There was a house and two apartments. She saw the house first. It was small and cramped. There was evidence of leaks in the ceiling and it smelled musty. It looked sad to Olivia, and the furniture in it was battered and drab. It looked as if it had been unoccupied for a long time and didn't appeal to her at all.

There was an extremely modern apartment, which looked industrial and trendy, but everything about the place felt cold, like a refrigerator. It had no soul. It was minimally furnished and looked like a cheap hotel suite. The location was excellent and the building clean and nice. It was owned by Italians who kept it as an investment property and occupied it briefly from time to time between renters.

The third option was in the sixteenth arrondissement, in a beautiful old building in good condition, with a broad spiral staircase in the main hall. It had a grand look to it, and the apartment was on what the agent called the "noble floor," or second floor, with high ceilings, wood paneling, beautiful old floors, and fireplaces. The kitchen was sparse and barely functional, and there was almost no furniture. If she rented it, she'd have to furnish it. It would be like camping out in the beginning, but the bare bones were beautiful, with high ceilings and good light. It was owned by a couple who had moved to Brussels for tax reasons and didn't want to part with their apartment. It had magnificent cream-colored satin curtains, but the rest of the furniture was dingy and inadequate. It was more of a commitment than the others because she knew she'd have to furnish it and decorate, but the place was so pretty and inviting that it was hard to resist, and the rent wasn't exceptionally high. The agent could see immediately how much she liked it.

"You could put in an Ikea kitchen for very little money," she told her. "And enough furniture to get by." Olivia was well aware of it, but she also wondered if she was crazy to be renting an apartment in Paris, and if she should just go home in a few weeks and face real life, instead of running away from it and playing house. But it was such a pretty apartment, and in good condition, in a lovely building in a safe residential neighborhood, that she was sorely tempted. She felt as though she was in a dream as they walked down the grand staircase.

"I love it. I just don't know if I should be doing this, renting an apartment for a year."

The agent gave her the expected sales pitch, that they rarely got apartments as nice as this one, it was a terrific deal, and she didn't have to spend much to furnish it. It had a big master bedroom, a smaller second one, decent closets, two good marble bathrooms, a pretty living room, small dining room, and kitchen. It had everything she needed, and it was nicer than her apartment in New York. She worked all the time and never entertained, and she used her apartment there to crash after eighteen-hour workdays, not to spend leisure time in. She could see herself entertaining in this apartment in Paris. It would be fun to furnish it. She could always ship the furniture to New York at the end of the year when she went back. It opened up countless horizons, and she wasn't sure what to do when she reached the street.

"I'd like to think about it overnight," she told the agent, who then told her that three other potential clients were seeing it that afternoon. She refused to be pressured and took a long walk, thinking about it on the way back to the Left Bank. Somehow it felt like a real commitment to spend a year in Paris. On the one hand she wanted to, on the other hand, she was scared to death, and felt slightly insane to be considering it. She had wanted to live her life, but maybe this was going overboard. But she loved the idea of living there for a year, or even longer. She knew that a year from now, if not sooner, she'd have to go back to work at some job or other, in New York. She felt as though she were becoming another person, being in Paris. It was not an entirely unpleasant sensation. It felt like a new lease on life—but whose life? Hers or someone else's?

The agent had suggested that she hire an assistant to help her furnish it, get all the necessary services signed up, gas, electric, and have the Ikea kitchen installed. It sounded like a big production. But she had a point. She gave Olivia the name of an agency to find someone to help her, and a cleaning lady, which she would need as well.

To confuse matters further, when she got home that afternoon, after buying groceries, she was still going around in circles about the apartment. It was so appealing, but a real commitment to stay for a year. She normally wasn't impulsive but felt as though she was being so now. Deciding to come to Paris had been spur of the moment, and renting an apartment for a year would be an even bigger leap. Just for the hell of it, she called the agency the realtor had referred her to, to see what an assistant and a cleaning person would cost. If it was insanely expensive, that might make the decision for her.

She called the number, almost hoping they

wouldn't answer. She felt as though she were being pulled along by a relentless invisible force that she couldn't resist and wasn't sure if she should. Was this her destiny or was it folly? She had enough money to live on for a year, a little longer if she was careful, but after that, reality would hit. She couldn't hide from it forever.

The domestic agency answered on the second ring. Olivia asked hesitantly if the woman spoke English, and she said she did. Not well, and with a heavy accent, but they understood each other. Olivia told her that she was thinking of renting an apartment for a year and staying in Paris, and if she did, she would need an assistant, at least to help her set it up, and someone to clean it, for a year. She said that the assistant would be short-term since she probably wouldn't need her once the apartment was up and running.

"Is there construction to do?" the woman asked her.

"Not really. I need to put in a kitchen, and it needs furniture. And I'll need to set up gas, electricity, phone, Internet, and I don't speak French."

"I understand," the woman said, making rapid notes of the address, the size of the apartment, and Olivia's contact information. "I don't supply assistants for an office. Only household help. The cleaner is easy. The assistant more difficult. Perhaps you need a secretary." That made sense to Olivia, and then the woman had an idea. "This may sound strange to you, and not what you are looking for.

I saw a candidate today. He is looking for a temporary job here for three or four months. He is overqualified for your job, but he is very capable. You might want to meet him or try him. He's a trained butler and was seventeen years in his last job, which just ended when his employer died. He ran two large homes for them in England, with full staff. He's Argentine, speaks four languages, and is legal to work in France, or anywhere in Europe." Olivia could easily imagine that he probably also cost a fortune, was undoubtedly ancient, and all she could think of was Carson in **Downton Abbey,** in white tie and tails. She wasn't Lady Mary, and this wasn't 1925.

"That sounds a little rich for my blood. I don't need anyone that trained. And I have no idea what I would do with a butler. He'd want to serve me breakfast on a silver tray. I need someone who could help me get the apartment organized if I rent it. I'm sure he's much too fancy for me. I don't even know what butlers do, except in the movies."

"I realize it's a problem, and will be for most of my clients," she said. "He's trained for formal service, and very few people still want that here. It's not adapted to today's way of life, particularly in France. People don't want a great deal of help, or formal training. He's aware of that. He says he's flexible, and it would be fairly short-term, so a project like this might work for him to set you up."

"Why did he leave England, or why isn't he

looking for a job there?" Olivia was suspicious and thought he would be a hundred years old.

"He wants to go back, and I think it's the only place where he'd find the right job and his training would be appropriate. But he has a mother here, and he says he wants to spend a few months close to her. She's quite old. He's staying with her, so he doesn't want a live-in position, and he doesn't mind working weekends. I have a copy of his reference from his employer's son, the Marquess of Cheshire. They raved about him and seem very fond of him. I can scan it and email it to you if you like."

"I just can't imagine hiring a butler. What does he wear? What would he do?"

"Whatever you need him to do, I imagine. He must be quite resourceful, if he ran two large homes. He came to see me in a smart gray suit, white shirt, and tie. I imagine he'll wear whatever you tell him to. He's young enough." She checked his application. "He's forty-two years old. He certainly could be an assistant, if he's willing to. I can ask him, and you can meet him if you wish, and see what you think. I can't think of anyone on my books at the moment who would be capable of what you're looking for. And since it's short-term, maybe you could both find a way to make it work," she said hopefully. Olivia was surprised by his age, but still couldn't get the vision of the butler in **Downton Abbey** out of her head.

"I need to make a decision about the apartment

tonight," Olivia said, feeling even more confused. "I'll call you tomorrow and let you know what I decide, and maybe you can think of someone else in the meantime. Do you suppose a maid would be able to do everything I need, a bright young one?"

"I can't think of anyone right now, but I'll look at my files tonight." Olivia thanked her, hung up, and spent the night tormenting herself. Did she want to stay in Paris for a year, or was that a crazy pipe dream and should she go back to New York to look for a job? If she stayed, should she rent that apartment or was it too grand for her, or too fancy and more than she needed? But the rent wasn't too high. And if she did rent it, could she find someone to help her set it up? Hiring a butler sounded totally insane to her, whatever he looked like. But what did it matter if he could do the job? And she had no idea what he'd charge. Probably a fortune.

She fell asleep with the lights on, with a pad and pen in her hand, and her thoughts spinning around and around. She felt as though aliens had taken over her mind. But the last thing she wanted to do was go back to her own depressing apartment in New York and start looking for a job, working for someone else, after years of working for herself, and having to explain why her magazine had failed. It still felt too fresh for that. And if she stayed in Paris, what would she do?

She had none of the answers when she woke up the next morning and went for a walk along the

Seine after she drank a strong cup of coffee. Her cellphone rang when she was on the way back. It was the real estate agent from Sotheby's to tell her that one of the people who had seen the apartment the previous afternoon wanted it. The owner was willing to give her priority since she had seen it first, but they wanted to know by noon. She almost cried when she hung up and said she'd call her back in half an hour. She hated to make rush decisions and was tempted to say no. She didn't have anyone to call for advice. Claire, her former assistant at the magazine, was already in L.A., and it was two-thirty in the morning for her, so she couldn't call her. And Olivia didn't want someone else making the decision. It was up to her. She wasn't usually confused, but this was a big leap for her, totally different from anything she'd ever done before. She was out of her comfort zone, on unfamiliar turf. It was terrifying and exciting too.

She stopped at one of the bridges on the way back and stared down into the swirling water below her.

"What should I do?" she said out loud, and the answer came as though someone had spoken to her.

"Take the apartment," the voice in her head said.

"Oh my God . . . are you sure?" She realized she was having a conversation with herself.

"You don't have to spend a lot on furniture, and you can always send it to New York when you go back. You're tired of what you have in New York anyway. The apartment here will open the doors to a whole new life. This is what you wanted. Now go for it!" the voice in her head said.

"Beware of what you wish for," she said out loud, and walked back to her apartment, feeling like a crazy person. She was talking to herself now.

She ran up the stairs and called the agent at Sotheby's.

"I'll take it," she said in one swift breath, feeling as though she was going over a waterfall in a barrel, or falling out a window, but once she said it, she was less scared, and felt more in control again.

"You're doing the right thing. You won't regret it. It's a terrific apartment." How did she know it was the right thing? She didn't even know her. And Olivia already regretted it, with classic buyer's remorse, but she was excited too. And it was only a rental after all. "It will be yours in two weeks. I'll come over with the lease for you to sign at six o'clock. Does that work for you?"

"Yes," Olivia said, feeling breathless, wondering what the hell she was doing and if she had lost her mind. But part of her felt happy about it, another part was terrified. She told herself that she could refuse to sign the lease and get out of it until six o'clock. But she didn't want to, and after she hung up, she called the woman at the domestic agency.

"I'm taking the apartment," Olivia told her, feeling slightly sick.

"Congratulations. And would you like to meet our butler?" she said, and Olivia laughed. Why not?

It was just as crazy as everything else she was doing, renting an apartment in Paris for a year, needing to furnish it and put in a kitchen, and interviewing a formal butler to hire as an assistant. It was the craziest thing she'd ever done, but she didn't have to hire the butler if she didn't like him. She had no obligation, and she did need help, and it would only be for a short time. For no particular reason, she assumed he was gay, living with his mother, and running a formal home. She didn't care either way. Maybe he'd be fun to work with. Although Carson on **Downton Abbey** wasn't gay. She remembered then that she had to give the woman an answer if she wanted to meet him.

"Yes, I guess I'll meet him. Will tomorrow work?" Signing the lease would be enough stress for one day.

"I'll see if he's available and interested. I'll call you back and let you know."

She called Olivia back while she was making a cup of tea to try to calm her nerves. "He can meet you anytime you like tomorrow." She didn't tell Olivia that he had sounded skeptical too.

"Perfect. How about four o'clock?" That way she could walk or shop or do errands, or go to a museum before she saw him.

"I'll let him know. Call me on my cellphone and tell me how the meeting went. I hope you like him. He seems like a nice chap. He's quiet and seems discreet." She didn't tell Olivia that he sounded tentative about it too. He hadn't expected her to line up an interview so quickly, and the project sounded odd to him. He was a butler, not an assistant, and the agency seemed to know very little about the prospective employer, except that she was American, and renting an apartment for a year. He imagined that she had probably just gotten divorced or was running away from something. They didn't think she had children, but they weren't sure. Or dogs. He was on edge and dubious about the whole thing. And he had forgotten to ask how old she was. Probably either some cranky old dowager, or a spoiled rich girl indulged by her father. Neither possibility appealed to Joachim.

He said as much to his mother that night when she got home from work. He was already sorry he had agreed to the interview.

"See what you think when you meet her," his mother said sensibly, smiling at him.

"I'm a butler, Mama, not an errand boy or an assistant."

"You've done lots of things that an assistant would do. And errands, when you were younger. She's a woman alone in a foreign country, renting an apartment, and she doesn't speak the language. It doesn't matter what she calls you, she needs help. That doesn't make her spoiled or cranky. It means she can pay someone to help her get the job done. She's probably a businesswoman, a lot of American women are. Don't get all worked up about it. Go with an open mind." As usual, she gave him good advice, and he put the interview out of his head and on the back burner for the night.

Olivia was sitting in her apartment on the quai Voltaire with the keys to her new apartment in her hand. She had ordered a wire transfer from her bank in New York for the first month's rent, and a security deposit, and the owner said she could go to the apartment and measure whatever she needed to. It had all gone smoothly, and she had done it. She felt calm about it now. She couldn't wait to see the apartment again and was planning to go the next day. She was smiling as she walked out onto the terrace and watched the Eiffel Tower sparkling. It was magical, and this was home now, for the next year.

Olivia went to her new apartment the next morning at ten o'clock. She had the outer code to the building, and there was an intercom she didn't need to use. No one stopped her, and she walked up to the second floor and let herself into the apartment. There was an alarm, but it wasn't on. She flipped on the lights and walked around the sparsely furnished rooms. There was a bed and a chest in the bedroom and nothing else, a dining room table with six chairs of one kind and two of another. There were two couches in the living room that were decent looking, and no tables. The second bedroom was empty, and she could use it as an office, a closet, or a storeroom, and there was a counter in the kitchen, a few cupboards and a sink, but no stove or refrigerator. The bones of the apartment were as beautiful as she remembered, but the furnishings were paltry and inadequate, as she remembered too. She needed to replace them, but not spend a fortune. She wanted the apartment to be livable, comfortable, and cozy, but she wasn't trying to replicate Versailles. She had been to the flea market once in Paris when she had come on a business trip and wondered if she could find decent things there at reasonable prices. The prices had seemed high to her, but the merchants were willing to bargain, and many of them spoke English, since a lot of Americans bought there. And Ikea was a great resource for basics, and simple, practical things.

She walked around the apartment, trying to figure out what she wanted to do. A coffee table in the living room, some lamps, some comfortable chairs to sit in, better dining chairs that matched. None of it had to be expensive, just pretty and practical. She noticed the curtains again and how handsome they were. And she could see trees from her windows, which gave the place a country feel. The floors were as beautiful as she recalled. She wanted to get started, so it would already be more inviting when she moved in. And she reminded herself that she had owned and run a decorating magazine for ten years and would figure out what to do.

She stayed for over an hour and had several ideas and written notes by the time she left. She had lunch at a bistro, and went for a walk in the Tuileries Gardens, and was back at her current apartment for the interview with the butler at four o'clock. Since he was coming from a reliable source, with supposedly excellent references, she felt comfortable meeting him at her apartment. She had no idea what to expect, but she had a better idea now of the help she needed with the apartment. She really wanted some assistance with the move. She wondered if he'd be too big a snob to go to Ikea or the flea market with her. If so, he'd be no use to her.

The intercom buzzer sounded at exactly four o'clock. He said his name, and she buzzed him in. She opened the apartment door to him two minutes later and was startled when she saw him. He didn't look anything like she'd expected. He looked younger than his age, was tall, blond, very attractive, and impeccably dressed in gray slacks, a gray turtleneck sweater, and a British-looking tweed jacket. He looked like an actor, and nothing like a butler, and even less like Carson in **Downton Abbey.** He wasn't wearing white tie and tails.

"I'm sorry not to wear a suit and tie," he said apologetically. "I wasn't sure what you preferred, but I thought more informal for a Saturday afternoon seemed appropriate. Of course, I can wear formal wear to work." Jeans would have been more appropriate to help with the move. She was wearing jeans, a black turtleneck sweater, and running shoes, and she noticed that he looked a lot more put together than she did. And he was wearing very good-looking brown suede shoes. He looked much more British than Argentine. And he spoke with a slightly British accent, as many Europeans did, not a Spanish one. It was an international accent and his English was perfect.

After they sat down, she told him about the apartment she had rented, where it was, and what she thought it needed. She told him that she had rented it for a year.

"The apartment is really beautiful, and it's in good condition. The furniture is very mix-and-match, though, and looks like it came out of someone's attic. I need to buy a few things. Like a bed, some tables and chairs. And it needs a kitchen. I was thinking Ikea, nothing too elaborate, just clean and functional, maybe in a fun color. I don't want to go crazy for a year, but I want it to be livable and pretty."

"I'm not a decorator," he said, smiling, "but I can certainly organize installing an Ikea kitchen for you. I put in several for my employers' children in England. It seems to be a universal convenience these days. They're inexpensive, functional, and durable, and they look great. They install them now. All you really have to do is go there once, pick what you like, and I or someone can get it installed for you. They can do it in a day unless you want something complicated."

"That's exactly what I want, someone to supervise

the installation. And phone, Internet, gas, electricity. I don't speak French. I want to hire someone to clean maybe twice a week. The agency said that wouldn't be a problem. And beyond that, I don't know what I'll need. I'd like to have friends over, when I meet some people, but wouldn't entertain formally, and I'd have to hire a cook for a dinner party. My cooking is awful." She smiled at him. "The agency said that you're a formally trained butler, but I don't know how much of that I'd need," she said. Probably very little. And she wasn't even sure what a butler did.

"I think I'm going to find, when looking for a new position, that a butler is a jack-of-all-trades these days. There aren't many formal homes left, which is why I'm not staying where I was. My employers' children no longer have the same lifestyle their parents did, and they're going to be selling the houses. I've been with the family for sixteen years, and worked for another employer for a year before that, on my first job. It's going to be a big change for me. I was twenty-six when I went to work for my recent employers. But things have changed since then, and the generation that wants formal service is dying out. There is a lot of human resources involved in the position, managing a large staff. But people don't want a lot of staff these days either," he explained. He had an easy, pleasant, polite way of speaking to her, expressing things simply in an unpretentious way. "It sounds like you have enough to keep me busy for a while. I'd like to be here for three or four months before I go back to England. My mother is very independent, but I'd like to spend some time with her, if she lets me." He smiled at Olivia, and she remembered wondering if he was gay, not that it mattered, but it didn't seem like it. He seemed like a regular guy, good-looking and with good manners. He looked intelligent, and it was actually hard to imagine him as a formal butler in white tie and tails, but she realized that he probably looked great when he played the part, and did it well.

"Actually, I just lost my mother," she said, "so I understand your wanting to spend time with yours."

"I'm sorry about your mother," he said politely. "Mine is still working full-time, and allergic to the idea of my hovering or taking care of her. So, she may throw me out before I want to leave," he said, grinning, and Olivia laughed.

"You're fortunate. Mine had dementia and faded away over several years. Yours sounds very lively."

"She is definitely that! I understand better now why you told the agency you wanted an assistant. It's hard to define a position like this, but butlers do things like this too today. It's all about maintaining a home and keeping things on track. What you don't need is formal table service or running other staff." And her apartment was tiny compared to what he was used to.

"That sounds about right," Olivia agreed.

"When would you want someone to start?"

"I have this apartment for four more weeks, and I can move things into the new one in two weeks. So I could use someone's help right away to help me buy what I need, since I'd be doing it in French, and I'm not sure where to go."

"Do you have a car?"

"No, I don't. I can rent one."

"A van would probably be more useful. Ikea delivers, but we can pick things up with the van, and I could drive you. You don't need a chauffeur to take you to Ikea, and the BHV, which is rather like Ikea, here in the city. It's a nightmare, massively crowded. You stand on line forever to pay, but they have everything practical you'll need."

"I was wondering about the flea market too."

"Good idea, though a little overpriced if you don't speak the language, and there's an excellent auction house you can check out." He was full of good ideas, and their minds were racing. "My mother used to love the flea market. She used to go every weekend and drag home all sorts of treasures, Chinese dragons from some restaurant, supposedly Marie Antoinette's slipper chair, or one just like it. She came home with the damnedest things, but somehow, they all worked. And she loved auctions too. I'll ask her where you should go."

"Has she given them up?" Olivia asked.

"There's not an empty inch in the apartment." He laughed. "If you hire me, she's going to be extremely jealous and want to consult."

"Does it sound like a job you'd want to do?" she asked him. He was easy to talk to, direct and straightforward, and she could tell that he was very capable, he sounded organized and willing to lend a hand at a multitude of tasks. She had expected him to be pompous and very formal, instead she found him very human, and not full of himself at all, although his previous position had been a very big deal. This sounded like fun to him, and she wasn't what he had expected either. He had thought she would be bossy and some kind of tough business-woman, and much older. Instead she seemed very nice and reasonable, a little shy, and younger than he'd thought. She was close to his age. He was respectful and spoke to her as an equal.

"It sounds interesting and like quite a lot of fun, and a challenge to get you all set up. Will you be working while you're here?" He was curious about what she did.

"I don't think so. I don't know. I've been nursing along a magazine that I started for the last ten years. It was my baby. It folded a few weeks ago. I haven't figured out the next step, so I told myself I'd take a year off. I'm not sure I'll stick to that. But I have no plans right now."

"That's more or less the same situation I'm in. Brave new world," he said. "I didn't want to go right back into a formal job. And my previous employers were so wonderful, it will be hard to match that situation, so I'm taking a break, and it seemed like a good time to visit my mother before I get buried in work again. Do you have children who'll be coming over to visit?" It had been one of his concerns about her. Wild teenagers, or badly behaved small children.

"I don't have children. With my mother gone, no relatives. I'm on my own." He nodded and was surprised by that. He wondered if there was a man on the scene, and maybe it was why she had come to Paris, but it didn't sound like that either, from what she'd said, which would also explain why she needed help.

"I'm normally not an impulsive person, and not very spontaneous. I work all the time. This is very unusual for me, to take a year off, come to Paris, and rent an apartment. I'm a little surprised at myself. It's scary as hell, but a nice change." She smiled at him.

"I just came back from Argentina, where I grew up. I hadn't been back in twenty-five years. I guess taking a break once in a while isn't such a bad thing. I've never done it before either."

"I'll probably start working again in a few months. I just don't know at what. But not another magazine." She asked him about his salary then and was pleasantly surprised at how reasonable he was.

"It doesn't seem fair to ask you for my usual wage.

I won't be doing most of what I normally do as a butler. This is really more of a jack-of-all-trades position, lending you a hand where I can. It sounds like fun, and it will be refreshing. I can go back to formal service when I go back to England if the right job turns up. And that might take a while. I don't want to rush into anything, and get stuck in the wrong position." Neither did she. She felt exactly the same way about her next endeavor.

"Would you like the job, Joachim?" she asked him directly, and he smiled.

"I'd like that very much."

"When do you want to start?" She was pleased by his answer, and he looked happy too. It seemed like one of those fortuitous moments when two people and an opportunity collide at the right time.

"How does Monday sound? That will give us both time to gather our wits, make some lists, and figure out where to start. I'd suggest Ikea on Monday morning to order the kitchen and whatever else we find that catches your eye. I can rent a van if you like."

"That would be terrific. Monday at nine o'clock?" she said and stood up. And he did the same. They shook hands on it, and she walked him to the door, and then he turned to her with a final question. He was just friendly and personable enough, and just formal enough to be respectful. He had clear boundaries and didn't try to pretend that they were friends. He knew where the line was and stayed well behind it.

"One last thing. Costume. Blazer and slacks? Black suit? I don't believe my livery would go over well at Ikea," he said with a grin, and she laughed.

"We can play it by ear. Blazer and slacks if we go somewhere nice, like a fancy antique store, or if I have someone over. Black suit if I give a dinner party. And jeans for Ikea. How does that sound?"

"Precisely as it should be," he said, and inclined his head slightly as a salutation of respect and left an instant later. She smiled as she locked the door behind him. Life was certainly galloping ahead. She had an apartment in Paris. **And** a butler. Her life was changing at lightning speed.

Chapter 7

Joachim picked Olivia up at exactly nine o'clock on Monday morning, in the van he had rented. They agreed to go to the new apartment first, so he could get a look at it, size up what they needed in the kitchen, and do some measuring. He brought a notepad, a laser to measure distances, and two industrial tape measures, with both centimeters and inches, since he didn't know which she preferred. He took photographs with his phone and looked around the rest of the apartment with her, measured some key spaces, for a new bed if she wanted one, coffee table, and some cabinets in the bathroom. He took the basic measurements in the kitchen and told her that once she selected the cabinetry she wanted, he would measure again more precisely. He was businesslike and professional, and half an hour later, they were on the highway to Ikea.

"It's a beautiful apartment," he said, as they drove

along. "You made a very good choice." Everything was in good condition and well maintained. The windows closed smoothly, the doors locked well, the alarm was a modern one. "You should be able to get it set up in no time." He doubted it would take her three months to organize it, and he'd be out of a job before that, which was all right with him. "I'm going to call the phone, gas, and electric companies this afternoon when we get back, or tomorrow morning." He seemed fast and efficient. She had called the agency to say she had hired him, and so had he, and they were very pleased. They had promised to send some cleaners for her to interview. She wanted to get the apartment clean before she moved in, and had decided to buy a new mattress. Joachim said he knew a place that would be better than Ikea for that.

"You can make the calls you need to from my apartment. There's a workspace you can use. I don't need it," she told him. He had brought a laptop in a briefcase.

They were both quiet on the way to Ikea, lost in their own thoughts. She didn't feel obliged to speak to him, and he didn't annoy her with small talk. He was respectful of her space, and his own position. He didn't attempt to become friends, although they had chatted amicably in the interview, but it was mostly to learn about the composition of her household, and his history.

They walked into the huge store together. He

picked up a large bag and they followed the yellow markings on the floor to the kitchen section. The choices were vast with every kind of counter surface from granite to the least expensive options, shiny lacquered cabinets, or wood ones, everything in a multitude of styles and colors and finishes, and dozens of different kinds of handles. All of it was displayed in a variety of attractive combinations, to show how the products could be used.

He was surprised by how quickly she made her selections and how decisive she was. She acted like a businesswoman after all, but not in an aggressive way. She showed him all the things she wanted him to order. White lacquer cabinets with a high gloss, simple brushed steel handles, a high-grade white plastic counter surface which he recommended. He had used it for one of the young Cheshires, and it had worked well. They picked light fixtures for the kitchen and he recommended a different store for appliances. They picked shelving, and everything they needed for the kitchen. They walked through the rest of the store then, and she picked kitchen plates and glasses, a big, powder pink, cozy armchair he would assemble for her bedroom, some mirrored cupboards for the second bedroom that could be set up for shelves or hanging, light fixtures for the bathroom, freestanding lamps, assorted tools, and practical things he said he would need for small installations. Two hours later, they were back on the road, with the van full. He was going to order the kitchen online, after he took the correct measurements, and they would install it within a week. Everything was moving quickly.

"You're a whiz, Joachim," she complimented him, and he smiled.

"I think that's what you're paying me for, if I'm not mistaken." They had spent astonishingly little at Ikea. He was mindful of her budget. "Next stop, Darty," he said, "for appliances." The apartment had a washing machine, dryer, and dishwasher, but she had to buy a refrigerator, stove with oven, assorted small appliances, and a vacuum cleaner.

They went back to the new apartment to unload it all afterward. The rest was being delivered. They stopped at a sandwich shop to buy lunch, ate it in the van, and then went to buy her a new bed, not just a mattress. Then they went back to her current apartment, so he could call about the utilities. She had never seen anyone as efficient. And when they had dropped off her purchases at the new apartment, he had taken the exact measurements for the kitchen, so he could place the order for everything she'd chosen.

"What about TV and stereo?" he asked her once they were back at her place on the quai Voltaire.

"I forgot," she admitted.

"I'll take care of it tomorrow."

"I love my new bed, by the way." She liked the store he had taken her to, and once again, the prices had been reasonable and the products high-quality.

"Maybe you should become a decorator, if you don't find a job you want as a butler."

"This isn't decorating yet," he reminded her. "This is basics." But they had covered them all in a single day in a matter of hours. He had set up many houses and apartments for his employer's children.

He made a quick run for groceries for her before he left, and left her at six-thirty, having accomplished three days' work in one. She couldn't believe how fast he worked or how capable he was. And she agreed with him, he'd have her new place set up for her in no time.

He was watching French football on TV when his mother got home. He looked energized and happy, and she was pleased to see it. She had shared some very heavy information with him only days before, and she was relieved to see he didn't seem depressed about it. Maybe the truth was a relief, and if anything, it had brought them closer to each other.

"So how was the first day of school? How do you like the teacher?" she asked him, as she took off her shoes and sat down on the couch next to him. He turned to her with a big grin.

"It was fun. Ikea, Darty, we bought a bed, picked out everything for the kitchen, and bought enough tools and practical items to build a house. Vacuum cleaner, microwave, toaster. She's all set. EDF for electric, Orange for the phone and Internet, and Engie for gas."

"My God. I'll have to send you out on all my errands. I need a new iron."

"Happy to do it. She's actually very nice to work for. Quiet, respectful, polite. She doesn't talk too much, knows what she wants, makes quick decisions, and she's very organized." He wasn't used to working for women like her. She was considerably younger and more efficient than the women he'd known in his job. The marchioness led a sheltered, protected life and handled no details about the home, except selecting menus. And the Cheshires' daughters and daughters-in-law had never had jobs or taken care of themselves. And their sons were equally indulged and inefficient. Joachim had organized everything for all of them.

"Is she married?"

He had told his mother on Saturday that Olivia had no children. "No. I don't know if she has a boyfriend or not. Probably not, or she wouldn't need me. But there's nothing helpless about her. She just needed someone to do all the things she can't, and she lets me do my job without sitting on top of me to check it. It's not a butler job, but it's actually quite a lot of fun. It'll be exciting to see it all come together. I'm sort of a project manager for her move and installation."

"At least it'll keep you from reorganizing my closets again. I can't find my red sandals, and I can't reach my hats on the shelf you put in. You can organize hers now." He laughed.

They continued buying small things Olivia needed for the next two days, he introduced her to the confusing wonders of the BHV, and on Thursday he took her to his mother's favorite auction house, the Hôtel Drouot. Olivia had a ball there. It was a treasure hunt in fifteen auction rooms, with new auctions every two days. Forty-five auctions a week. They placed bids on two very handsome leather chairs, and a white lacquer chest for her bedroom. On Friday, she found out that her bids were successful. She had had a very enjoyable week, and Ikea was installing her new kitchen on Monday, the same day the bed was due to arrive. The owner didn't mind her having things delivered or installed a few days early. She wasn't rushing to move in. She wanted to set everything up first, so she wouldn't be moving in to chaos. She had found very decent dining room chairs at Ikea. They were exact copies of some she had and liked in her New York apartment, for a fraction of the price.

On Saturday, they went to the flea market together, and walked for hours poking through shops and stalls in the various markets that were a jumble of junk and some beautiful objects all thrown in together. All of it was negotiable. She found a very handsome coffee table, in good condition, two more vintage leather chairs that would look well with the first ones she'd bought at auction, and two paintings she loved. One for the bedroom, and a good-sized one for the living room. Joachim liked them too, and complimented her on her choices.

"I think even my mother would love them," he said when they stopped for a cup of coffee. They had walked for miles.

"Does she enjoy art?" Olivia responded.

"She's an art expert," he said quietly. "And my stepfather was an expert at the Louvre. He did the authentication of all their new acquisitions. That's how they met. My mother was a curator at the National Museum of Fine Arts in Buenos Aires. He got her a job at the Louvre when she first got here after they married. And then she went to work for a different organization. They work in conjunction with the Louvre at times. She researches stolen paintings to track down the rightful owners."

"How interesting. That must be fascinating."

"It is, and heartbreaking sometimes. She works on finding the art that was stolen by the Nazis and returns it to the heirs of the original owners, whenever possible." He was even more proud of her now that he knew why she did it. Olivia looked at him for a moment over their coffee, sitting on two chairs outside one of the flea market stalls.

"If it's not rude to ask, how did you end up a butler?"

"By accident. I finished high school when we came from Argentina. I got my baccalauréat degree and went to the Sorbonne. I was studying art and literature, and feeling lost. I have a brother I was very close to, and he stayed in Argentina. Nothing made sense or was fun without him, so I dropped out of school and did odd jobs for a while. I saw an ad for a butler school in London and signed up for six months on a lark. And much to my surprise, I liked it and found my calling. I could use a variety of skills and learned many new ones. Being a butler is both hands-on and a managerial job. I like the combination. It requires precision and perfectionism, which is a constant challenge. And resourcefulness. I took a job with an earl, who lost everything a year later, and then I got the job with the Marquess of Cheshire. I thought I'd stay a year or two and go back to Paris. Fast-forward the film, sixteen years later, I'd wound up as the head butler within a few years and stayed until they both died. It became addictive. I liked my job, and I loved them. I never saw the time fly by. And now here I am, starting over, or I will be when I go back. I would have stayed if they hadn't died, and the houses weren't up for sale. It won't be easy to start again," he said with a wistful look. "This is a nice change of pace in the meantime. I'm enjoying it," he said, and she nodded.

"I am too. It's been a good week. I'm in the same boat you are. I'm not quite sure what I'm going back to when I go back to work. I put my heart and soul into my decorating magazine for ten years, all for nothing. I don't know whether to go to work for someone else, another magazine, or start something of my own again. It was a beautiful magazine, but this isn't a good time for magazines. The Internet is putting them out of business. Mine was too high-quality and too elitist."

"I'm not so sure it's a good time for butlers either. The great houses are all being sold to people who don't know how to run them or what a butler is, and don't want one, or they're being run as commercial ventures, for tourists or conventions, or rented out for TV shows. There are only a handful of great houses left, and no one gives those jobs up. They stay there until they keel over. I slowly became obsolete while I was working for the Cheshires. It's a very special kind of life. It doesn't suit most people. And you give up your personal life to do it. The two aren't really compatible."

"A lot of jobs are like that," she said thoughtfully. "I gave up my personal life for work too. I thought it was worth it. Now I wonder. One day you wake up, years have gone by, and you're alone. And if the business fails, then what do you have? Not much." Or nothing at all, in her case. That was how she felt now.

"It sounds like you did the right thing coming here and doing something different for a while." She nodded agreement.

"And in a year, then what? I have absolutely no idea what I'll do after this," she said seriously.

"You'll find something. Or it will find you. My

mother is very philosophical about those things. She's had a remarkable life. She fell into the job she has now, and loves it. She's been doing it for twenty-five years, and she works as hard at eighty-one as she did at forty or fifty. I think caring about it as much as she does keeps her young. I loved my job too."

"So did I." She smiled at him as they both stood up, ready to explore the antiques stalls again. "I try to think of it as chapters in my life. Or maybe it's a trilogy of some kind. A ten-year chapter is now over. Now I'll just have to see what the chapters are about in future. I agree with your mother. It will find you."

"And in the meantime, thank you for the job, Ms. White. I mean that sincerely. I was driving my mother crazy, reorganizing her closets. She's grateful to you." Olivia laughed as they walked into the next stall, where she found another painting. It was a graceful ballerina that looked like a Degas, and she bought it for her bedroom. It made her think of the work his mother did, which touched her profoundly.

She asked him about his brother in Argentina on the drive back to the city. "Did you see your brother on your recent trip to Buenos Aires?"

He took a long time to answer. He kept his eyes on the road when he did. "I haven't seen him in twenty-five years," he said in an even tone, and she didn't press him about it. She could see that it was a painful subject. He was a man of many facets and contradictions. His choice of working as a butler seemed like an odd one, but he seemed to like it. And he was good at what he did. He was fast, bright, resourceful, and efficient, and he seemed to have a wealth of knowledge on many subjects. She wondered what the story was with his brother but didn't ask him. It was clearly off-limits, and she had no desire to pry. She had her own taboo subjects and painful family secrets.

They rode back to Paris in comfortable silence, with her new acquisitions in the van. They dropped them off at the new apartment on the way back to the quai Voltaire.

"Do you have enough food for tonight?" he asked her, and she smiled and said she did.

"Thank you for a fun afternoon, and for giving up your Saturday. Have a nice day off tomorrow," she said, and closed the door of the van. She waved as he drove away, and went upstairs to make more lists of things she needed for the apartment. They were installing her new kitchen on Monday. They were moving ahead at full speed. She was well aware that she couldn't have done it without Joachim. Their respective needs had dovetailed nicely. She was filling a gap for him, and he was helping her set up her new life in Paris. The timing for each of them was perfect, and just what they needed. In a way, it was almost too good to be true. And very exciting to have a beautiful new apartment in Paris.

Olivia met Joachim at the new apartment on Monday. He was overseeing the installation of the Ikea kitchen. The workmen were making an appalling mess, but they seemed to know what they were doing. They were leaving fingerprints everywhere, and she cringed when she saw the chaos in the kitchen.

"Don't worry. It'll be perfect when they're finished. Their installers are magicians," he reassured her. It was too soon to tell, and she was interviewing three cleaning women that morning. Two of them were very young, and only had short-term references. The third one was slower, older, but had worked for twenty years for the same woman who had recently died. So she had no reference, but she was immaculate and Olivia liked her. She looked trustworthy, and as though she knew her job. She was fifty years old and had worked for the Plaza Athénée before her long-term job. Olivia's instincts told her she was the right one, and she hired her, to start immediately. They had managed with Alphonsine's minimal English and Olivia showing her what needed to be done. And the agency had provided translations of her references. Olivia wanted the whole apartment scrubbed before she moved in. Alphonsine promised to start the next day. Olivia told Joachim over lunch that she had hired her.

"You didn't like the younger ones?" he questioned her.

"Neither of them has stayed in a job longer than six months and that didn't look good to me. Alphonsine worked for twenty years for the same woman. She just died so she has no reference, but she looked spotless and seemed serious." He nodded.

By the end of the day, the kitchen was fully installed, and looked perfect other than the mess everywhere, which the new maid could deal with the next day. Joachim was very pleased with the kitchen installation, and Olivia was happy with it too, and liked the way it looked. The whole kitchen was lacquered white.

He drove her back to the seventh arrondissement, and then left for the night. He said he had promised to make dinner for his mother.

"She doesn't eat well if she doesn't have anyone to eat with. She says it bores her."

"My mother was that way too, and once her mind started slipping, she couldn't remember if she had eaten or not. I had to have nurses for her eventually. Losing your mind is a terrible thing." Olivia had noticed that he was cool with her when they met again on Monday. She wondered if her mention of his brother had made him retreat. She had inadvertently touched a nerve, but by the end of the day he had warmed up again.

"What did your mother do before that?" he asked her.

"She was a book editor. Eventually, she only edited one very famous author." She looked out the window, thinking about George, and their cowardice at not telling her the truth before he died so she could speak to him about it, and his selfishness in taking over her mother's life, stealing her youth, and feeding her addiction to him. She didn't mention any of it to Joachim. He could sense there was more to the story. They each had their secrets. But they weren't friends, or just a man and a woman. She was his employer, so different rules applied, and there were only certain questions one could ask. He had very careful boundaries, and never crossed them.

For the rest of the week, deliveries arrived. Her new bed came, they sent the old one to the owner's storage and threw away the old mattress. Alphonsine cleaned the bathrooms and kitchen until they shone. She scrubbed the floors after the deliveries and used a special leather cream on the four vintage chairs. The new Ikea dining chairs improved the dining room, and made the existing table look better. And the coffee table from the flea market looked handsome in the living room. The Ikea cupboards they'd bought turned the second bedroom into an efficient dressing room and storage space.

Joachim hung the three new paintings she had bought, and spent a whole day installing light fixtures. He was good with his hands and was undaunted by anything they needed to do. And Olivia was thinking about shipping the few pieces she'd kept of her mother's furniture to Paris from the storage facility where she had sent them. She didn't need them in New York, and she thought they'd look well in the new apartment. She gave Joachim the relevant information to research the shipping. There was nothing he couldn't do.

Within two weeks the apartment was well set up, and livable. She began packing what she had at the apartment on the quai Voltaire, and Joachim moved it all to the new place, and she gave up the temporary apartment a week early.

She bought fresh flowers and set them around the new apartment and unpacked all her things. Joachim asked her if she wanted a safe, and she hadn't thought of it, and told him it was a good idea. He arranged to have one installed, but they were booked solid for two weeks. They said there had been a number of burglaries in the sixteenth recently, and the demand for home safes had increased. Olivia didn't own any major jewelry, just a few pieces that had been her mother's, and she was going to use the safe for them, and whatever documents she brought with her.

She'd been sleeping at the new apartment for a week when she decided to get out of her work clothes and put on a decent outfit for a change. She put on black slacks, a white cashmere sweater, and high heels. Joachim noticed it but didn't comment. It wasn't his place. She was a strikingly pretty woman, and close to his age, which made it all the more inappropriate for him to remark on her looks. He knew his place and he always respected the limits. He saw her walk into her bedroom and come back with a strange look on her face, as though puzzled by something.

"Is everything all right?" he asked her in a businesslike tone. It was his job to notice what went on around him, and he had a sharp eye and a keen awareness of people's moods and reactions. He could see that Olivia was upset about something.

She had gone into her bedroom to put on a pair of pearl earrings and the diamond band her mother had worn as her pseudo wedding ring from George. It was the first time Olivia had wanted to wear it, but when she opened the small jewel case where she'd been keeping them, it was empty, and neither the ring nor the earrings were there. She'd been keeping the jewel case in her underwear drawer until the installation of the safe. She opened the case several times, as though her mother's jewelry would materialize, and it didn't. Alphonsine was busy scrubbing the bathroom, and she didn't want to accuse her of anything. There had been many workmen in the house, and deliveries, and she hadn't checked the jewel box since she'd moved. If someone had stolen her mother's jewelry, she had no idea who it could be, and she didn't want to accuse anyone unfairly.

She walked out to the kitchen and poured herself a glass of water. Joachim walked in, and looked at her closely. She seemed near tears and looked distracted.

"I don't want to pry," he said quietly, "but I get the feeling something's wrong. Is it anything I can help you with?" She didn't answer at first, not sure what to say. And if they'd been stolen, he could have done it too. He was at the apartment more than anyone else. She didn't think he was a thief, but she didn't really know him. They were all strangers to her. And for all she knew, he could have written his glowing reference from the new Marquess of Cheshire himself. Who knew if it was real? She had never called to check his references. She trusted him, perhaps wrongly so.

"No, I'm fine," she said to him, and left the kitchen, and he noticed that Alphonsine had emerged from the bathroom and was watching her closely too. He had seen incidents like it before, and could guess what had happened, or thought he could.

At the end of the afternoon, he spoke to Olivia again. "Are you missing something?" he asked her. She hesitated and then shook her head. How did he know? Except if he had taken the jewelry.

"No, it's fine. My drawers are still a mess since

the move." But he already knew her better than that and was trained to learn his employers' habits. Nothing she touched was ever a mess. She was an extremely tidy person, and a creature of habit. She always put things back in the same place. Too trusting perhaps, but definitely not messy.

He nodded, and didn't insist, but she didn't speak to him again before he left. He could see distrust in her eyes when she said good night.

Olivia suddenly felt surrounded by strangers and people she didn't know if she could trust. There was no doubt in her mind now. Someone had taken her mother's jewelry. A workman, a delivery person, maybe Joachim, although she hated to think that. She liked him and had trusted him implicitly. Alphonsine didn't seem like a likely candidate. She looked like an honest woman, and a sweet little grandmother. Olivia would have sworn it wasn't her.

She had a sleepless night over it, and felt terrible. Her mother had loved her pearl earrings and wore them almost every day, and the ring from George was her most treasured possession. George had rather sarcastically called it her "unwedding ring" but her mother had loved it. Olivia had taken it off her finger before they buried her. And now her mother's treasures were gone, forever. She should have put them in a vault in the bank, but she had been careless and too trusting.

She looked tense and unhappy the next morning when Joachim came to work. He had spoken to his mother about it the night before, disturbed by the expression on his new employer's face. He had been through it before, but they were in such close quarters and she seemed so alone in the world that it pained him for her.

"She thinks I stole something from her," he told his mother over their dinner in the kitchen.

"How do you know? Did she accuse you of it?"

"She didn't have to. I've seen that expression before. She looked panicked, and she didn't look me in the eye when I left."

His mother looked worried. She didn't want it to be an unpleasant experience for him, or end badly. "Is it something of great value?"

"I have no idea. Maybe not. But it's something she cares about deeply. She was almost in tears. And she looked as though she suddenly couldn't trust anyone. She's among strangers in a foreign country. I feel sad for her."

"I remember when Francois's cleaning woman took a gold locket I had with pictures of you and Javier in it, as babies. It disappeared right after we arrived from Buenos Aires. I looked everywhere and it didn't turn up."

"Did it ever?" Joachim asked, worried.

"Francois made a huge fuss and threatened to call the police. And he very cleverly offered a huge reward to the person who would find it. It turned up the next day, mysteriously under a chair where I had looked, and the maid claimed the reward.

We fired her almost immediately. But I got the locket back." Joachim nodded. He had done similar things in the Cheshires' homes with the staff, usually with good results, but not always. He just hoped he could bring about a good outcome for Olivia. He hated seeing her so unhappy and worried. And he didn't want her thinking it was him.

When he got to work the next morning, he watched her face carefully, and waited until they were alone in the kitchen. Then he spoke to her in a low voice so no one could overhear, although Alphonsine's English wasn't fluent, but just in case. For all they knew, she spoke better English than she let on.

"I know you've lost something, and you don't know who to suspect and who to trust right now. I'd like to help you with it. Is it something of great value?" he inquired. She hesitated and then shook her head and decided to trust him.

"It's of great sentimental value. They were my mother's two favorite pieces of jewelry. I had them in a small jewel case in a drawer. I was going to put them on yesterday and the case was empty. It could have been anyone. I haven't opened the case since I moved, and there have been a million people in and out of the apartment." He was relieved that she was telling him. He thought it was a good sign. She had to trust someone, or her life would be untenable, and he was glad she had chosen to confide in him.

"Let me handle it. Trust me. I know we don't

know each other well, and you have no reason to trust me. I'd like to handle this in a way that I think will get results."

"Are you going to accuse someone directly?"

"I don't think I'll have to. And with any luck, you'll get your jewelry back. It's worth a try." She nodded, and for some unknown reason, she thought he was being honest with her, although she had been almost certain it was him, the day before.

"Come with me," he said quietly, and she followed him to her bathroom, where a plumber was working on a leak under the sink. Joachim had called him to do some repairs and adjustments. He asked the plumber to go to the living room and wait for them there. He then went to Olivia's bedroom, where Alphonsine was making the bed. She was coming every day while they got settled. She looked frightened and startled when they walked in together, and Joachim used a harsher tone with her, and told her to go to the living room. There was a window washer hanging out the dining room window, and Joachim sent him to join the others and then he and Olivia walked into the living room and sat down.

Joachim was wearing an odd expression and used a tone that Olivia hadn't heard from him before. He looked and sounded harsh, merciless, to the point of frightening. He suddenly looked like the head butler, a man to fear, or the police. He eyed each of the three people seated across from them, and then he spoke, as Olivia observed their faces. The plumber looked confused, the window washer clearly had no idea why he was there, and Alphonsine looked terrified and was shaking in her seat.

"I have a very disappointing announcement to make to all of you. There has been a theft in the house, of two pieces of Madame White's jewelry. Of course, I have no choice here, I am obliged to notify the police. You may not leave the apartment before they arrive. They will want to speak to each of you, and probably fingerprint you. We cannot take this matter lightly, and the insurance company will want to question you too. I will be very grateful to any of you who have information on the theft, if you saw anything unusual, or saw someone take them. If the items reappear, there will be a reward to any of you who find them. Five hundred euros, and no further questions will be asked. In the meantime, and until the items are returned, we will wait for the police." There was shocked silence in the room, as Olivia waited with them, and Joachim disappeared, presumably to call the police. She was sure he would, in order to terrorize the three suspects further.

Joachim returned a few minutes later to tell them that the police would be with them shortly.

"Can I go back to finish the windows?" the window washer wanted to know, and Joachim said he could. The plumber went back to the leak under the sink, and Joachim and Olivia walked into the kitchen. Alphonsine had been crying when they left the room.

They were sitting in the kitchen, talking quietly, when Alphonsine rushed in, shrieking that she had found the missing items. She said they had been swept under the corner of the rug, and she hadn't seen them previously. "Someone must have dropped them," she said. Her hand was shaking violently, as she held them out to Olivia.

"Are those the missing items?" Joachim sounded fierce when he asked Olivia, and she nodded with tears of relief in her eyes and took them from Alphonsine.

"Thank you," she said softly, although it pained her to be grateful to a thief.

"Do I get the reward?" the maid had the nerve to ask him, and he nodded.

"Yes, you do," he said quietly, took out his wallet, and handed five one-hundred-euro bills to her. She looked pleased but still shaken, as she slipped them into her apron pocket, and left the kitchen.

The police showed up twenty minutes later, and Alphonsine had mysteriously vanished.

"She must have gone down the back stairs," Olivia said when they went to look for her and couldn't find her coat or her purse.

"She won't be back," Joachim told her. He explained the situation to the police and apologized for bringing them out for nothing. They asked if

Olivia wanted to file a report or a complaint against the maid, and she said she didn't. Alphonsine didn't have keys to the apartment, and Olivia agreed with Joachim. Alphonsine wouldn't be back, if she had to face the police. She had probably done things like it many times before, with her previous employer who was elderly, and at the hotel before that. The police had suggested that too. It was a common occurrence.

The police departed quickly, and the plumber and window washer left when they finished their work. Joachim called the safe company and told them it was an emergency and they had to come that afternoon. They agreed to, for an additional charge. Joachim reported Alphonsine to the agency. They apologized profusely, and promised to find better candidates, and said they would take her off their books. Olivia was smiling when he hung up, and was wearing her mother's earrings and ring. She had mixed feelings about the ring, but her mother had loved it, and it was pretty.

"Thank you. I'm sorry I was short with you yesterday," she said to him. "I didn't know what to think."

"It's all right. You're among strangers here. You don't know me. I'm sorry it happened. I had a bad feeling about her. She was a little too sweet."

"You can hire the next one. And don't forget to list her reward with your expenses. And by the way, Joachim, you're pretty damn scary when you put your head butler face on." The look on his face, and his tone, had been worthy of Carson after all. She smiled when she said it.

"I only do that when absolutely necessary," he said, laughing. "It always works."

"You scared me."

"I scared her. That was the important thing. Amazing how she had the cheek to collect the reward. But she's gone, and she won't be back. She thought you'd be an easy victim. Be careful, Ms. White, and I'll keep a closer eye in future."

"Thank you," she said quietly, ashamed that she had thought he was the thief. She knew now that he was trustworthy, and she had at least one person to protect her among strangers. She had an ally. She was grateful to have her mother's jewelry back, and that Joachim was an honest man. She was glad to have a butler after all.

Chapter 8

They worked hard on the apartment, and Olivia bought more than she expected to. Joachim knew Paris well, and took her to interesting places where she found things she liked. It was taking shape nicely and had a distinctive style to it. She liked vintage pieces and antiques, and mixed them well with contemporary ones. She had a great eye for what would bring a room to life, after all her experience with her decorating magazine. Her new home had style and personality. Some of it was very subtle, as she was. The more Joachim got to know his new employer, the more he liked her. She was honest and straightforward. They respected each other. He wasn't overly personal, nor was she, and they were together constantly, while she continued to decorate the apartment. She often asked his opinion before she bought something. He never volunteered it when she didn't ask. Some purchases she was sure of the minute she saw them, others she was less sure of. And some were frankly awful, or very odd, but somehow, she made them work when she got them home, which always surprised him. She had a good eye and very definite taste.

He usually left work by dinnertime, but occasionally he stayed late to help her work on a project she couldn't do alone. She had a passion for antique books and had bought a whole collection of vintage fashion and decorating books in an auction at Drouot. She found innumerable treasures there.

He stayed late one night to put together a bookcase and help her put the books away. She could have done it herself, but it was easier with his help. The bookcase was ten feet tall, dwarfed by the high ceilings, and she was up and down a tall ladder all night. It was ten o'clock when they finished, and neither of them had eaten. They were too engrossed by what they were doing, and he could tell that she didn't want to stop and would have been teetering on the high ladder all night alone in the apartment, so he stayed. He offered to make dinner when they finished. They both admitted they were starving. She had bought a roasted chicken at the supermarket. He made a quick bowl of pasta and she made a salad to go with it. He was an adequate cook for himself, but had never worked as a chef, and didn't want to.

They sat down at the kitchen table together. She had set it simply with colorful placemats she'd bought at one of the shops he'd taken her to. She set a bouquet of white tulips on the table. She used linen napkins and had a nice touch about the way she did things. She was very visual about her surroundings and had an eclectic style. It wasn't grand in the way he was used to, but she had a good sense for fine things, and he had learned that her home was important to her. She was having fun with the apartment.

"I used to come home from work so tired, I'd eat a salad out of a plastic box, or wouldn't eat at all," she volunteered, as he served her the simple pasta he had made with fresh tomatoes and basil. "It's lovely having time to actually sit down and do things nicely. Great pasta, by the way," she complimented him. "My mother always insisted we sit down to a proper meal." She had always set a pretty table for George, with candles and flowers on the table. She had everything ready whenever he dropped in and acted as though he was expected. She would have been the perfect wife if he'd ever married her. It still angered her that he never did.

"What was your father like?" he asked, curious about her. She talked about her mother, but had never mentioned her father. Eating together, at a late hour, after working side by side all day dropped some of the barriers between them.

"I never knew him," she said bluntly. "Or actually, I did. But I didn't know he was my father until after he died. I thought my father had died when

I was a baby." It was an odd admission to make to someone she barely knew, who was her employee. Joachim was quiet for a minute, as he digested the information.

"That must have been painful for you, when you found out about your father," he said. "I never knew mine either. He died when I was three. I only found that out recently. He left us before that. It was just me, my brother, and my mother. She remarried when I was seventeen. That's when we came to France from Buenos Aires. My stepfather was a wonderful person. I only lived with them for a few years, and then I left for England, and stayed there. It'd odd never having known your father. My mother did a good job with us for all those years before we came here. She's a remarkably strong woman."

Olivia was pensive, thinking of her own mother. "Mine wasn't. She gave up her whole life for one man. They never married. She spent every moment waiting for him, and only came alive when he was with her. She was like a ghost in a way, or a shadow. She never materialized until he was in the room. I hated it for her. It made me gun-shy about ever being dependent on a man. So I became addicted to my work instead," she said. "I suppose we all have our addictions."

He nodded, thinking about it. It explained why she wasn't married at forty-three. He had less of an excuse, other than the nature and demands of his job. He had dedicated himself to his career too, to the exclusion of all else, with the exception of occasional passing romances that he never allowed to become serious involvements. But he never let them get in the way of his work. They had that in common too.

"My mother met my stepfather when she was fifty-four," he said. "She was almost forty when she had me. He was the love of her life, so I suppose it can happen at any age. I remind her of that now when she tells me I should be married." He grinned at Olivia. It was easy opening up to her, and unusual for him. He always kept his distance, but in many ways their circumstances were similar. They were each at a crossroads in their lives, during a pause between jobs, with previous single-minded direction. Olivia seemed very vulnerable to him, and his instinct was to protect her, as he had from the dishonest maid. That was part of his job too. He had shielded the Cheshires, particularly as they got older and more fragile. He had been at his side with the marchioness when the marquess died. Their children had never been very attentive. They had grown up in boarding schools from an early age, and weren't close to their parents, except when it suited them, which wasn't often. But he supposed the same could be said of him, working in England now that his mother was alone. She never complained, and made it easy for him, and he felt guilty about it.

Olivia wondered about his brother, but didn't bring it up, despite the confessions of the evening. It had seemed so painful to him the last time it came up, when he said he hadn't seen him in twenty-five years. She assumed that they must have had a terrible falling out for that to happen. And she was impressed by his dedication, and obviously deep affection for his mother. He always spoke of her with a warm smile or a look of concern. She hadn't been as warm with her own mother. She had so hated her mother's willingness to give herself up to George until there was nothing left of her. He had always come first, above all else, even her daughter. He had destroyed her mother's life, and she had let him. She was his willing slave. Olivia still shuddered at the thought of any relationship like that. She would never let it happen to her. She would rather be alone than a slave.

Olivia and Joachim enjoyed dinner together, and the relaxed atmosphere between them. Most of the time they were too busy to talk much, and concentrated on the task at hand, whatever it was. Their dinner had led to confessions.

He had hired a new maid for her, a Portuguese girl who was hardworking and seemed honest, so far. But Olivia kept her few valuables in the safe now, at the back of one of her closets. She had learned her lesson. She even locked up her purse.

*   *   *

As she got to know him, Olivia had become aware that Joachim was a very private person, with clear boundaries. He always kept in mind that he worked for Olivia and acted accordingly, which made their conversation over dinner unusual. He never said how he spent his days off. He never talked about a girlfriend, which didn't mean he didn't have one. Because of the nature of the job, he knew more about Olivia than she did about him, which occasionally made her uncomfortable. She had never had anyone in a comparable position in her home life, or even her assistant at the magazine, although there wasn't that much to know about her, except her history, which she had never shared with anyone, but had talked about with Joachim.

It had bothered her all her life that she was illegitimate, and her mother had been the mistress of a married man. It bothered her morally, but it also made her feel less than others, and she never told the men she dated. She would have told someone she intended to marry, but she had never even come close to that. She knew that all her romantic relationships were temporary, and most of them were a dead end, for one reason or another, geographically or socially, or she just didn't think the men were good enough. Her mother had had the prejudices and snobbisms of her Boston family, who had shunned her on moral grounds for having a child out of wedlock with a married man, and punished Olivia for it by disapproving of her whenever they saw her. Even as a child she could feel their icy disapproval of her.

Her mother had never liked a single boy Olivia dated when she was younger. Later, she never bothered to introduce them to her mother. There was no point. She wasn't planning to stay with them anyway. But at least none of them were married. That was one trap she had never fallen into after watching her mother's agonizing loneliness all her life, and her pain whenever George was with his family. Holidays were days of mourning for Margaret, and became that way for Olivia too, with her mother always too depressed to celebrate anything, except when George showed up. In recent years, Olivia had spent Christmas and Thanksgiving with friends, and she no longer needed an excuse once her mother had dementia. She didn't know what day it was anyway, and holidays went unnoticed and unacknowledged. Margaret's longstanding affair had touched every area of their lives. It was almost a relief to Olivia when George died. They no longer had to wait for him to show up, and she didn't have to see her mother disappointed. But his death hadn't freed her either since Margaret never put her life back together. It was too late by then. She didn't have the energy or emotional strength to do it.

It made serious relationships seem dangerous to Olivia. They could ruin your life if you let them.

Joachim had always had the same feeling, although

his mother wasn't bitter. She was vibrant and alive, and refused to be defeated by poverty or solitude, or her losses, and things had turned out well for her in the end. It made Joachim feel that he had his whole lifetime to meet the right woman. He had never had a strong desire to have children, and he didn't have biology to contend with, as women did.

Olivia's childhood felt like a long span of gray years to her, tainted by her mother's constant depression, and later her drinking and dementia. She had no desire to inflict that on a child, although she couldn't conceive of a life like her mother's. She preferred her freedom to being tied down to anyone or anything, except her work. Being alone left her free to work as hard as she wanted, with no one to complain to her about it. It was when she wasn't working that she didn't know what to do. The free time she had in Paris was unusual for her, and she kept busy with the apartment. But she needed to meet people and find things to do. She went to museums and galleries and liked going to movies. She knew Joachim did too, but she would never have invited him to go with her. It seemed too forward. She never asked him what he did on the weekends, and he didn't say.

So she was startled after the following weekend, when he said he had been to London for two days.

"To see old friends?" she inquired, which seemed nosy even to her, but she was curious why he had gone, and suddenly worried. She had conveniently forgotten that he was still looking for a job. She had hired him for three months, and four weeks of it had already rushed by.

He was open with her about it. "I had an interview and stopped by to see the new marquess. He's expecting a bid on the Sussex estate soon. He and his wife want to buy a house in the South of France. They seem to be enjoying themselves." He had just commissioned a yacht and a sailboat in Italy. He liked living well, just not in the same way as his father had, who preferred staying on home turf.

"How did the interview go?" Olivia asked with a knot in her stomach. Quite wrongly, she knew, she felt as though she owned him now, and interviewing for another job felt like an infidelity to her. She was well aware that she had no right to feel that way. He could see how anxious she was.

"The interview went well, but it's not a job I want. It's an American film star who just bought a big manor house in England, but the lifestyle's not for me." The actor was well-known for his drug use and wild parties. He wanted a fancy English butler, and was already planning to give house parties every weekend. Joachim could easily imagine the mess that would be, with staff either dragged into it, or expected to turn a blind eye to inappropriate behavior. It was everything Joachim was determined to avoid. He was hoping to find an older couple, whose pastimes were similar to the Cheshires', but then there was always the risk that the job would be short-term if they died. What he'd had with the Cheshires had been ideal, had suited him perfectly, and the agency had already told him it would be hard to replicate.

In the meantime, he wanted to reassure Olivia. She looked panicked as soon as he'd said he had gone on an interview. "I feel obliged to at least go on some interviews," he told her, "or the agency won't take me seriously and will forget about me. But I'm very happy here, working for you." He hadn't missed living in Paris for almost twenty years, but now he was enjoying being back again, ferreting out interesting shops and galleries to take her to, and working on the apartment, which had taken shape nicely so far. "I won't surprise you, Ms. White," he said formally. "If I find a serious possibility, I'll give you plenty of warning, and I won't leave before the time we agreed on. If they want me, they'll have to wait until I complete my commitment to you." She was terrified that someone would snatch him up and hire him for a long-term job. If they had any idea how efficient he was, they would hire him immediately, and give him whatever he wanted. She had no idea what his requirements were, or his salary, for a full-time head butler's job.

"Would you consider extending your time with me, if we still have work to do?" she asked him.

"I would, but I think another two months will do it, as we planned. I think you estimated it very correctly. We might even finish before that. And I don't want to waste your money or time."

"You don't. You help me with so many things, Joachim. I don't know how I'm going to manage without you, when you leave." She was genuinely sad about it, and it hadn't happened yet. And she didn't want it to. She had grown more dependent on him than she expected to. Language was part of it, since she didn't speak French, and had only learned a few words. But more than that, he was so resourceful and intelligent, it was easy to rely on him, and they worked together so smoothly. There was never tension or dissent between them. He was so professional that even after the night he had made dinner for her and they had talked about their fathers, when he came to work on Monday, it was as though they had never spoken of them. He returned to work in his usual professional form, with no sign or mention of the confidences they had shared. He retreated back behind the lines of his boundaries.

Two days later, after his weekend in London, she came back to him and asked him to stay for three additional months, for a total of six months in her employ, and offered him a raise. He answered her on the spot.

"In theory, yes, I'll stay another three months, under certain conditions. If I find the job of a lifetime, I'll tell you and give you a decent notice, but those jobs are rare, and I don't want to pass up an opportunity that might not come again. And the second condition is that if we see that eventually I really have nothing left to do for you, that we agree to wind it down. At a certain point, you won't need me. I don't want to become useless to you, so let's see as we go along. But yes, in theory I would be very happy to stay three months longer than our original agreement. And I refuse the raise. It's a very generous offer, but it's not necessary. I'm not worth that to you. You are already paying me very handsomely for what I do, and I'm grateful for it." She was shocked when he refused the raise.

"That's not businesslike, Joachim," she chided him. "You're worth every penny of it. I'd be lost without you. I **will** be lost without you when you go. And I hope you find a wonderful job you love, just not too soon," she said sheepishly, and he smiled.

"There's no risk of that. If I'd taken the job I was offered this weekend, I'd probably wind up in jail for drug trafficking, or running an opium den." There had even been signs of it during the interview. The potential employer had offered him a joint, which he declined. And he appeared to be on coke or some form of speed or upper during the interview. He had recently been arrested in the States for possession of cocaine and crystal meth. He had adult children who were drug addicts too. "You're safe for now," he assured her, "and I'll let you know if I see any serious contenders in London. So far, there is nothing I want at all."

"I'm relieved," she said, and looked it.

A week later, she had a new project for him. She'd gotten an email from a very important American decorator, Audrey Wellington. They had met several years before when the magazine interviewed her for a cover story, and she had kept Olivia's personal email address. She was an older woman, had decorated the White House for two presidents, was a greatly respected interior designer, and had taken a liking to Olivia. They stayed in touch, she had heard about the magazine folding and that Olivia had moved to Paris right after it did. She wrote to say how sorry she was about the magazine and said how much she had always enjoyed it and read it religiously. She was coming to Paris and hoped to see Olivia while she was there. She was in her seventies, and still very active. She said she had a longtime client who wanted to redo her apartment in Paris, and she was coming on a reconnaissance mission to see what needed to be done. Olivia was happy to hear from her, answered her immediately, and said she'd love to have her over for tea. She went to find Joachim as soon as she pressed send. He was checking under her bathroom sink for another leak, and he had promised to hang another painting she had bought at Drouot. The apartment was becoming a much bigger decorating project than she had originally planned. She kept finding things that she loved, and it already felt like home.

She talked to him while his head was still under the sink. "I have a friend coming from New York. I'd love to have her over for tea. I mean, a really lovely English tea, proper tea service and all, little cucumber or watercress sandwiches. You playing butler, all of that." He stuck his head out with a smile.

"I think I can manage to 'play butler' rather well." He sounded very English when he said it and she laughed.

"I know you can. I just wanted to warn you. We can use the tea service I got at the flea market." It was a beautiful antique English silver service and she had gotten it for next to nothing. "Maybe I should go back for a tray."

"I can borrow one from my mother. She'll be happy to lend it to you. She has a nice one I got her from the silver vaults in London. You don't need to buy one."

"Thank you." She was touched and appreciated the offer. "Maybe scones and clotted cream too."

"I'll give you a sample menu. Egg sandwiches too, I assume."

"Yes, that would be perfect. I know it sounds silly, but I want to impress her. She's one of the most important interior designers in the States. Kind of a 'grande dame' and she's very chic."

"Don't worry. We'll do it up royally for her. Black suit and all." He was still wearing jeans to work every day, which made the most sense given what they were doing. His mother kept asking him if he was sure it was all right with his employer and he wasn't slipping in his standards. He promised her it was fine. "My mother will be relieved. She's been worried about my workman's clothes." He smiled. He was looking forward to doing something fancier for one of her friends. "I'll give the tea service a good polish before she comes."

"Thanks, Joachim."

Olivia heard from Audrey Wellington the following week. She called Olivia at home, on the number she had given her, and was delighted with the invitation to tea.

"Would you mind terribly if I bring a friend? I've known him for years. We're going to look at a job together. I want his advice. His name is Jean Beaulieu. He's a wonderful decorator. He does mostly yachts, but the occasional chateau." Olivia had heard of him, and said it was fine to bring him. They were coming to the apartment in two days, and Olivia rushed to tell Joachim as soon as she hung up.

"There will be three of us. She's bringing another decorator. Another very famous one, from here."

"We will impress them to death," he promised her. "It will be pure **Downton Abbey**," he said, and she laughed. She had confessed to him how much she liked the show and wondered before she met him if he would be like the butler on the show. "I will do my Carson act," he said with a grin, and had a sample menu for her half an hour later. She approved it, and she saw him polishing the tea service that afternoon. He enlisted Fatima's help, the new Portuguese girl. She was proving to be immaculate, scrupulously honest, and a hard worker. Joachim had chosen well, a lot better than she had with the ill-fated Alphonsine she had hired.

The apartment looked beautiful. Everything was in order, the wood surfaces shone. The curtains looked splendid, Olivia had arranged white flowers in a silver bowl, and bought an orchid plant for the entry hall. All her new furniture, art, and decorating touches added to the charm of the apartment, and Joachim had everything in control in the kitchen. He had brought his mother's tray, and his black formal butler's suit, which he was wearing with a perfectly tailored white shirt, a black Hermès tie, and impeccably shined John Lobb shoes. He looked strikingly handsome and like a butler in a movie when Olivia saw him.

"Carson never looked that good," she said to him, and he laughed. His tall, blond, Teutonic looks served him well, and were an asset along with his training and skills.

Audrey Wellington and Jean Beaulieu arrived five minutes later. She was visibly impressed when Joachim opened the door. She was wearing a navy-blue Chanel suit, with her still-trim figure and perfectly groomed blond French twist. She'd had two very well done facelifts over the years, and maintained them with Botox shots. She looked younger than her years, was energetic and very chic, as she sat in Olivia's new Paris living room, while Joachim served an exquisite high tea. Jean Beaulieu admired her tea service and her utterly perfect butler, as Audrey smiled at her, holding one of the Limoges cups Olivia had bought with Joachim at an auction at the Hôtel Drouot. She had gotten a service for eighteen, with only two butter plates missing.

"I was feeling very sorry for you, my dear, when I heard about the magazine. You did such a good job with it. I really enjoyed it. But now that I see you in your divine new Paris apartment, prettier than ever, **with** a most impressive butler," she added, "I don't feel sorry for you at all. In fact, I'm quite envious of you! Are you moving here?"

"I don't know yet," Olivia said. "I haven't decided. I have the apartment for a year. Everything happened at once, the magazine folded. We had to do it, we held on as long as we could. My mother died at the same time, I emptied her apartment, and now I'm here. I haven't figured out the next step yet. I'm keeping an open mind and seeing what happens."

"Well, you're certainly doing that in ideal surroundings, and well-staffed," she said, eyeing
Joachim, who had been the most dignified and professional Olivia had ever seen him. He really did
look like a butler in a movie, and his formal service
had been flawless. Then he discreetly disappeared
to the kitchen. She didn't tell Audrey that she only
had her "staff" for six months, and after that, like
Cinderella at midnight, the coach would turn into a
pumpkin and the coachmen to white mice. Joachim
would become a real butler in England again, for
someone else. But he had definitely impressed her
guests. Jean Beaulieu was a huge snob, and they
had snowed him too. He was a little younger than
Audrey, and a big deal in Europe. "I might have
a project for you if you're interested. Jean and I
looked at it this morning, and I can't take it on.
I can't run back and forth to Europe and do justice to my clients in the States. I do something in
Europe every year or two, but this one's not for me.
And Jean can't do it either."

He chimed in immediately. "I'm finishing two
boats in Holland, one in Italy, and another one in
Turkey, and a huge house in Saint-Jean-Cap-Ferrat.
I absolutely cannot take on a massive chateau on
top of that. It would kill me. And all of the boats
will launch before the summer."

"I know you're not a decorator," Audrey continued to Olivia, "but you have a great eye, wonderful taste, and this isn't a traditional job anyway. It's

for a Russian. He lives in Moscow and bought an enormous chateau less than an hour outside Paris. He's never even seen it. He wants it to look like Versailles. That's asking a lot. It needs a little reconstructive work, but it's not in terrible shape. But it needs everything, decorating-wise. The floors need to be buffed up and restored in a few places, there are marble fireplaces all over the place. You need a good curtain man. And you need more furniture than for the Ritz. But if you want to, I think you could do a terrific job with it, if it amuses you. Most decorators won't have the time. The Russians pay well, but it probably won't ever make the cover of **Architectural Digest.** They're fun to work with, but they go off in funny directions sometimes, and love flash."

"And they either pay you three times what you ask, or not at all," Jean Beaulieu added. "They never show up when you want them to. Or they don't come to see it for three years after you finish it, or sell it to a friend. They call you at four A.M. to see how it's going. I can't deal with Russian clients," Jean said, looking exasperated.

"Neither of us has the time," Audrey explained more calmly, "and maybe you don't either. If I had nothing else to do, it might be fun. I'm not taking any new clients. I have too much work from the ones I have. They keep buying houses. Now they're all moving to Florida to reduce their taxes. They're selling their houses in Mexico."

"And buying yachts," Jean confirmed. "Thank God."

"Are you interested in doing any decorating?" Audrey asked her directly. "You have the taste and the talent, but not the credentials. Most Russian clients don't care about that. I don't know why someone recommended me for the job." Audrey could be very grand at times, and she accepted another delicately trimmed egg salad sandwich from the silver tray Joachim offered her. And the tea he had chosen was delicious. The cucumbers were sliced paper thin, and the scones were the best Olivia had ever tasted. He had produced a high tea they would never forget. Olivia was very pleased with him. He had made her look fabulous to Audrey, not like someone whose business had just gone down the tubes and had left New York in defeat. She was to be envied, not pitied, which was just the effect she had wanted to achieve, and Joachim had done it for her.

"It sounds very interesting, and challenging," Olivia said, thinking about it. "I'd like to see it before I give you a definite answer."

"Of course," Audrey said, "I think it looks more daunting than it really is. With the right contractor, I think you could knock it out in under a year. The bones are there. You could stretch it out of course, but the Russian owner is very eager to have it finished. He's more interested in speed than fine craftsmanship. See what you think, and then let me know. I thought of you, because I wasn't sure what you were doing now. This might be a fun next step, and it could be an entrée into decorating here in Europe. He probably has a million friends who would hire you if he likes the results. They tend to follow each other in groups. It can be **very** lucrative," she said, lowering her voice discreetly. Olivia was more excited than she wanted to admit, but she wanted to see it first so she didn't get in over her head or start something she couldn't finish before she went back to New York.

They chatted about the New York decorating scene for a little while. Half an hour later they left. Audrey was staying at the Ritz, paid for by her client, who had a jewel box of an apartment at the Palais-Royal that she wanted freshened up. She wanted to redo all her upholstery for a bright new look. Audrey had done it years before. The client was ninety and a famous socialite in New York. She still came to Paris twice a year for the couture shows, to order her clothes, and entertain her Parisian friends.

Olivia promised to call Audrey as soon as she saw the chateau. Audrey said she'd email her all the access and alarm codes and warn the caretaker that they were coming. Olivia said she'd contact her as soon as possible and hoped to get out to see it the next day. And she thanked Audrey again for the opportunity. She was very flattered that Audrey even thought her capable of it. Maybe if it went well, decorating would be the right avenue for her in the future. She had considered it before and enjoyed it. Audrey said the chateau in question had an open budget, in other words she could spend, and charge, whatever she wanted. It was very tempting. Everyone knew that Russian clients paid well, even if their payment schedule was sometimes erratic and unpredictable, but they were very generous if the job went well.

Olivia let them out herself, and then went to the kitchen to see Joachim and compliment him on the beautiful job he had done and tell him how impressed they were.

"You made me look like a fairy princess or queen of the castle," she said. "They were very envious of me. And I might have a new project as a result. A Russian who bought a chateau just outside Paris. She's recommending me as the decorator. It sounds like a big job, but maybe it's feasible. I have to look. I want to go tomorrow." He nodded and saw no problem with that. They had no appointments for the next day. "Let's go early," she suggested, "so we have plenty of time to nose around. We can take lots of photographs," she said, looking enthusiastic.

"I'm happy for you," he said, and genuinely meant it. He was curious about it now too. She had made decorating her apartment fun for him, but the chateau sounded like it was on a very grand scale, which would be exponentially more work to repair and decorate.

He left on time that night, saw to it that Fatima

put everything neatly back in its place, with the silver in felt covers as he showed her. And he took the big silver platter home to his mother. He was pleased with the way things had gone with their first entertaining in Olivia's new apartment. It was gratifying to help her, she was so appreciative, and maybe now she'd even get a job from it. It made him feel useful, which was what he loved best about his job. He had been a butler again and had gotten high marks for it. He always did. And now Olivia had seen just a little taste of what he could do. He was happy she had. If she got a job out of it, all the better. She deserved it. He hoped he would be as lucky soon. He was beginning to miss his work, although she kept him busy and he liked working for her.

Chapter 9

Olivia and Joachim left the city at nine o'clock Monday morning as soon as he arrived for work. It took them just under an hour to get to Barbizon, even with Monday morning traffic. Joachim drove her in his car, an Audi station wagon. It was an easy drive, and the setting was pastoral enough to give one the feeling that one was in the country, much farther from Paris. It was a tiny village near Fontainebleau and the area had been known to be the home of many artists. There were several galleries still there on the main street in the town. The chateau was a few miles beyond it. Olivia had to remind herself that the new owner had never seen the place and bought it from photographs they had sent him and videos on the Internet. He had purchased it for many millions of dollars and was now planning to decorate it from a distance too. It was a strange way to do things, and Audrey had said he was going to give the person who decorated it carte blanche.

When they arrived at the address, there were huge gates between two imposing stone posts, and a small forest of trees obscured any view of the chateau, so the owner's privacy was ensured. They punched in the code and the gates swung open. There was a slightly eerie feeling as they followed the driveway. The trees were thick, and one somehow sensed that the property was uninhabited. There were stone outbuildings along the way, and more recently built stables, in contrast to the eighteenth-century chateau. The previous owner had owned racehorses. The property had been foreclosed on a year before and was sold by the bank.

Joachim was observing the property closely with a practiced eye. "They need groundskeepers," he commented. The place hadn't been kept up, and she could see that he was right.

The keys to the chateau and the stables had been delivered to Olivia by the realtor who had made the sale. When they got out of the car, and walked up the front steps, there was a keypad. They put in the code they'd been given, and then turned the big old-fashioned key, and the door creaked as it swung open. Olivia looked at Joachim.

"I feel like we're going to be attacked by ghosts," she whispered, and he smiled.

"Or something worse." The chateau hadn't been lived in or renovated in a long time, and they were glad they had come in daylight. There were no lamps or working light fixtures anywhere. The electricity had been turned off. They walked through a front hallway into a massive living room with high ceilings and a fireplace Joachim could stand up in. There were handsome ceiling beams, and carved wood paneling. You could see that the chateau had been beautiful but not for a long time. Olivia understood why Audrey hadn't wanted to take on the project. It was going to be a lot of work for someone, and would have been nearly impossible to manage from New York. It would have been hard enough from Paris, let alone Moscow, where the new owner lived. One would need to be near at hand to make constant decisions and communicate with the contractor one chose, hopefully a reliable one.

When they looked closely, they noticed the beautiful details. The main living room and several smaller ones beyond it had good proportions and many windows. The aristocrat who had built it originally must have been a very rich man, judging from the exquisite craftsmanship, carved moldings, wood paneling, and many windows. There was a wood-paneled dining room that looked like a banquet hall. She could imagine a long table running down the center of it, for fifty people or more.

"I hope he has a large family, or many friends," Joachim said. The kitchen was a huge room with nothing in it. They looked at each other and said at the same time, "Ikea!" And they both laughed. It was daunting, but not quite as overwhelming as it had looked from the outside. There were two floors of countless bedrooms, which led into one another, and seemed to turn into a maze. Many bathrooms, but probably not enough. They all needed to be modernized. The servants' rooms were on the top floor, and there were utility rooms and a vast wine cellar in the basement. Audrey was right, Olivia realized. It was going to be a huge amount of work. But she loved the idea of turning something so ancient and unloved into a beautiful home for its owners to enjoy. She could imagine house parties there, and music and dancing, exuberant meals in the great hall, and ancestral portraits that the Russian didn't own, but could buy. They went for very little at Drouot, particularly the enormous ones that would have been the right scale for a house that size. People sold their relatives for only a few hundred euros. They would add dignity to the entrance. Olivia could see many things she would do if she took the job. What the place needed was to have a lot of money thrown at it, and a good contractor. It wasn't destroyed or badly damaged, it was just very old and hadn't been lived in for a very long time.

Joachim could sense her mind going at full speed as they walked around. She jotted down a few notes and made some sketches, which he glanced at over her shoulder. And he took photographs for her with his phone. They saw a dead bat on the floor, which made her shudder.

"Oh God, I hope there are no live ones."

"They sleep in the daytime," he said to reassure her.

"That is **not** comforting." She scowled at him.

"You'd have to have the place cleaned up by a professional company before you start any work." But it all looked feasible. The windows weren't broken, the leaks didn't look recent and had been repaired, the floors needed buffing but were in decent condition when one looked closely. She looked at the views from all the windows. There were lovely trees all around the property, and orchards in the distance. After a thorough walk through the house, which took them an hour, they locked up, set the alarm again, and went to explore the stables, which were relatively modern and had been expensively built.

There was a good spot for a very large, modern pool and patio area closer to the chateau. There were guesthouses, and some cottages. It was practically a village of its own. Joachim could imagine seminars there, or a school, as many great houses in England had been transformed into for more practical use. Turning it into a vacation home for one man seemed excessive to him, and he wondered if he'd ever use it. Many of the Russians who bought property renovated it and never even came to use it. They just liked knowing they owned it and could arrive at any time. It seemed sad to Olivia to treat it that way, and if she did take the project on, she hoped he would spend time there and enjoy it. Otherwise, it seemed like a waste to her too.

After they had seen the house and the stables, they walked around for a little while in the overgrown grass. She stumbled over a few hidden rocks.

"The gardening alone will cost a fortune here," Joachim said from experience. "They'll need a dozen gardeners, or at least ten good ones. The Cheshire property in Sussex is about this size, which is why the children don't want to keep it. It's too much upkeep and expense for them. It would break my heart if a Russian winds up buying that too. The marquess kept it in such good order for his heirs. I don't think it ever occurred to him that his children might sell it. I always thought they would. They never had the passion for the land that he did. His family had worked for generations to keep the estate intact. That will all change now. Only billionaires and foreigners want these properties now, and can afford them." Some of the British families gave tours of their homes, and treated them as paying tourist attractions in order to be able to maintain them, but the French had allowed almost anyone to buy them, and often had no choice. Americans had bought them for a while. Then the buyers from Russia and the Middle East moved in, with unlimited money to spend, and more recently Chinese buyers.

"What are you thinking?" he asked her, as they walked slowly back to the car.

"That it's a huge project. Audrey was smart not to take it on."

"And you?" He could see a gleam in her eye, and a distant look as she mulled it over, trying to remember everything they'd just seen, and he had taken dozens of photographs for her to study when she got home.

"I don't know," she said, as she got into the car. "I'm tempted to do it. It's such a challenge and I have nothing else to do here."

"It could take you two or three years, if the workers run into roadblocks or hidden problems."

"Money is no object to the owner, but he wants it done fast."

"I suppose if you pay enough, you can get people to work faster," Joachim said cautiously, but that wasn't always true. And the quality of the workmanship might suffer as a result. "It's a huge commitment, of your time and his money." She nodded agreement and they left the property in silence. She thought about it all the way back to Paris, and called Audrey when she got home.

"So? What do you think?" Audrey asked her.

"It's not beautiful now, but it could be."

"I thought that too," Audrey confirmed. "Most

people can't see it. He probably got it for a fairly decent price because of that. He wants an answer," she told Olivia. "And just for the record, my feelings won't be hurt if you don't do it. I gave you the opportunity, but I have no investment in whether you do it or not."

"I love the challenge," Olivia said in an undervoice, and before she could stop them, like unruly birds, the words flew out on their own. "I'll do it," she almost whispered, and then said it with more conviction. "I'll do it. I'm probably crazy and I might regret it, but I would love to try to make it into something wonderful."

"I can understand that," Audrey said. "You're a lot younger than I am. It makes a difference. A project like that would probably kill me, especially with everything else I'm doing. My hat's off to you, if you take it on. You could never have done it if you still had the magazine to run," she reminded her, which made her freedom now seem like more of a gift than a defeat.

"I know. And right now, I'm between jobs or careers or whatever I'm going to do. If I'm ever going to try my hand at something like this, now is the time."

"You could try your hand at something smaller," Audrey reminded her. "Something more bite-size. That chateau is one hell of a big bite. But it could launch you on a new and very lucrative career." She liked Olivia and wanted to help her.

"That's what makes it exciting," Olivia said, and thanked her for the referral.

"I'll pass the word on to Moscow. He has a designer now. He'll be very pleased."

"I am too," Olivia said simply. She was still glowing when she went to the kitchen to find Joachim. He knew the moment he saw her. Her eyes were alight and looked like emeralds, and she was smiling.

"I smell trouble coming," he said, laughing. "In the form of a three-hundred-year-old chateau. Am I right?"

She nodded with an impish, mischievous look that made him laugh harder. "I think I can really make it into something beautiful."

"You probably can," he said. He had great faith in her, even after the little he'd seen. She had vision and talent, and energy, but he wondered if she had any idea how much work would be involved. She shocked him then with a question she hadn't dared ask him so far.

"If they hire me to do the project, will you help me?" He stood very still when she asked him. He wanted to turn her down flat, but he didn't. He just stood there, looking shocked.

He didn't know what to say at first. There was the obvious answer, and the one she wanted to hear, that he would. "I'll tell you what, I'll help you until I get a real job as a butler and go back to England."

She mulled it over and then nodded. "That's fair enough. Then I'll just have to finish it before you find a job. Or keep you locked in the dungeon. There must be one."

"I didn't see one," he said, smiling. He still couldn't believe she was going to do it. One woman, alone. She wasn't a contracting company, or an architect, or a licensed designer. She was just going to do it and figure it out as she went along. "Well, we'll have our work cut out for us now." And he thought they were finished with her apartment.

"First, I have to get an agreement from him, and negotiate what he'll pay me."

"It should be a lot. Don't settle for too little," he advised her. "He can afford to pay you well, if he bought a place like that."

"I hope he remembers that." She smiled at him, satisfied that Joachim would at least be there for a while. Hopefully a long while.

The Russian owner called her as soon as he got the word. He had a deep, booming voice and a strong Russian accent, and told her that he was sure she was going to do a beautiful job for him. He said he felt it in his bones and in his veins. She promised him progress reports and ongoing photographs, and he repeated what Audrey had said in blunter terms.

"You make beautiful, I pay more." He quoted an amount for a monthly payment, which staggered her. It illustrated to her how foolish she would have been to turn it down. She still looked dazed when she saw Joachim in the kitchen.

"It's official. I'm a high-end prostitute now. What

he offered to pay me is obscene." She quoted Joachim a number that she would pay him for as long as he worked on the project. She couldn't expect him to help her with it for what she was paying him for the short-term job to set up her apartment.

"Will that make me a prostitute too?" She didn't answer, and he laughed. "So be it. Why not? It's more lucrative than being a butler. We're in it now," he said, and chuckled on his way home. Life had certainly been interesting since he met Olivia White. He was a decorator's assistant now.

Chapter 10

The first payment was made on time by Nikolai Petrov on the first of the month, and she gave Joachim his portion of it. He had been interviewing contractors for her, and had already hired grounds-keepers to clear away the brush, and arborists to trim the trees. They went back to look at the house again, and she saw no major structural changes she wanted to make. It was mostly refurbishing wood paneling and boiseries. They'd polish up the floors in the end. She had to figure out what bedrooms to use, and what to turn into dressing rooms, guest rooms, and a fabulous modern gym, at the owner's request. She had two notebooks filled by the time the first check came in. And they sent the contractors' estimates to Moscow, to leave the choice to him. He picked the most expensive one, which didn't surprise Joachim, who said that to a man like Petrov, the more money he spent, the better he thought it would be, which wasn't always the case.

They had just returned home from their third visit to the chateau when Olivia got a call from her realtor in New York. She had an offer on her mother's apartment. It had been on the market for three months. It wasn't a fabulous offer, but it was respectable, and Olivia wanted to sell it. She had a small apartment of her own, and living in her mother's would have depressed her. She had already emptied it, sold what she didn't want, and put the rest in storage, so she didn't have to deal with that now. There were a few pieces of furniture in storage that she was thinking of bringing to Paris, and after thinking about it that night, she made a suggestion to Joachim the next morning.

"I have an offer on my mother's apartment," she told him. "I think I'm going to take it. And I want to bring a few pieces of furniture to Paris. Do you want to come with me for a few days and help me organize it?"

It sounded like fun to him, and a change of scenery. "I'd like that."

"I only need a few days there, but it would help me if you take care of the shipping, while I sign the papers and wrap up the apartment. It'll be a weight off my shoulders. My mother was so sad there so much of the time, especially since her . . . friend . . . died, and even before that—the place feels like bad karma to me. I want to get rid of it." He nodded, it didn't sound like a happy memory to him either.

"I haven't been to New York in a long time. I took a brief holiday there about ten years ago. I don't know the city very well," he commented.

"I'll put you up at a hotel near my apartment. I live in SoHo. There are lots of hotels there. It's downtown. My mother lived uptown, on the Upper East Side." He had a vague idea where all of it was and told his mother that night where he was going. He had told her all about the chateau too. She was intrigued by the woman he was working for. He seemed to be more of a property manager these days, or a secretary, than a butler. But he kept telling her it was only a stopgap until the agency found him a suitable job in England.

"She sounds like an interesting, enterprising woman," Liese had commented. She was busy with her own job at the moment, hot on the trail of the heirs to the Monet. She'd had one false start, but thought she was on the right track now. She'd been working on it for a long time. She never gave up until she had explored every possible avenue. Olivia struck Joachim that way too. Liese was seeing less of her son these days. His new employer was keeping him busy, but she thought it was good for him. She had wondered at first if he was attracted to her, but then decided he wasn't. It appeared to be strictly business for both of them. Although they seemed to have the same phobias, or similar ones, about close attachments. And as she had guessed at first, Olivia was a businesswoman above all. The job she was doing for the Russian billionaire sounded intriguing, and she could see that Joachim was having fun.

Olivia bought business class tickets for both of them. They sat together, and watched movies and slept on the plane, and didn't exchange much conversation. She had brought her notebooks with her and made numerous notes about the chateau on the flight.

When they landed in New York, they had to go through separate lines at immigration, since she was a citizen and he wasn't. He had gotten an ESTA visa for the trip online. The lines for foreigners were so long that an Air France ground crew member told Joachim to go through immigration with Olivia, since they were traveling together.

They were still standing in line, waiting, chatting with each other, when two huge Homeland Security officers approached them and asked to see Joachim's passport. He handed it to them, and looked very respectable, traveling in a suit and tie. Olivia was nicely dressed too. The senior of the two officers studied his passport closely, and then nodded at his partner, and addressed Joachim and Olivia.

"Come with us," they said curtly. It had never happened to Olivia before, and she had no idea why they were being removed from the line. It didn't look like some kind of ground assistance to her, it seemed more like a detour and neither of the men had been friendly. She wondered if Joachim's visa was in order.

They were led to a small office behind immigration. The officers waved them into two chairs and took Olivia's passport too. Then they left them sitting there for half an hour, and returned with two more officers, one of whom had a file in his hands. Neither Joachim nor Olivia could guess what it was about. They both looked like ordinary business people, not terrorists or smugglers.

"Why are you coming to the United States?" the senior officer asked Joachim, and Olivia thought his tone was unnecessarily harsh, since Joachim hadn't been aggressive with them, or even complained about the delay. He knew better. Customs in any country were not people to quarrel with, and he never did.

"I'm here to assist my employer," he said simply.

"And who is your employer?" one of the other officers asked.

"Olivia White." He pointed to her.

"What are you assisting her with?"

"I'm going to help her ship some furniture to Paris."

"What kind of furniture?"

"I don't know. I've never seen it." Joachim remained calm and polite.

"Where is it located?"

Olivia spoke up then, and she had a slowly forming knot in her stomach. She had a feeling that this was about more than her mother's furniture. And why had they singled Joachim out? "The furniture was my mother's. She died recently. It's at Franklin Storage on the Lower East Side. I'm sending it to Paris, and I asked Mr. von Hartmann to help me. Is there a problem?" The agent didn't answer her question.

"What is his job as your employee?" he fired at her.

"He's my butler," she said, sure that it sounded odd to them, it did to her too.

"And what does he do?"

"It's a temporary position. He helped me move into a new apartment in Paris."

"And what do you do?" they asked her.

"I'm currently unemployed. I owned and ran a magazine that went out of business a few months ago. I'm between jobs at the moment. I'm doing some freelance decorating in Paris. Mr. von Hartmann is my assistant." They stepped out of the room and conferred in whispers for a minute and then returned and focused on Joachim again.

"What do you do as a regular job?"

"I'm a trained butler. I've been employed by the Marquess and Marchioness of Cheshire for sixteen years. The marchioness recently died, and I accepted a temporary position with Ms. White in Paris, as she described." There was a deadly calm about Joachim. He refused to let them rattle him, and if they had, it didn't show, despite their decidedly aggressive tone as they fired questions at him. The impression they gave was that they didn't believe him.

"You're traveling on an Argentine passport," they said accusingly. They had gotten their information from the manifest. The passenger list of all flights into the United States was carefully checked against the FBI's No Fly List before they were given clearance to take off. Passengers on the list were removed from the plane before departure or sent back to the country of origin when they landed. And those on a questionable list were interrogated on arrival, as they were doing with Joachim.

"I was born in Argentina. I'm a dual national, with French citizenship as well, and I have legal residency in England, where I work." They flipped through his passport and looked at the stamps in it without comment for several minutes.

"You were recently in Argentina. Why?"

"I hadn't been back in twenty-five years, and I wanted to see it again. After my previous employer's death, I had the time." His answers were straightforward and honest, but Olivia noticed that he was perspiring, and so was she. The room was small and hot, the lights were bright, and there were six of them in it, she and Joachim and the four Homeland

Security officers. She was nervous, and frightened, and hoped she didn't faint, which wouldn't look good to them.

"Did you see relatives in Argentina when you were there?"

"No, I didn't. I was there for a week, and then I went back to Paris, where I'm currently staying with my mother."

One of the officers who hadn't spoken up yet addressed Joachim in a surly tone. "Is she your girlfriend?" he asked, pointing at Olivia, and Joachim looked shocked, and wondered if they were trying to trip him up.

"No, she's not. She's my employer."

"Are you sure?"

"Absolutely."

"Have you had sex with her?" the officer asked him right in front of Olivia, and she blushed and looked shocked.

"No, I have not. May I ask why you're asking us these questions?"

"You can ask, but we don't have to answer. We'll get to that later." Joachim guessed that there was a reason for it, but he couldn't guess what it was. "Is the name on your passport an alias?"

"No, it's not. It's my legal name." He was careful not to say he was born with it, now that he knew his mother had changed their name to his grandmother's maiden name when his father left them, and his grandfather was arrested for war crimes.

There was no way these people would ever understand that. And it was none of Olivia's business.
This was humiliating enough, without adding to it.

"Have you ever been arrested for drug trafficking,
or smuggling?"

"No, I haven't. I've never been arrested."

"Have you been in prison?"

"No, I have not." At the last few questions, he
began to suspect what it might be about, but he was
not going to ask them any questions or volunteer
any information.

They left them alone again then. This time for
an hour. They had been in the small, airless room
for almost two hours by then, with no sign of re-
lenting, and Olivia wondered if they were going
to put them back on a plane to Paris, and not let
them into the country. But she had no idea why.
As the minutes ticked by, she began to wonder if
there was something dangerous in Joachim's past
that he hadn't told her. Nothing like this had ever
happened to her before. They avoided talking to
each other while they waited, not knowing if
the room was bugged and who was listening, or
watching them.

The officers periodically drifted back into the
room to repeat some of the same questions and got
the same answers. And they kept an eye on them
through a two-way glass window the entire time.

When they had been there for four hours, Olivia
was feeling sick, and she was wondering what was

going to happen to them, and if they would be arrested. She was wondering if Joachim had brought drugs with him. Maybe there was a whole side of him she didn't know. Anything was possible, and there had to be a reason for the interrogation they were being subjected to.

A fifth officer joined them then in plainclothes. He was more polite than the others, and he ignored Olivia while he honed in on Joachim, and sat very close to him, to unnerve him.

"Why are you traveling under an alias?" was his first question.

"I'm not. Joachim von Hartmann is my true name."

"No, it's not," he accused, never taking his eyes off Joachim's for a second. "Isn't your name **Javier** von Hartmann? Why the fake first name?" Joachim knew his guess had been right then. And this would only be the beginning.

"Javier von Hartmann is my brother. My identical twin brother. I haven't seen him in twenty-five years." The officer looked surprised by that but tried not to let it show. He glanced over his shoulder at one of the others and then back at Joachim. Olivia was staring at Joachim.

"If that's true, do you know where your brother is now?"

"No, I don't. I've heard rumors from time to time when I inquire, that he's in Colombia now, and has been there for many years. The last time I spoke to him was twenty-three years ago. My mother and I moved to Paris when I was seventeen. My brother stayed in Buenos Aires to finish school, fell in with bad associations, and disappeared. No one I know has seen him in more than twenty years. I saw him the last time when I was seventeen and spoke to him for the last time at nineteen." Joachim was fighting back tears as he said it, which he didn't want Olivia and the officers to see. Losing Javier had been the heartbreak of his life, and now his brother was still causing trouble for him.

The man in plainclothes pulled a large photograph out of a file then and threw it on the table in front of Joachim. It looked like a photograph of Joachim in prison garb, with a heavy beard. But it was the same face. Olivia could see it too, and she was shocked.

"Is this you?"

"No, it's not," Joachim said in a hoarse voice.

"If what you say is true, are you aware that Javier is a member of one of the most powerful drug cartels in South America? He has escaped from prison twice. Our agents have died at his hands."

"I'm not aware of it, and I'm sad to hear it, but I'm not surprised. I think he was pulled into whatever he's doing by some very bad people, and he's one of them now. Neither my mother nor I have heard from him in all these years."

"How do you know—and how do I know that this photograph isn't you? It's a great story, about an identical twin. Maybe that's you," he said with his face an inch away from Joachim's.

"I know it isn't," Joachim said quietly. "We are not exactly identical, we are what's called mirror twins. We have the same marks on opposite sides." He gently picked up the photograph and pointed to a black spot on the subject's forehead. "My brother has a dark mole on the left side of his forehead, I have the same mark on my right side." He pushed back the hair at his hairline then and showed them the mole. All the officers stared at the photograph and then at Joachim's head. The evidence was there, plain to see. "He has another mark on his shoulder, a small birthmark. You can see it in the photograph, in the undershirt he's wearing. I have the same one on the opposite shoulder." Without being asked, he took off his tie, unbuttoned his shirt, slipped it off his shoulder and showed them. There was dead silence in the room, and in spite of the four hours of terror they'd just been through, Olivia felt sorry for him. It was terrifying, humiliating, and heartbreaking all at once.

"The only good news in what you've told me," Joachim said quietly, "is that if you are searching for him, and you thought I was Javier, then he must still be alive. I haven't been certain of that in years. Although what he's doing and the choices he has made are hardly something to celebrate, but at least his colleagues haven't killed him yet. That's something, I suppose. Although he has been dead to my mother and me for many years."

The five men left the room and conferred again. They took the photograph with them. Joachim didn't look at Olivia or say a word, and neither did she. She had no idea what to say. She couldn't even be angry with him, and she remembered easily when he told her that he had a brother in Argentina that he hadn't seen in twenty-five years. It was his mirror twin.

The man in plainclothes entered the room again ahead of the others and spoke harshly to Joachim, probably to cover his own embarrassment. He didn't apologize, instead he was aggressive with him.

"We could send you back to Paris if we wanted to. We can put you on the next plane. Your twin brother is on our list of people who are not allowed to enter the United States. We've checked while you were here, under the name of Joachim von Hartmann. You have no criminal history." And the photographs spoke for themselves, by how they matched the marks on Joachim's body. "Keep it that way. If your brother contacts you while you're in the United States, you have an obligation to report it to us, and his whereabouts, if you are aware of them. You're free to go," he said and stormed out, obviously frustrated. He thought he had caught a prize but wound up with an innocent man, and made a fool of himself.

One of the officers stayed to lead them back through immigration and customs and left them there. Their luggage was still sitting next to the carousel, and no one said anything more to them. Joachim and Olivia left the terminal. She thought her legs were going to buckle under her. They hadn't even offered them a sip of water in four and a half hours. Once outside the terminal, Joachim hailed a cab for them, and helped her in. She gave the driver the name of the hotel where Joachim would be staying and told the driver there would be a second stop after that, and then she heard Joachim's voice next to her.

"I can't even begin to tell you how sorry I am, Olivia. They put you through hell, because of my brother."

"I'm sorry for you too," she said quietly. "I didn't know you had a twin, you just mentioned a brother." It was the first time Joachim had called her by her first name, but in the circumstances, it seemed appropriate. He had been sure for the first four hours that they would be arrested, although it had taken him a while to link it to Javier.

"He's a terrible person, as you just heard. I used to love him more than anyone on earth, even more than my mother. There is poison in his veins. He's been dead to us for all these years. He broke my mother's heart, and mine." She felt deeply sorry for him when she saw the look on his face, and tears in his eyes.

"You have each other," she reminded him, and he nodded, and finally had the courage to look at her.

"I am so, so, so sorry for what I just put you through. I never expected something like this to happen or I wouldn't have come with you."

"You couldn't know. We both need a good night's sleep and we'll feel better tomorrow." She didn't want to talk about it now, but she was suddenly afraid of him, and the baggage he carried with him. What if his brother found them and killed somebody, or kidnapped her, or killed Joachim? It was so enormous that she couldn't absorb it yet. They were silent on the drive into the city. She lay her head back against the seat and closed her eyes. Joachim looked at her and didn't speak. When they got to the Standard hotel in SoHo, he got out, and said the same words again.

"I'm so sorry."

"I know," she said softly. "Get some rest." Then she left him to check in to the hotel and the cab took her home. It had been the most frightening experience of her entire life. And his. But there was a flicker of hope in his heart from what he'd heard, which mattered more than anything. Javier was still alive.

Chapter 11

Olivia was still feeling shaky and slightly sick when she got to her apartment that night, after the scene at the airport. She had never been treated like a criminal before or come so close to being arrested. She hoped that Joachim had been able to check in to the hotel without a problem, but she didn't want to call and find out. She needed a break from him, at least for the night, and from the heavy baggage he carried with him. An identical twin brother deeply embedded in the Colombian drug cartels was more than she wanted to deal with. She felt sorry for their mother too. But she had to think of herself now.

And coming back to her apartment was depressing. It looked so sad and gray and faded now. She hadn't realized how bad it looked when she left. It didn't feel like home anymore. It reminded her of all the bad times and sad times of watching her mother deteriorate and her magazine go under slowly. She missed the pretty, happy apartment in Paris. It was fresh and new, and felt more like home now. She suddenly couldn't imagine coming back to her dreary New York apartment after a year in Paris. Now she had the chateau to do, but she didn't want to think about that either. She just wanted to go to bed and try to forget what had happened at the airport with Joachim.

She'd been gone for months, so there was nothing in the fridge, and she wasn't hungry anyway. She didn't even unpack. She went straight to bed in her clothes, and tossed and turned all night, and had nightmares about going to jail.

In the morning she met her realtor at her lawyer's office and signed the papers to sell her mother's apartment. It took them an hour to sign everything, and then she sat and talked to her lawyer, Eric Parks, for a few minutes. She had known him for many years and trusted his advice. She told him what had happened at the airport and said that she believed Joachim was an honest man. But this was not a small incident like Alphonsine stealing her mother's jewelry, when she suspected him. He had a twin brother who was seriously involved in the Colombian drug trade. What if he showed up in Paris and tried to kill Joachim? Or her? Or took her hostage? Or if one of his dangerous cohorts mistook Joachim for Javier one day and killed him, or assassinated everyone around him, including her? These were highly dangerous people. And by blood, Joachim was at risk. His entire family was, and Olivia didn't want to be in the wrong place at the wrong time with him. The scene at the airport had been terrifying enough.

She explained the whole situation to her attorney, and he didn't disagree with her. Hiring the identical twin of a dangerous Colombian drug lord didn't sound like a good plan to him, even on a short-term basis. She told him that Joachim was only going to work for her for a few months.

"You need to run a criminal investigation on the twin who works for you. You know about the other one now, but you need to be sure that this one isn't working underground for the same organization, or that he's not a terrorist, or has a criminal history. The truth is you don't know enough about him." She realized that now too. She liked him, and he was a terrific employee, but she wanted to know more than that now, about his background. The Homeland Security agents at the airport had checked and said that Joachim had no criminal history, but she wanted confirmation of that.

Eric offered to contact a detective agency he had used before. They had international contacts, and he promised to get a report for her as soon as he could. She didn't want to fire Joachim before that. Maybe he was totally clean. But she needed to know and then decide if she wanted to keep him or not. If there was anything smoky at all in his history, she was going to let him go. She couldn't afford to do otherwise. She was a woman alone, his brother was a dangerous criminal, and she couldn't take the risk. She had no one to protect her, and she didn't want to be looking over her shoulder all the time, wondering if she was going to be killed.

She met Joachim at the storage company, after her meeting with the lawyer. They were both subdued. He looked like he'd had a bad night too, and he was mortified seeing Olivia again. They kept the conversation to the items she wanted to send to France for her apartment there. He had taken the measurements she'd asked for, and said they'd fit in the Paris apartment. They had a quick sandwich together afterward, and neither of them mentioned the incident at the airport. It was too painful for either of them to discuss. Joachim felt terrible for putting her at risk with the authorities. She felt guilty about the criminal investigation of him that she had just authorized, although it was the sensible thing to do, in the circumstances. They only talked about the furniture she was shipping, and then she let him go to explore New York on his own. She wanted to pack some more things at her apartment, but she told him she didn't need his help. It wasn't entirely true, but she wanted to be alone, and think about what to do.

She picked him up at his hotel on the way to the airport the next day. She had thought they might have some fun together in New York, or a meal at least. But she didn't want to see him after the incident at the airport, except for work. She didn't want to call any of her work contacts or friends either. She was still smarting from the blow of losing her business. So she kept to herself. And they said very little to each other on the way to the airport. She was worried now that they would have a problem when they checked in at Air France, but they didn't.

Joachim felt like a criminal himself when he boarded the plane and was panicked that they'd stop him again. He was sure that there would be something about him now in the computers. The authorities were aware of his existence now, and his relationship to Javier. Being the identical twin of a man on the No Fly List was not a good thing, and he thought there might be repercussions again, but there weren't. Everything went smoothly when they checked in and boarded the plane.

Olivia slept most of the way back to Paris. She was exhausted by the trauma of the trip. And seeing her apartment had been sad. She had never realized how dreary her life was there, and how bad her apartment looked. And selling her mother's apartment was emotional for her. She felt drained.

Joachim dropped her off at her apartment in Paris and went home. His mother was waiting for him, to hear all about the fun he'd had in New York. The minute he came through the door, she could see that something was wrong. He had burst into tears when he got to his hotel room in New York, and he almost did now. The humiliation of the four-and-a-half-hour interrogation had been a nightmare, particularly since he was with Olivia. He told his mother about it and she looked shocked.

"They thought you were Javier?" The whole story sounded awful to her.

Joachim nodded. "Yes, they did. Thank God they finally produced a photograph of him and you could see the mole we both have, on opposite sides, and the birthmark on his shoulder. Otherwise I'd probably be in prison by now, as a drug dealer, and he'd be scot-free." He had loved being an identical twin as a boy, and they had played tricks on everyone, their teachers, their friends. The only one who could always tell them apart instantly was their mother. But it was not fun being the twin of a criminal like Javier. The federal agent said he had killed several American agents, and probably a number of other people as well. He had become a very dangerous man.

"At least we know he's still alive," Joachim said with a sigh, sitting next to his mother on the couch. It felt good to be home. "That's some small consolation."

"It's no consolation at all," she said with a ravaged look. "He's no longer the man we knew. The Javier we loved is gone. He might as well be dead," but she was glad he wasn't too. He was still her son, no matter how bad he was.

"I should probably quit my job." He'd been thinking that for two days. "I'm an embarrassment to Olivia. I'm surprised she didn't fire me in New York."

"She needs you," his mother said simply. "And walking out on her and quitting is cowardly. You're better than that. You embarrassed her, and probably terrified her. Now you have to stick it out until it calms down. You don't walk away when things get hard," she admonished him.

"I never have before. But she doesn't need the headache I represent."

"No, she doesn't. But she does need your help. You owe it to her to stick around. If she wants to fire you, she will. Then you can go. Not before." His mother was very firm about it, and in the end, he promised her he wouldn't quit for now, and went to bed.

The atmosphere between Joachim and Olivia was still tense the next day, on their first day back. They had returned to real life and were together all the time. And he knew his mother was right. It would take a while to settle down again. He thought Olivia still looked scared and maybe she was. It had terrified him too. He didn't know how his brother could live like that, always on the wrong side of the law, wanted all over South America, and in the United States, with criminals just like him who wanted to kill him and maybe his family. He was amazed his brother was still alive.

Olivia was as uncomfortable with Joachim as he was with her. She thought she would probably fire him before anything else happened, but she wanted to wait for the results of the criminal investigation to come back. Maybe he was as innocent as a lamb. She wanted to be fair, which was one of the things he liked most about her. He could sense how torn she was, but knew nothing of the investigation she had launched. He just thought she was jumpy. And he didn't blame her. It had unnerved him too. It was the undiscussed elephant in the room whenever they were together.

They both felt a little more normal when they had the distraction of the chateau to keep them busy. They were sifting through assorted estimates from subcontractors that week, and other workmen they were hiring. They consulted with each other constantly and went out to the chateau three times. It was a relief to have a project to focus on, and little by little, they began to feel normal with each other again. He even made her laugh once or twice, which broke the tension.

Olivia finally said something to him about it at the end of the week. It took her that long to be able to talk about it. They were sharing a sandwich at the chateau, and she looked at him calmly. "Are you okay?" she asked him, and he looked surprised. They'd had a nice morning, working together, with no trace of the malaise that had plagued them since New York.

"Yes. Why?"

"I was scared to death in New York. You must have been even more terrified than I was. I thought they were going to put you in jail."

"So did I." It was a relief to talk about it, and

he was glad she had. "I felt so awful putting you through that."

"I'm sorry about your brother. It must be terrible for you and your mother." He nodded agreement and looked at her.

"I thought you were going to fire me in New York. I wouldn't have blamed you. You were incredibly decent about it."

"It's not your fault. It must be a heavy burden for you to carry."

"I've never been accused of being him before. That was a little too much reality for me." He still looked shaken.

"I've never heard of mirror twins before. Lucky for you."

"It's the only way our mother could tell us apart. I think it's pretty rare."

"It must have been fun being twins," she commented.

"It was, as kids. Not anymore. Once we were teenagers, he was always tougher than I was, and meaner. He used to beat the shit out of me sometimes. My mother says now that he was always different, that he has no heart. I loved him anyway. I think that's how twins are, it's a special bond. I would have died for him then. But not anymore. I have no intention of taking the rap for him. I hope that's the last time that anyone ever gets us confused."

"It's a little bit like Cain and Abel, isn't it?" she said pensively.

"Yeah. A little too much so." They turned to other subjects then and went back to work. By the end of the following week, things felt normal between them again, except that Olivia was still waiting for the report on him.

She was surprised to hear from Jean Beaulieu that week, Audrey Wellington's decorator friend who had come to tea. He was giving a dinner party on Saturday and invited Olivia. She was grateful for the invitation. She still wanted to meet people in Paris and hadn't yet. He said he was having twelve people over for dinner.

"It won't be as elegant as your place, with your fancy butler," he teased her. "But I have a pretty good cook I hire for parties." She wanted to find one too that she could have cook for dinner parties, once she met some people. She accepted Jean's invitation with pleasure. It was her first step into a Parisian social life.

She wore a simple but sexy black dress when she went to his dinner party. He had a very fancy apartment on the avenue Montaigne, with a view of the Eiffel Tower. His apartment looked like a yacht since that was most of what he did. But the people were interesting and pleasant. She was seated next to a very charming architect, Charles de Prex. He spoke excellent English and was mesmerized by her. Jean told him about the chateau she was renovating and decorating and he was impressed. He appeared to be at the dinner on his own. And just before the party ended, he asked her if she would have dinner with him sometime. She had enjoyed his company all evening.

"I'd like that very much," she said, and meant it. She'd had a very good time talking to him, and he was clearly very taken with her. He hadn't left her side all night. It was only when they collected their coats that a very pretty redhead in a short black dress sidled over to him, and told him to stop misbehaving, it was time to go home. She was his wife. He looked mildly embarrassed but not very, and Jean told her after they left that he was a bit of a player, but a great guy. His wife was a very successful attorney and they had four children. Olivia was incensed by how misleading he had been. He had never once said he was married or mentioned his wife. And what was he going to do about the dinner invitation he extended? Just take her out and cheat on his wife?

She took a cab home, which was how she'd arrived. And Charles, the infamous cheater, called her ten minutes after she got home. She had given him her number when he invited her to dinner.

"I'm sorry about that little unpleasantness when we left the dinner," he said smoothly. "Normally she's quite good about these things. We have an agreement. She has the occasional fling too."

"How nice for her," Olivia said icily, furious that she had fallen for it and been duped all evening. "I'm afraid I'm a little more straightforward than that. I don't get involved in other people's 'arrangements.' I'm not interested in that."

"You sound so charming when you're angry, Olivia. I would kiss you if I was there. Americans are so funny about these things. This is Paris. The city of love."

"Actually, if you were here, you wouldn't kiss me because I wouldn't let you. I think cheaters are disgusting. You'll have to find someone else to play with," she said and hung up. He called two more times and she didn't answer. She was furious at herself for getting fooled, even for the length of a dinner party. And his wife was gorgeous. Why cheat on her? All she could think of with men like that was George Lawrence and how he had ruined her mother's life. Olivia had never gone out with a married man, and she didn't intend to start now. She knew where that path led. She had seen it firsthand. She would have preferred to be alone forever than to date a married man. But it was disappointing. He had been so handsome and intelligent and seemed so nice. She'd enjoyed meeting him and been excited about dinner with him.

She was still angry about it on Sunday, when she got an email from Eric Parks, her lawyer in New York, with a large attachment. It was the criminal report on Joachim that she'd been waiting for, and she could see that it was long. She didn't know what to expect and was almost afraid to read it. But she couldn't avoid it any longer. She climbed into bed with her laptop, opened the attachment, and began reading.

It began at the beginning and said that his father was the heir of an aristocratic family in Buenos Aires, and had been a banker at a respected financial institution owned by his family. His mother, Liese, was born in Germany. Her mother, Joachim's maternal grandmother, was killed in the Allied bombings of Germany, and Liese's aristocratic father had moved from Berlin to Buenos Aires with Joachim's mother after the war. She was five years old at the time. She had grown up in high social circles, married, and gave birth to twin boys at the age of thirty-nine. Joachim and Javier were mentioned by name.

It then went on to say that Joachim's maternal grandfather, who had enjoyed high social standing in Buenos Aires for thirty-four years, and had a considerable fortune, was exposed four months after Joachim's birth as a Nazi war criminal. Further investigation had revealed that in exchange for secrets, information, and documents relating to other war criminals of the German High Command, he had made a very lucrative deal with both the Americans and the British, who had paid him a very large sum, and allowed him to leave Germany on the condition he never return to Europe or the United States. And he had been allowed to take several very valuable paintings as his personal spoils of war. The agreement had been top secret, and he was discovered and exposed by a well-known hunter of Nazi war criminals.

His agreement with the Allies was disavowed and rendered null and void, and he was extradited to Germany at the age of seventy-three, where he was convicted, served eight years of his fifty-year sentence, and died in prison. Joachim and Javier were four months old at the time their grandfather was extradited. Their grandfather's fortune and art collection were reclaimed and sent back to Germany. Within weeks afterward, Joachim's mother had been abandoned by her husband, Alejandro Canal. He gave up all legal rights to their twin sons. They were divorced within a year, with no financial support for her or the twins. Joachim's mother had been left penniless, with no remaining family, other than her father in a German prison, where he died several years later. Joachim's father remarried a year later, another local socialite, and he was subsequently killed in a polo accident when Joachim and Javier were three years old. And according to their sources, Joachim and his brother had never known or seen their father after the age of four months.

Their mother had been left destitute when her husband left her, and moved to a poor slum area of Buenos Aires. And she supported her two boys by working at the National Museum of Fine Arts, as a curator in the department of French Impressionists. According to his school records, Joachim had been a good student, his brother less so, and reports of locals who still remembered her informed them that Liese had been a devoted mother.

It went on to say that when Joachim was fifteen, his mother, then fifty-four, met Francois Legrand, an art expert at the Louvre in Paris. They married two years later, and Liese and Joachim immigrated to Paris to be with Mr. Legrand. His twin, Javier, remained in Buenos Aires, supposedly to finish his studies there, living with family friends. According to all reports, he fell in with bad company, and within two years became involved in the drug trade, and eventually moved to Colombia, where he remained to this day, deeply embedded in the drug cartels. He was considered to be highly dangerous, and had been in prison several times in Mexico, Venezuela, and Colombia, and escaped each time with the help of his powerful connections.

When Joachim got to France at seventeen, he attended the lycée with high marks, obtained his baccalauréat degree, and spent two years studying art and literature at the Sorbonne. He then began to lose his focus, according to professors' comments, dropped out, and had assorted minor jobs for five years in Paris, until he attended a respected butler school in London, obtained a job with the Earl of Ashbury, where he remained for a year, and was then hired by the Marquess and Marchioness of Cheshire, eventually became head butler, ran both of their homes, and remained in their employ for sixteen years until the recent death of the marchioness. He left the family on good terms at that time, and was highly thought of by the heir and current marquess. For the past four months he had been living with his mother in Paris, the widow of Francois Legrand. She remained employed and was eighty-one years of age. Upon arrival in France, she obtained a job also at the Louvre and within a year, went to work for an international organization that tracked down important works of art stolen by the Nazis and returned them to the heirs of the family they were taken from. She continued to be employed by them, and was active with the organization, to the present. She lived in the same apartment in Paris she had lived in for twenty-five years. Mr. Legrand died eight years after she came to France. The whereabouts of Javier von Hartmann were currently unknown, but he was believed to reside principally in Bogotá, Colombia.

The report itself was surprisingly bloodless and cut and dried. Given its content, it was very un-emotional and listed tragedy after tragedy that had occurred in Joachim's life and his mother's. It was chronological, appeared to be well researched and documented, from a wide variety of sources. It also stated that Joachim had no criminal record, had never had a problem with the law, had a clean driving record in England, and paid his taxes and was in good standing and had legal residency and a current work permit in the United Kingdom. All his documents were in order. The report concluded that everyone they had contacted spoke highly of Joachim as an honest, trustworthy person of high morals, with an excellent work ethic and reputation.

Olivia already knew some of it. She knew all about Javier now, more than she'd ever wanted to know, and Joachim had told her that he'd never seen his father. He hadn't said that he'd been abandoned and renounced by him almost at birth, that his grandfather had been a Nazi war criminal, and had died in prison, or that his mother had lost both her father's fortune and her husband's support and within weeks had descended from a lifetime of comfort and luxury to abject poverty in the slums of Buenos Aires, where Joachim had grown up. Somehow, they had survived it, and she had supported them. The story it told was a sad one, but also a triumph of the human spirit, with a mother who had done everything possible to protect and nurture them, successfully with Joachim, and who had been unable to save Javier, who had defected to the drug lords in Colombia as soon as he could and had been unsalvageable despite all attempts to contact and rescue him.

Olivia had profound respect for Joachim and his mother. The person to fear in all of that was Javier, which had become clear to her in New York. It seemed unfair to punish Joachim now for the sins of his brother, and she didn't want to fire him. He was an upstanding, honest man, and a terrific employee. But clearly, if his twin ever surfaced, which seemed unlikely, he posed a danger to them all, and particularly Joachim and his mother.

Just reading the report saddened her, and made her wonder how they had survived, and how he had turned into such a decent, honorable human being after so much adversity. And his mother was nothing short of remarkable, even at eighty-one.

There were tears running down Olivia's cheeks when she finished reading. She printed it out, put it in an envelope, and put it in her safe. She was glad she'd had it done. It put her mind to rest about him forever. No harm would come to her at Joachim's hands, which was what she had wanted to know. There was no similarity between him and his twin and no connection in twenty-five years.

Her own mother's sad life seemed paltry in comparison. She had been weak but not cruel or dangerous. And George Lawrence for all his faults didn't compare with a Nazi war criminal, a father who had abandoned both his sons, and a Colombian drug lord. Whatever she had been through didn't match for an instant the tragedies Joachim had survived, and he had still come out of it a decent human being. It would seem that, entirely by accident, she had crossed paths with an extraordinary man. For as long as he was willing to work for her, his job was secure. And it didn't sound as though his dangerously criminal brother would ever surface in his life again.

Chapter 12

After she'd read the report, there were no longer any questions in Olivia's mind about Joachim. She had no intention of firing him, in spite of his criminal brother. Javier hadn't come near Joachim in twenty-five years and had turned his back on him. Why would he surface now? As they continued to work side by side at the chateau, they became closer and more at ease with each other again. They were accomplishing a great deal in a short time, with the chateau owner's willingness to spend vast amounts of money to speed the process along. And Joachim could tell that Olivia was comfortable with him and trusted him again.

"He must have an incredible fortune," Joachim commented to Olivia one night about the Russian owner of the chateau. They were working late going over their expenses. Nikolai Petrov never challenged their bills or scolded them for what they spent. His check to Olivia arrived on time every month, and he kept more than enough money in the account from which they paid their suppliers. Olivia was very pleased with how the chateau was progressing. It already looked like a different home, with all the grand glory of the chateau in its original state, and the fine workmanship and every modern convenience that money could buy. She had ordered the fabric for the upholstery and curtains, and there was an entire workroom set up to receive it, with some of the finest curtain makers in Paris waiting to work on the order.

Audrey called her from time to time to see how it was going and was impressed that Olivia was managing it so well. It was beginning to look like they would have the chateau ready for the owner in under eight months, although the pool area might take a little longer. They even had twenty-two very imposing ancestral portraits to hang in the entrance.

And through the entire process, Petrov hadn't come to Paris once. Olivia sent him frequent photographs, and he assured her that he trusted her completely, and was pleased with her results, which was very gratifying. He was always nice to her on the phone and by email, expressed the utmost confidence in her and treated her well.

It was an exhausting project, but Olivia loved doing it, and Joachim was enjoying it with her.

It was an ideal combination of unlimited money, Olivia's good taste, and a beautiful house, which they were making even more beautiful every day.

The one thing she always found odd was that whenever Petrov called her, the number he called from was blocked so that she could not see it, and she didn't even know what country he was in. She had no phone number to reach him, only email. Supposedly he lived in Moscow, but Audrey said she'd been told that he moved around constantly, and had an elaborate security system, and dozens of bodyguards. Every pane of glass in the chateau was now bulletproof, at his instruction, and his bedroom and office suite were missile-proof. There was an entire floor of bedrooms for his bodyguards, also at his request. There were to be twenty-four of them, bunking two to a room.

Olivia and Joachim spent many nights working late at the chateau. He was mostly in charge of keeping all of the crews working hard at full speed, and he dealt with the outdoor crews who were trying to make the gardens look like Versailles, at Petrov's request. They had even brought in a fully grown twelve-foot-tall hedge cut as a maze, which cost a fortune. And the stables were being refreshed for horses he wanted to buy and bring in from Saudi Arabia. They added some additional touches, but few were needed.

Olivia concentrated more of her efforts on the inside of the chateau and coordinating the artistic side of it. Joachim oversaw the construction and outdoor landscaping. Together they formed a formidable task force. They even worked on many weekends. There was still much she wanted to do in Paris, but she had no time now until they finished the chateau. And looming in the distance was the end of her lease on the Paris apartment. She already knew she wanted to stay, but hadn't told her landlord yet, and hoped he'd let her. She didn't want to move again, she loved her new home, and had no desire to go back to her dreary apartment in New York. It seemed part of the past now and wasted years of her life. But she hadn't let it go or sublet it in case she decided to move back at the end of the year in Paris.

They were driving back to the city from the chateau on a Friday night when Joachim asked her a question she constantly asked herself.

"What do you want to do after the chateau?"

She'd been thinking about it a lot lately, as the project neared completion. "Maybe the same thing on a smaller scale. A lot of Americans still buy chateaux in France. I've loved refurbishing this one. Maybe something less extreme. I'll never have another client with this much money, but it adds a lot of pressure too, although he's certainly easy to work for." They both agreed on that. Petrov was an invisible, undemanding presence with unlimited funds.

"Too much so. I hate to think where the money comes from," Joachim commented. A job as a butler still hadn't come up in England for him, and he'd done nothing about pursuing it lately. He was having too much fun working with her, and he couldn't make this kind of money as a butler. She was paying him a very fair portion of her earnings, in consideration for all the work he was doing. They both knew she couldn't have done it without him. There was far too much work for one person to handle, too many component parts, and workers you constantly had to chase to show up and threaten and cajole. He was better at that than she was, and she liked the artistry of it better. Their combined talents made for a very efficient team.

"What are you doing tonight?" he asked, as they entered the sixteenth arrondissement.

"I was going to soak in a hot tub and go to bed." She had helped carry some of the lumber that day since the workmen were shorthanded, and rocks for the garden. Each rock was individually selected. Nikolai Petrov wanted the most beautiful garden in France. And Joachim was constantly impressed by how hard she worked. Nothing stopped her or was too hard. "But I think I'll go to a movie. There's a new one on the Champs Élysées I want to see, the original version in English. I get homesick once in a while, but not very often."

He smiled. Her French had improved in the last few months from speaking to their workers. Her accent was pure American, but she knew the words she needed to speak to the workmen, and they understood her.

"You can't go to the Champs Élysées alone. It's dangerous." He frowned at her. "There are juvenile delinquents all over the place, and Gypsies." She still hadn't made any friends or met anyone, other than the people she worked with, and Joachim. They had a good employer-employee relationship that had developed into an artistic partnership, like war buddies, but he was careful to maintain a respectful distance, which was comfortable for her too. They were both people who shied away from close relationships, although it manifested differently. He had said to her once that signing on for a life of service was like joining a religious order. You gave up your personal life for your job. To do it well, you had to give up your freedom, independence, and other loyalties. The job would always have to come first and the family you worked for, and your own family, personal pursuits, and girlfriend would have to come last.

"And no woman likes that," he had said, and she agreed.

She had sacrificed her own personal life for her work, for a magazine that didn't even exist now, so what had that gotten her? Ten years of hard work and long nights and an empty pot of gold at the end of the rainbow.

They both agreed that if they'd been dating anyone,

they couldn't have devoted the same intense amount of time to the chateau. But as a time-limited project, they were both willing to do it, and the rewards were considerable.

He argued with her again about the movie when he dropped her off at home, and offered to take her and she finally gave in. He wasn't entirely wrong about the Champs Élysées, but she didn't want to monopolize all his time, and she said she didn't need a babysitter, to which he always responded that she sounded like his mother.

"I'll go home and change. I've been crawling around in dirt all day. And I'll pick you up at eight. That still gives us time to buy popcorn," he said, and she grinned, and took a bath and changed into clean jeans herself. He was slowly becoming her best friend in Paris.

When she talked to Claire, her old assistant, in L.A., occasionally, she always asked Olivia if she had a crush on him and she insisted that she didn't. They were work friends and nothing more and Claire didn't believe her. She insisted that wasn't possible with no sexual undercurrent at all.

"Maybe I'm a freak then," Olivia said. She hadn't slept with anyone since she'd come to France, and for months before that, since she had dated a photographer briefly in New York. Like most of her relationships, it ended because she had no time to see him and didn't really care. She had decided she was too old for casual sex and had never liked that anyway. The only men who had invited her out on dates so far in Paris were married, which she liked even less. She gave them a sharp rebuff every time, and they told her she was too American.

Joachim's mother had asked him the same question, if he was attracted to Olivia, and he said the same thing as Olivia had to Claire. He added that it was out of the question. They were employer and employee, and once in a while in their off hours, they enjoyed a casual friendship, or friendly conversation, with no physical overtones whatsoever. Liese didn't believe him either.

"One day you're going to wake up and figure out you're in love with her," his mother said matter-of-factly, which annoyed him. She seemed certain of it.

"Never," he said confidently.

"Men and women can't be friends in that way," she said wisely.

"Yes, they can. Everything in life doesn't have to be about romance, Mama," he said stubbornly.

"Well, something does, or it's a damn sorry existence, and a lonely one. Francois and I started out as friends, and I wanted to keep it that way. He wouldn't have it, and he was patient and persistent, and I'm glad he was. He was my soul mate." Her first husband, Joachim's father, had been dashing, handsome, and superficial, and had deserted her the minute the chips were down. Francois would never have done that. He never even gave up on Javier completely, and always hoped he would find his way back, for Liese's sake. And Joachim knew that about him. Francois had been such a good man and the love of his mother's life.

"I can't live a life in service, and go around falling in love with my employers, Mama. Besides, I don't see her that way, as a sex object. I see her as a person."

"And the woman you're in love with can't be a person? Who dreamed that up? I may be an old woman, but I remember what love is. You're not a priest, Joachim. You didn't take holy orders. At least I hope not." She doubted that she'd ever have grandchildren, but at least she wanted her son to be happy, and not sacrifice his entire life for his employers. He had always put them and all their needs first, and Liese wished he wouldn't, or he would be a lonely old man one day, if he wasn't already. Olivia sounded as if she'd been cut of the same cloth, from what he said. Joachim had mentioned that she was badly marked by her mother's relationship with a married man, so she was careful not to get too deeply involved with any man. It didn't sound like a fulfilling life to Liese. It sounded like both her son and Olivia were afraid of love. She secretly wished that Joachim would sleep with her. She had said it once, and Joachim was outraged, and said that even saying that was disrespectful. In Liese's opinion, they were both running from the best part of life.

"She's not a vestal virgin, for God's sake, or a

fourteen-year-old. She's a forty-three-year-old woman."

"She's only interested in working," he confirmed. And so was he. It made it easy and safe for them to be together. The most they could ever be was friends.

"Then she needs a good shaking. And so do you," his mother scolded him, and hadn't mentioned it lately. She was coming close to the end of her search for the Monet's rightful owners, and was working on two new paintings, a Pissarro and a very unusual Picasso that Goering himself had taken out of Paris on his famous art train, on one of his raids on the Louvre. He had put it there for safekeeping after taking it from a well-known Jewish family. Liese was looking forward to working on them when she finished with the Monet. But she also worried about Joachim. He had lost his brother and never known his father, and she knew he was terrified to love.

As promised, Joachim came back to pick Olivia up in time to get to the movie and buy popcorn. She liked it with sugar now, as they did it in France, instead of salt.

"I forgot to ask you what movie it is before I so gallantly offered to be your bodyguard," he teased her.

"It's a love story with Meryl Streep and Robert De Niro," she said, as he found a parking space down a side street from the theater and she noticed that he was right. There were gangs of teenage boys cruising everywhere, and little clusters of Gypsies begging and eyeing people's purses.

"Oh God, I should have asked," he said. "Isn't there something violent, or a science fiction movie with robots beheading each other?" She laughed at him.

"I hope not," she said happily, as she got out of the car. It was nice having someone to go out with. She usually went to the movies alone or didn't go at all.

Joachim pulled her close to him, so no one snatched her purse, and his broad frame protected her. They got to the theater two minutes later, bought popcorn on the way in, and found two seats together, which was rare on a Friday night. He looked around and saw with amusement that there were a number of older couples seated with one arm around the other. Given the age of the stars, it had attracted an older audience, even older than they were.

"I think I'm too young for this movie," he complained, as the previews came on.

"Shut up and eat your popcorn," she told him, and he laughed and put an arm around her shoulders.

"Just so people don't think we're strange or don't like each other."

"I don't think they care," she said, smiling and eating her sugared popcorn. But it felt nice to have a warm arm around her. It made her feel more human and not just like a work machine that went nonstop with no affection to fuel it. She had forgotten what that felt like, it had been so long.

The movie came on then, and Joachim kept his arm around her until the end. He enjoyed the film more than he wanted to admit, and Olivia loved it and said she wanted to come back and see it again sometime.

"You can get the DVD or stream it."

"It's not the same as in the theater," she said, as they walked back to the car. They'd had a nice evening together. He was good company and they were comfortable with each other.

"Do you want to stop and have a pizza? I'm hungry," he said, as he started the car, and a teenage boy pounded on the hood, and ran away laughing with his friends. "That's why I don't want you here alone. Pizza?" She thought about it and nodded. Neither of them had had dinner, just popcorn. There was a pizza restaurant a few blocks from her apartment. They were fancy pizzas, and delicious.

They shared a truffle pizza and talked about work and the movie, and she was sleepy by the time he took her home and dropped her off.

"Have a nice weekend!" she called out to him and waved. "Thanks for the movie!" He had treated her. She was upstairs in her bed half asleep ten minutes later, and he drove back to his mother's apartment with a smug look on his face, determined to prove that his mother was wrong. He wasn't in love with Olivia. They were just friends. She was probably the best person he knew and he admired her and wanted to protect her from any harm. And he loved working with her. But that didn't mean he loved her. He was absolutely certain he was right. She was beautiful and fun to be with and smart, but that didn't sway him. They were work partners, and she was his boss, and nothing more. He couldn't wait to tell his mother as he drove home. For once her intuition was way off base.

Chapter 13

When Joachim came home from the movies with Olivia, he heard voices in the living room, and thought his mother had fallen asleep in front of the television. It was late for her to be up, and he walked in to gently get her to her bedroom and stopped in his tracks. She was wide awake, sitting on the couch, and Javier was sitting across from her. His left upper arm was wrapped in a towel soaked with blood, and there was a gun lying on the coffee table in front of him. He grabbed it and stood up the minute he saw Joachim walk in. He pointed the gun at Joachim's heart, and their mother's voice rang out strong and clear.

"If you hurt so much as a hair on his head, Javier, I swear I'll kill you myself. Put the gun down. You don't shoot your own brother. You're in my home. Have some respect. You come here after twenty-five years, with a gun? What's happened to you?"

But she could see what had happened. He was an entirely different person. There was nothing left, no morals, no compassion, no humanity. There was nothing he cared about. It was Cain and Abel in the end.

"What are you doing here?" Joachim asked him, walking into the room slowly, not wanting to startle him. Javier's eyes were wild, with the pain of his wound, and probably because he was on drugs. "I'd been told you were in Colombia," Joachim said calmly, and sat down next to his mother on the couch. Her eyes were steady as she looked at Javier, but her hand was shaking in Joachim's. It was deeply emotional for her to see Javier again, and for Joachim too.

"What are **you** doing here?" Javier spat back at his twin. They still looked exactly alike, one filthy, one clean, same face. "I thought you were a servant in England," Javier said in a mocking tone. Joachim had no idea how he knew about that, since he had gone to London long after Javier had cut off communications with them. But news traveled both ways. It surprised Joachim that his twin had made inquiries about them. Maybe he was human after all, but he didn't look it, with his hair a matted mess, a heavy beard, and his arm bleeding in the towel. It was his left arm, and Javier was left-handed, so it would make him a less accurate shot if he fired at either of them, and Joachim didn't want it to be their mother.

"Why don't you put the gun away. I don't think you need it to defend yourself against Mama." The irony wasn't lost on Javier, and he shrugged and put it in his belt. If Javier shot anyone, it would be his twin brother, not their mother. "Why are you here?" It was a cruel way to meet after twenty-five years.

"I have business here. It's a new market for us."

"Are you married? Do you have children?" Liese asked him, struggling for normalcy. She wanted to reach out and touch her son, but she didn't dare. He looked like a wild animal ready to strike. Joachim was deceptively calm, watching his every move.

"No, Mama," Javier answered her, sounding like her son again. "I don't have kids, or a wife." It was an absurd question in the circumstances, but she wanted to know. A long, long time ago, he had been her baby, and would be until the day he died. "Do you have whiskey?" he asked Joachim in a rougher tone. Joachim decided not to argue with him, walked away, fished a bottle out of the cupboard, and handed it to him. Javier turned the cap with his teeth to open it, let the blood-soaked towel fall, and poured whiskey over the bullet wound in his arm. It was nasty looking and Liese cringed. He wrapped it in the blood-soaked towel again.

"One of your new business associates must have gotten pissed off at you," Joachim surmised. "That looks ugly."

"I can't go to a hospital," he said roughly.

"No, you can't," Joachim agreed.

"We have doctors. I can see one tomorrow if I need to."

"You can't stay here, Javier. It's too dangerous for Mama, if someone finds you here. Whoever did that will try again." Whoever did it had been aiming for his heart. Joachim wasn't afraid of his twin, he was soaking up the look of him. As it always had been, it was like looking in the mirror, except there was something missing. As his own mother had said about him, no heart. He didn't look happy to see them, or moved by their mother, who was an old woman now. She had been middle-aged, in her fifties, the last time he saw her. Now she was eighty-one, but the fire in her eyes was the same, and her spirit was just as strong.

"Where will you go?" she asked him, still his mother. She didn't want Javier to die or be killed, no matter how bad he had become.

"I'm staying here," he said belligerently to Joachim.

"No, you're not. You're not safe here. I spent five very unpleasant hours in the airport in New York, where they thought I was you. You're on the No Fly List in case you didn't know. You're barred from the United States."

"I don't care. I never go there. Why did they think you were me?"

"They have your picture and your name in their computers, they thought I was using an alias."

"Why did you go there?"

"My boss took me to work. She didn't enjoy

being interrogated for five hours either. So they know where our mother lives, they know who I am, and they know a lot more about you than I do. If anyone knows you're in France, they'll come here and kill you. Either your business associates, or the police." Javier thought about it then stood up. He pulled out the gun and pointed it at his twin again.

"I could take you with me as a hostage, for safe passage."

"I don't think they'd care. I'm expendable, to get you. They want you badly. Our mother lost one son, she doesn't need to lose two. You have to go." Their mother didn't argue with Joachim. She knew it too. Every minute he stayed there, they were all at risk. The police might even already be on their way, or the bad guys Javier knew, who wanted him dead.

Javier took a swig of the whiskey and walked across the room. He stood inches from the brother he had once shared a womb with. They had been like one person with one heart while they were growing up. But the heart had been Joachim's, not Javier's. He knew that now just looking at him. "I cried for you every night for ten years," Joachim said to him, and Javier made a sound like a low growl. "And then I stopped, because I knew you weren't there anymore."

"I never was. You didn't know me. You never knew who I was. I wasn't you, the perfect little boy, kissing everyone's ass and getting good grades in school. I'm not like you." That they all knew. "I'm

important now, while you're a servant to the rich."
Joachim didn't try to answer him. There was nothing left to say. "I spit on you," Javier said with a mur-
derous look in his eyes and spat at his brother's feet.

"I loved you," Joachim said quietly, "and Mama
still does." Javier glanced back at her and she was
crying as she watched them.

"If you tell the police I was here, I'll come back
and kill both of you," he said to the room in gen-
eral, and then with his right hand, he opened the
door, walked through it, slammed it behind him,
and disappeared down the stairs. Joachim knew in-
stinctively that he would never see him again. And
what they had just seen was a ghost. A man in the
final stages before someone killed him, either his
enemies or his associates. A man like Javier had no
friends, not in his world. None of the normal rules
of humanity applied.

Joachim put the chain on the door after Javier
left, but he knew that they could shoot it off if they
wanted to get in. He gently took his mother to her
bedroom and tucked her into her bed. Her cheeks
were still wet with tears as she looked at Joachim.
"They'll kill him. Maybe that would be easier for us
all. He looks like a hunted animal." Joachim nodded, he couldn't disagree with what she said, or tell
her she was wrong.

He sat on the chair in her room all night while
she dozed and woke with a start periodically, and

then drifted off again. He wanted to be near her in case Javier came back. But he didn't think he would.

The police rang the doorbell at eight the next morning. It was Saturday and Joachim was already up. They knew Javier had been there, and wanted confirmation from Joachim, and he didn't deny it. He said he and his mother had no idea where Javier was going, he didn't say. Joachim said that they hadn't seen him in twenty-five years until last night, and he had held a gun on their mother until Joachim got home, and then on him. The police knew he was wounded. They said it had happened when a delivery went wrong and an informant had tipped off the police. He lived in a hard world, on the razor's edge, at the edge of the abyss at all times.

"We got information that he was killed in a gun-fight last night," the police officer told Joachim, but he said they didn't believe it, and neither did Joachim. Even Liese said she was sure he was still alive. He and his cohorts had put out the word to get the police off his trail, but it hadn't worked.

"Call us if you hear from him again," they said, and Joachim agreed. They had cooperated fully with the police.

"He won't contact us." Joachim was sure of it. "I don't know why he came here. Maybe for one last look at his mother. I think he knows he's a marked man. Everyone's after him, even his own people."

"That's how it always ends with them. The only

one safe is the man at the top, and he's not it," the chief detective said, and Joachim nodded.

"I want protection for my mother. Here in the building or just outside to watch who comes in. I have to go to work during the week, and she goes to work too. I want someone here for her at night." The detective promised to arrange it by later that day.

Joachim stayed with his mother all day. They stayed in the house, and he told her about going to the movies with Olivia the night before, putting an arm around her, and nothing had happened, so she was wrong. She looked at him in exasperation and shook her head.

"Then you're either a zombie or a fool." But she was too wrapped up in thoughts of her other son to worry about Joachim's love life or lack of it.

They saw it on the news that night at eleven o'clock, and this time they believed it. It had happened an hour before and was breaking news. Javier had been shot and killed by one of the SWAT teams from the drug unit. He had been supervising the unloading of a boat in Toulon with five hundred tons of heroin in it. The entire shipment had been seized, and nine men had been killed, one of them a member of the SWAT team. Javier had been the first man down. In his world, he was a hero. To the rest of the world and his family, he was a lost soul.

Liese felt a shiver run through her as she watched it. And this time she knew it was true. She sat silently watching the news report on TV, and held

Joachim's hand, as the tears slid down her cheeks and fell on her bleeding heart.

Olivia had seen it on CNN too. They described the men and showed photographs of the more notorious ones. She saw Javier's photograph come up, the same one she'd seen with Joachim at the airport in New York. She knew that it was another grief for them, for Joachim and his mother. She turned off the television and said a prayer for his mother.

Joachim called Olivia on Sunday night, and told her that he wouldn't be able to come to work on Monday, and possibly Tuesday as well. He had some appointments at the chateau that he said he would cancel. She knew why he wasn't coming in. It wasn't hard to figure out.

"I'm sorry for your mother. How is she?" He knew then Olivia had seen it on the news.

"The way she always is. Strong, wise, loving. He showed up here on Friday night while we were at the movies. He held a gun on her. He'd been shot. He wanted to stay here, and I told him he couldn't. They might have come here and possibly shot all of us. He must have gone to Toulon last night. Someone had bungled a shipment on Friday night and he got shot. But the big shipment was due last night in Toulon. Five hundred tons. He was handling the operation. One of the SWAT teams killed him as soon as the ship docked. They're going to let me collect his body tomorrow. I want to make the arrangements, so my mother doesn't have to. She shouldn't have to deal with that. He was a different person from the boy we knew. He was filled with venom, and hate. It's ugly to see. I'll come to work as soon as I can. Tuesday, or Wednesday at the latest. We'll do a service for him on Tuesday."

"I can manage," Olivia said calmly. As he listened to her, he knew what he had to do. He had thought the same thing after New York and should have done it then.

He told Olivia he'd call her when he could.

Joachim wore a black suit, white shirt, and black tie when he went with the undertakers to collect his brother at the morgue. The police had taken all the photographs of the body that they needed. There was no need for an autopsy to determine the cause of death. Joachim was having him cremated and had arranged for a small graveside service the next day, performed by a priest they didn't know. His mother hadn't been to church in years. She said she had her own agreements with God, and they understood each other.

Joachim refused to look at his brother's remains in the casket before they cremated him. There was nothing there he wanted to remember. The identification of the body had been made by the police, and it was certain, with fingerprints from Interpol to confirm it. Joachim sat quietly with his mother that night. She was peaceful. She knew where her son was and she had nothing to fear for him anymore. She had been mourning him for years, and so had Joachim.

On Tuesday afternoon, they went to the cemetery together. She wore a black dress and a hat, and they stood together, as the box with his ashes was lowered into a small grave. It was marked with a simple cross, and later there would be a plaque with his name.

The service only took a few minutes. The priest said a prayer, they each threw a handful of dirt into the grave, and then the priest shook Liese's hand. He told Joachim what a brave woman she was, and he didn't know the half of it. She was braver than anyone could have imagined. She left a single white rose on her son's grave, and then they went home and she cooked the dinner that had been Javier's favorite meal as a child. It was her tribute to him, as a boy, not the man he became. Joachim remembered it perfectly. She used to cook the same dinner for them on Sunday nights. Rice and beans and pieces of chicken and spices. Sometimes it was the only time all week that they had meat, and very little of it for three people. And it tasted the same when he ate it. But this time it had the bitter taste of loss and regret added to it, which was all too familiar to his mother. Joachim had no tears left for his brother. He had shed them all years before. The cord that had bound them had been severed. He was free of him at last.

Chapter 14

Joachim went back to work on Wednesday, after a two-day absence, and so did his mother. She was eager to get back to work. She had put so much effort into her project, she wanted to see it through to completion. They both looked somber when they left the apartment, and Joachim was relieved to see that there was a plainclothes policeman stationed outside, dressed as a street cleaner. He met Joachim's eyes as they walked by, and Joachim nodded slightly. He knew what he was, but others wouldn't have.

He dropped his mother off at the place where she worked. She insisted she could have taken the metro, but he wouldn't let her.

"One of them could follow you, Mama. If even one of his enemies doesn't believe he's dead, they could follow you to see if he shows up. A lot of people lost money from that failed delivery in Toulon.

They won't swallow that easily. Someone will have to pay for it, in blood if not in money. Javier was a fox and I'm sure he has pretended to be dead many times before." But not this time. This time it was for real. He could see how low his mother's spirits were when she got out of the car and walked into the building. She didn't look back at him and wave, as she would have normally.

He drove to Olivia's apartment then and was only a few minutes late. She looked relieved to see him the moment he walked in. She could see in his eyes all that he'd been through since their night at the movies five days before. Years and years of loss and worry had finally come to their inevitable conclusion. He accepted it. He had no choice, but he was sad anyway. She made him a cup of coffee and handed it to him. They both sat down at the kitchen table.

"How's your mother?" she asked kindly.

"Brave. She always is. She's had to be too often. I'm not sure it's real to her yet. I never expected to see him again. I gave up years ago. I'm not sure she ever did. It's an ugly thing having a son like that. She must wonder where she went wrong, what she should have done differently. It wouldn't have changed anything. I think some people are born like that. There's something missing, or one enzyme too many, or a subtle poison that releases into their veins slowly, and one day takes over their body and their mind. He had no soul." Olivia nodded, and he set his coffee cup down, and looked at her. She had the feeling that something bad was coming. But how much worse could it get than what had just happened? "I'm going back to England," he said in a low voice. They were words she didn't want to hear and he didn't want to say. "It's better if I go now. I should have done it after what happened in New York. You were good to let me stay, but I should have known better."

"You don't have to leave because of this, Joachim," she said in a gentle tone. She thought he was embarrassed and wanted to do the honorable thing for his employer, but it was so much more than that.

"Yes, I do." There was no doubt in his voice this time. He had made his mind up as soon as Javier left their mother's apartment. He was even more sure of it now. All of his instincts told him he was doing the right thing, and she wouldn't change his mind. "I'm a death sentence for both of you, you and my mother. If even one of his enemies doesn't believe he's dead, they'll come after us, and when they see me, they'll think they found him, and they'll go crazy.

"The police are probably not the only ones who didn't know he had an identical twin. It's the weak link in the chain of all of this. Without wanting to, I will draw those people to you. They'll stop at nothing. I'm the red flag that will put you in danger. I have no right to do that to you. I want to get as far away from you as I can get."

He was doing it out of respect and loyalty to her and because he cared about her. He didn't want to be a danger to her, or his mother, or to anyone. "For the rest of my life, for those who know what just happened, I will have to explain that I'm not him. But the kind of people he did business with don't wait for explanations. They believe what they see, act, and think about it later, if they ever do. I don't think any of us can conceive of how low he sank or imagine the things he did to others. I understand that better now. I saw him. Who knows, if I hadn't been there, he might have killed our mother so she couldn't tell anyone she'd seen him. I don't think even she realizes that. He went there for his own safety, not because he cared about her and wanted to see her. If that was true, he'd have showed up long ago. It was a desperate move to get a few hours out of the line of fire and was probably the only safe place he could go." The degree of brutality and inhumanity was hard for Olivia to imagine, and she knew that Joachim was trying to do something noble, leaving them, but she didn't want him to go.

"They'll forget about it eventually. When he doesn't show up. They'll figure out that he really is dead."

"Possibly not for years. People go underground for a long time in that world. And in the meantime, I'll be walking around, like a living poster of the man they're looking for. You never know who's watching or what they see." He knew little of his brother's world, but he could guess, and even in his innocence, he had walked into the middle of it. "My face alone puts you at risk, Olivia. I can't let that happen."

"I need you," she said unhappily. "I can't finish the chateau without you. It's a ten-man job, not even a two-man job. I don't know how we've gotten it this far." With their careful coordination and relentless hard work, they were way ahead of schedule. Even Petrov was impressed, when they emailed him the weekly progress in pictures. He had promised them a big bonus if they finished early, but she wasn't thinking of that now, only that she didn't want Joachim to leave. She saw it as a defeat for all of them if he did. She wanted to finish the job with him. Leaving now was giving in to the forces of evil, as she saw it. Javier and the people around him would win if Joachim left. They would rob him of a life and a job. He saw it differently, as the only choice he had to do the right thing. Because he looked so exactly like his brother, he thought there was a good chance that sooner or later he'd be killed, and he didn't want the people he cared about anywhere near him when that happened.

"The police can protect you," Olivia insisted. Her face was troubled, she sounded angry, but her eyes were sad.

"I don't think they can. I'm hoping they'll protect my mother. But they won't protect you. And if it goes wrong, it will happen in an instant, with no warning. They'll see me in a supermarket, in a car, at the movies with you like the other night, and it will be over. I can't bring that kind of danger close to you. I don't think I understood that fully in New York, which is why I didn't quit then. Now I do understand it. I can still lead my life in England the way I did before. Maybe not in London, but on some remote English country estate, they're not likely to see me. On the streets of Paris, I'm a walking target. They'll be looking for me here, and in London." He knew he was going to be having the same conversation with his mother that night. Olivia was trying to convince him otherwise, but he was sure she was wrong this time. The people he was worried about weren't human, they were animals, and Javier had been too.

"How soon do you want to go?" Olivia asked him, wondering how much notice he was giving her. Logistically, it was going to be a nightmare for her, and throw off progress on the chateau dramatically. She couldn't manage all the crews the way he did and install the interior too. Aside from the fact that she liked him and had grown fond of him, she needed him to do his job or it would take much longer to finish hers.

"Tonight, tomorrow," he answered her. She looked shocked and angry for a minute.

"Are you serious? It'll shut down the whole project."

"If I get killed, it will too. Or if you do," he said coldly. This wasn't an argument he was prepared to lose. He was giving her no choice. He was telling her what he was going to do. "I shouldn't even have come here, but I wanted to tell you in person. That's only fair. This is about saving your life, Olivia. Not about the chateau." But there was nothing fair about any of it and they both knew it. It wasn't fair that he had to give up a life, a job, a golden opportunity for the next steps of his career, and it wasn't fair that his mother's heart was breaking again and she had lost a son, and could lose another, or that she had to spend her final years alone and wouldn't have the comfort of a loving son near her. It wasn't fair that it had come to this, and that Javier had managed to damage all their lives with the poisonous way he lived his own. "I don't want you killed," Joachim said heatedly. "I won't put you at risk."

"I don't know how you can call this fair," she said angrily to Joachim. "What am I supposed to do?"

"It's not fair to any of us. I have no choice. Call the agency. They'll send you someone else," he said. It only made her madder.

"People like you don't stand on every street corner waiting for a job." She'd never had another employee like him. It wasn't just about his training, which was really not adapted to his job with her anyway. It was about his common sense, his dedication, his fine mind, his ability to solve problems and make everything work, to fit the puzzle together in just the right way, and work endless hours in the process, making everything easier for her. It was about how much he cared. She knew she'd never find that again. He loved his job with her. He didn't want to give it up either, but he knew he had to, and all thanks to Javier. He had won in the end, and Joachim was the loser, and so was Olivia, and his mother. It infuriated Olivia as she sat looking at Joachim. "And what are you going to do for a job?"

"What I was doing until I met you. There aren't many butler jobs these days, as you know, but I'll try to find one. Maybe for another Russian who wants to look important to his friends. I can make anything work if I have to." He had with her. He was flexible and could adjust to any situation, and he was willing to.

He had no personal life he cared about, so he could do whatever he wanted. There was no one dependent on him to complain about the compromises he made. But he didn't live entirely in a vacuum. He knew that his mother would be deeply affected by his leaving. And now Olivia would be too. But in the end, it was just a job for him and Olivia, and he reminded himself of it now. They'd been working together for a few months, and it had always been temporary. He hadn't intended to stay. That had only changed recently, when she asked him to stay on. But she wasn't even sure if she was going back to New York to get a job there, after she finished the chateau. Nothing had been sure, and both their lives were up in the air. They were equally unattached and independent, and very similar in that way. The similarities between them were coincidental, but they understood each other because of them.

"You're running away, Joachim," she said in a low voice. She was angry at him and it showed. "You're scared."

"Yes, I am," he admitted freely. He was an honest man, and never tried to hide his flaws. "I have to run away. And I have a right to be scared, for you, and for myself. You're going to be better off without me. You'll see that one day."

"Don't make it sound so noble. You're leaving me in the lurch and you know it. Can't you at least wait till I find someone else? That would be the decent thing to do, even if this is just a job to you. And I thought we had become friends." She looked hurt as well as angry, which went straight to his heart, but he had to put a shield up to protect himself from her too, and he already had. He had spent the past few days bracing himself for what he had to do, even if it meant hurting her. He was willing to hurt her, if it meant saving her life.

"And what if they find me before that?" he said, angry too. "And yes, we're friends, as much as the job will allow. We both have the same fears. We've both spent our lifetimes avoiding deep attachments, you know that as well as I do. Being attached to anyone is dangerous. You've seen it in your life, and I've seen it in mine, and now here it is again, only this time the danger is real. You need to remember that now. You don't know me. We don't own each other. In the end, Olivia, even if we were friends for a while, I'm an employee, and this is just a job, for both of us." That hit her like a slap in the face. He wanted to tell her to toughen up, but he didn't dare. "Don't forget how strong you are," he reminded her, for her own sake.

"I guess I forgot that for a minute," she said and stood up. "You're right. We're both strong and we'll find our way, and it's just a job." She smiled coldly at him and he knew she didn't mean it. He had hurt her, and he knew it, but he had to in order to let her go, and make her let go of him. He couldn't allow her to have a hold on him. It would be too dangerous for them both. "I hope you find a job you like in England. They'll be lucky to have you."

"Thank you," he said politely. "And I hope you find the right person for the job."

"I'll send you a reference, if you want one," she offered, decent to the end, and gracious. But he didn't need one from her. His reference from the Cheshires, and the length of time he'd worked for the family, would get him any job he wanted. His few months with her was just a sidebar and wouldn't carry much weight.

"Good luck, Joachim. Stay safe," she said, and held out a hand for him to shake, which he did, looking her in the eye with everything he couldn't say.

They had both respected the boundaries between

them right to the end, and she was glad they had. He was right about them, because of all the things that had happened to them, neither of them was able to attach, in their personal lives or their professional ones. She hadn't spoken to her past employees at the magazine in months, except for Claire. They had gone on with their lives, and so had she, and drifted apart, no matter how close they appeared to be while working together. And now it was true of him too.

He was a solitary person and had chosen jobs until then that had reinforced that. It was a spell put on them that neither of them would ever break, and she knew that now. It was both a blessing and a curse, and the protective covering they wore, like a suit of armor, but the blows of life still found a way in from time to time. She couldn't allow him to hurt her, or herself to care.

As she watched him go through the door of her apartment, it was hard to believe that only five days before they had gone to a movie and had sat with his arm around her and they both had the illusion that they were friends. It was only an illusion, she realized that now. She couldn't allow herself to be sad or miss him when he was gone. She put his coffee cup in the sink for Fatima to put in the dishwasher, and she went to her work area to call the agency. She didn't want a butler this time, she needed a real assistant, and she wouldn't make the same mistake, of allowing herself to believe that they were friends. It was just a job, as Joachim said.

The woman at the domestic agency was surprised to hear from her.

"I thought it was working out so well, for both of you. I spoke to Mr. von Hartmann when we found Fatima for you, after that nasty little business with the girl before her," she reminded Olivia of Alphonsine. "He seemed very pleased with the job working for you, even if it was somewhat out of the ordinary for him. And the last time I called him to check on how Fatima was doing, he said he was helping you refurbish a chateau. That was quite beyond the scope of what we originally discussed. And he said he was enjoying it very much. I'm so sorry he's leaving."

"So am I. I'm still working on the chateau and need help. I think he missed being a butler and is going back to England to find another job using that skill set. This was probably too much for him," she said, not knowing what else to say.

"It didn't sound like it," the woman said, disappointed, and she was shocked that Joachim hadn't given her any notice. Olivia didn't volunteer that his brother had been killed in a drug deal gone awry, and he was saving her from danger by association. The woman at the agency didn't need to know that. "That's how these people are, though," she said with a sigh, "even the good ones. People who do domestic work, particularly at a high level, can be temperamental, and don't always leave the way they should. I hear this more often than I like, or about someone who's been in a job for twenty years, doesn't have the courage to say they want a change, and just up and leaves one day with no notice, or they leave a note for their employers who've been good to them for years. It's the nature of the beast, I suppose. Would you rather go to a business agency to find an assistant? I'll see who I have on my books, but no one comes to mind. Do you care if it's a man or a woman?"

"Not at all. It's probably easier working with a woman, but a little muscle wouldn't hurt at the chateau. Joachim was quite good at that, and he never thought he was too important to do menial work." Nor did Olivia.

"That's useful. I was worried that he might be a little grand, because of his experience in England."

"I was afraid of that too, when I hired him, but he wasn't." She gave the devil his due in spite of being upset about Joachim leaving her with no help at hand, and no one to replace him. She was determined to get over it, just as he said. But she was sad anyway. It was a loss, whether they admitted it or not. She had grown attached to him, just as he was to her.

"Well, it was always going to be a temporary job,

and he stayed past the three months you required in the beginning. Is that still the case now?" She had her apartment for another four months, and she still hadn't decided whether she was going back to New York, or wanted to stay for another year. She had no reason to go back, and she liked living in Paris. It was a happier life for her than in New York, and her life there still had the smell of loss and defeat to her after losing the magazine, and her mother. And her apartment in New York had looked so depressing after the two days she'd spent there when her mother's apartment sold.

"I'm not sure," she told the woman at the agency. "I think I should hire someone for four to six months, with the possibility that it could become permanent. I'll have to decide soon if I want to extend my lease. I should have finished the chateau by then if Joachim's leaving doesn't put us way behind schedule now."

"I'll see who I can find, as quickly as I can," she said sympathetically, but the options she sent Olivia in the ensuing days were all wrong.

She had a twenty-one-year-old American girl who had dropped out of college. Her mother was French, and she had dual nationality, so she was legal to work in France. She wanted to be an assistant, but had never been one, she was also willing to be a nanny, but admitted that she didn't like kids much, and she was currently working as a maid at a hotel. She would have been fine for Fatima's job, but not

Joachim's, not by a long shot. And the woman at the agency kept warning Olivia that Joachim would be nearly impossible to replace. Olivia knew that anyway. He had spoiled her.

She had another girl from Serbia, who was slightly older, and had been a secretary. She had followed her boyfriend to Paris, and spoke perfect English, but not a word of French, so she was useless to Olivia, whose French had become basic. But she needed someone fluent to help her.

There was an older man who had run his own business and failed and was working as a janitor, but he seemed slow and not too bright. An Irish boy who seemed energetic and willing, and had been in a dozen different jobs, and admitted to Olivia in confidence that he was wanted by the police in Ireland for some "unfortunate incidents," so he had come to France. And the business agency she called as well had a lineup of colorless, uninteresting girls who had worked in offices, knew nothing about construction or decorating, and thought it sounded like too big a job. Most of them wanted to work from home on their computers, which was of no use to her, and a problem she'd had in New York in recent years at the magazine too. No one seemed to want to go to an office if they could avoid it.

The domestic agency came up with the most viable option, although it wasn't a perfect solution, but Joachim hadn't been an obvious fit in the beginning either, as a butler. Since his departure, she had been fending for herself, and was totally swamped. She was stuck at the chateau fifteen hours a day, meeting with subcontractors and supervising workers. She was using a car service with a driver, so she could make calls on the way there. The job hadn't slipped but it was eating up her life and more time-consuming than before with only one person juggling everything and no one to share the responsibility with her.

She hadn't heard from Joachim since he left, and didn't want to now, although she had had to text him several times to ask him for details and information she didn't have. He answered immediately every time, and said nothing personal in his responses, nor did she in her messages. The boundaries between them had been firmly set, as they always were, and readjusted further for an **ex**-employer and **ex**-employee who had not parted on the best of terms. She didn't ask if he'd found a job and didn't care. She was sure it wouldn't take him long, with his previous experience.

The best candidate the domestic agency came up with was a man. He was thirty-five years old, had worked in an art gallery, and wanted to become a chef. He was listed with the agency because he wanted to hire out to do parties, and eventually open his own catering business. The woman who ran the agency said he was supposedly a fabulous cook, which was of no interest to Olivia. He had some background in art, so her decorating might not be totally foreign to him, but he was looking for a job as a chef, to give him a base income. He couldn't survive so far on what he made doing parties from time to time. He was hoping to cook for a family or a business, until his catering jobs were more regular. The agency was trying to help him find both a full-time cooking job and work as a party chef when they got requests for one. But he was the only person that she could think of who could work as an assistant, after his gallery experience.

Olivia agreed to meet him, and he seemed pleasant, polite, and shy. His face lit up whenever he talked about cooking. He was particularly interested in Asian cooking, anything organic, said he could prepare vegan and vegetarian meals, and had bookings for two small weddings and a bar mitzvah in the coming months, and he often had catering jobs on weekends. But he lived in the city and said he didn't mind late hours. He was very disappointed to hear that she wasn't interested in his cooking skills, and fended for herself, usually with a salad. He was so gentle that she couldn't imagine him arguing with their stoneworkers, carpenters, glaziers, and other workmen that she had to deal with every day at the chateau. He seemed very precise and had arrived punctually, but he looked like he might cry or run if one of their workmen shouted at him or insulted him. Joachim had gone toe to toe with them every day, and he did it a lot better than she would have. Anatole, the young chef, didn't seem equal to the task, and said he hoped she would try his chocolate soufflé one day.

She didn't know what to do after she saw him, discussed it with the agency at length, and finally decided to hire him and give it a try. For the time being, the job was only temporary, and he might tide her over for a while. No one else had turned up, and there were days when she hated Joachim for leaving her in the lurch. She was holding her own at the chateau, but she felt like she was fighting for her life, and they were slipping backward in the schedule. The workmen she had to deal with didn't respect a woman the way they did a man, and they tried to pull all kinds of stunts on her, left early, didn't show up, left work undone, lied to her when they thought they could get away with it, or padded their bills. She was trying to be tough with them, which was the only thing they respected, but she knew she was no match for them, and they were going to eat Anatole alive.

Chapter 15

Liese took the news that Joachim was leaving even harder than Olivia had, when he told her the same night he'd told Olivia that he was going back to England the next day. He didn't want to frighten her, but explained that because he and Javier were identical, for those who didn't know Javier had a twin, any sighting of Joachim, and his ongoing presence at his mother's home, might convince the wrong people that Javier's death was a fraud, and inadvertently bring danger to his mother's doorstep. For her safety, he wanted to stay away from her, at least for a while. Living with her and having a regular job in Paris seemed fraught with danger to him. Liese didn't like his theory, but she could see his point.

"I'm not afraid, Joachim," she said quietly. "He was associated with the wrong people for years, they never showed up here."

"They didn't need to. They knew where he was. He kept his activities limited to South America. For some reason, he seems to have branched out recently. So, they'll be looking for him here if they don't believe he's dead. And I'm sure he faked his death many times before, to get his enemies and the authorities off his scent. The authorities know he's dead. The bad guys don't and might not believe it, even if they were told. Eventually, when time passes, they'll figure it out. But probably not for a while. We need to give it some time." But at eighty-one, even in good health, who knew how much time she had? Every moment she could spend with her only surviving son was precious. She had no one else, no other children, no grandchildren, no spouse, and few friends. Many of her friends had already died. She had her work, but nothing else, except Joachim, and she had loved having him near her once he took the job with Olivia. Knowing he would come home every night, and she would see him in the morning before they both left for work, or for a meal on the weekend, added immeasurable joy to her life. And now he was taking that away from her.

"I'm willing to take the risk of your being here," she said, with tears in her eyes, but she would not allow herself to cry. She wanted to be stronger than that. "But I don't want you at risk. What happened to Javier and who he became is bad enough, for both of us, but I don't want it to kill you too. The price is too high. I want you to be safe. I've lived my life. You haven't yet. The rest of your story is not yet written. Mine is almost complete. If they kill me, they will only steal these last years from me."

"And from me," he said sadly. He didn't want to lose her, at any time, it would be the greatest heart-break of his life, even if she died at a hundred.

"But you have many, many years ahead of you. I will not bury a second son." And when she said it, the tears spilled onto her cheeks, and he put his arms around her and hugged her tight. Leaving her was unbearably hard, even more than he thought it would be, now that he was living with her again, which he hadn't done since his early twenties. He enjoyed her company, and how smart and sensible and sharp-witted she was. She was clever and in-terested in life, and wise. He was going to miss her terribly, much more even than his job with Olivia, which he had hated to leave too.

"I just want you to be safe, Mama. I don't want to put you in danger. It would be different if I didn't look exactly like him. But no one will be able to tell the difference. They will think I'm him, if they're looking for him."

"I know they will," she agreed. It made perfect sense. It was a cruel turn of fate. She had always loved the fact that they were twins, and identical, but it had slowly turned to a heartbreak over the years. And she had been shocked to see that even with time and distance, and very different lives, they still remained completely identical when she saw them together the night before Javier died. Joachim had noticed it too. They were the same weight and build. There were little wisps of gray in their hair now in the same places. Their faces were identically lined in spite of Javier's beard and their different lifestyles. Javier hadn't led a good life, and Joachim had, but time had marked them identically, and no one could have told them apart, even at the end, except their mother. Their enemies certainly couldn't.

"Did you tell Olivia?" she asked him, and he nodded.

"This morning."

"What did she say?"

"She wasn't pleased. I've never done that in my life, left a job with no notice. It leaves her badly stuck with the construction at the chateau, but I can't do anything about it. I don't want to put her at risk either, or increase the danger to you, by staying longer in the job until she finds someone. And the police have promised me that they will protect you, they'll have a man downstairs night and day, no one will get in the building without their notice, so I feel safe leaving you here. Safer than if I was here with you, luring the bad men toward you." But she wouldn't even have the protection or comfort of her son. "I **have** to leave, I have no other choice. For a while anyway. And Olivia is a casualty of our situation. I can't let the job color my decision."

"Is it just about the job or is it more than that?"

she asked him gently, and he didn't answer her for a minute.

"I told her it's only a job," he said in a raw voice.

"That must have been hard to hear. And is it true?"

"Not entirely," he admitted. "Of course, it's not just a job. No job is. I care about the Cheshire offspring too, although some of them annoyed me severely, for their lack of care for their parents in their final years, but I had no voice in it.

"Olivia is a woman alone. She's strong but vulnerable. She's had her share of disappointments and losses, like all of us. She just lost her mother, and the magazine she put her heart and soul into for ten years. She's lost her anchor, and I told her that we're very much alike.

"Because of what's happened in our lives, neither of us seems able to attach to anyone. I've chosen a career that makes it impossible. There's a reason why old-fashioned butlers never married in the old days, and people in service rarely did. It leaves you neither the time nor the energy to give to anyone if you do it right. You **belong** to the job and the family you work for, you **are** the job. I wonder now if I chose it because of that. It gave me an excuse never to get attached to anyone or tied down, except to my work. It would be a constant tug-of-war to be a married butler, or one with children. I know some people do it now, and live out, but they probably don't do as good a job as the old butlers used to. Head housekeepers, head cooks, butlers, great nannies were always spinsters and bachelors. The ones who weren't were giddy young girls sleeping with the footmen."

"It's an antiquated lifestyle, Joachim, from another century. I grew up in a house like that. It doesn't exist anymore, and it probably shouldn't. You can't give up your life for a job, or your employer. It sounds like she did it for a magazine, not even a family."

"She did it for the same reason I did. So she wouldn't get hurt. Her magazine must have been a place to hide from having a life. Her mother was a married man's mistress, and it sounds like he destroyed her life and she let him. He was Olivia's father and she never knew it. Her mother never told her until after he died. She's been hurt, so she protects herself, and doesn't trust anyone.

"I'm no different. I was hurt by Javier, and the father who abandoned us, and even the grandfather who hurt you so badly and I never knew. It's all connected, and it leaves some of us unwilling to risk our hearts. Olivia is like that too. It created a kind of unspoken bond between us. We are similarly flawed, and we respect or even admire each other. She's a very smart, honorable, intelligent, kind woman. So, we became friends, no more than that. We feel safe with each other. But now the risks are too great. The price to pay would be too high if she got hurt, or you did. So, it's time to move away from each other again. Olivia and I never attached, or allowed ourselves to, so there's no torn flesh, no bleeding wounds. That's the advantage of never getting too close," he said in a tone that was almost bitter. "So, it becomes just a job, which is what I told her. And the friendship was a perk of the job, so that's over too." He said it matter-of-factly, as his mother watched him closely.

"The friendship was not a 'perk of the job.' It was a gift to both of you, and maybe the only form of love that either of you can tolerate. For the moment, at any rate. You're both wounded people, but that doesn't mean you will never attach to anyone, to her or someone else. I was wounded too when I met Francois. I did everything I could to discourage him and chase him away. He persisted for two years and refused to listen to me. He was my soul mate and he became the love of my life. Don't cheat yourself of that one day, when it comes along. Don't be a coward, Joachim.

"The reasons you list for being friends with her are the same reasons why people marry, and in many cases they marry for far less than that. You trust and admire each other. It's a wonderful foundation for a friendship and could grow to be more one day. And you can't just cancel the friendship when you leave the job, like a membership to a club or a library. You are scarred by your losses. So am I. So are we all. Francois loved me anyway, and I learned to love again. You are marked by your losses, and wounded, and losing Javier now is just one more loss for both of us. But you are **not** irreparably damaged. Don't hide behind that. I don't know this woman, but seen through your eyes, she appears to be a good person. Don't run away too far, or too harshly, or you'll regret it one day. It is never a good thing to leave people unkindly or even cruelly."

He felt guilty now because he knew he had been unkind to Olivia, maybe even cruel when he told her it was just a job to him, which wasn't true. But what else could he say? What point was there to staying linked to each other in some way when he had to leave now, and their lives were headed in opposite directions? All he was for her now was a danger, and a handicap. He disagreed with his mother on one thing. He knew that he was damaged, but he believed he was irreparably so. And perhaps Olivia was too. He was not willing to take the risk of caring about anyone, or no more than he had with Olivia. He hadn't wanted more than that and he was convinced that she didn't either, despite his mother's romantic notions. Whatever he had said to her, it was too late to fix it now. Olivia had become another casualty, part of the rubble left in the wake of his twisted, misguided, evil brother. And Joachim was convinced that no matter what the reason for their friendship, Olivia would be better off now without him. It was the last and only gift he could give her, to remove himself entirely from her life, no matter how he had to do it.

*   *   *

His parting from his mother was bittersweet and painful. He made her breakfast before she left for work, fighting bravely not to cry after she hugged and kissed him. He tidied up the apartment for a last time after she left and made it neat as a pin for her. He laughed softly after he did it, realizing that it would annoy her and she would claim that he had made something disappear or misplaced it.

He had the strange sensation as he was doing it that Javier was going to appear at any moment. It seemed inconceivable to him that his twin was finally gone forever, and nowhere on the planet. He kept expecting the doorbell to ring, or the intercom to buzz from downstairs, or a frantic pounding on the door, and Javier would be standing there, desperate, angry, broken, still rebellious, perhaps injured and bleeding, as he had been the last time Joachim had seen him. He wondered if he should have looked at his bullet-riddled body at the morgue to make sure he was dead but he couldn't bring himself to do it. He couldn't have borne it. It would have been one blow too many. But if he had, maybe he would believe his twin was dead now. He still didn't. Some part of him was still linked to Javier and always would be. Perhaps the tie that bound them even transcended death, which would be a terrible life sentence for Joachim. He could even imagine opening the door to Javier, and having him shoot him, or stab him, which was why he wanted to put distance between himself and their mother. If his associates believed that Javier was still alive, and they injured Joachim instead, he wanted his mother nowhere near that. The only way to protect her was to remove himself, since he was what would attract them. It was a curse now to be an identical twin. Maybe it always was, and he just hadn't seen it.

He looked around his mother's small, cluttered apartment for a last time before he left, and sent all his love to her in thought. He remembered Javier sitting on the couch with his gun, only days before. He thought of Olivia, and what he'd said to her the last time he saw her.

He couldn't wait to get to England now, and to get lost in another job, so he didn't have to think of all of it. He had his whole life packed into two suitcases, which he carried downstairs to his station wagon. He saw the plainclothes detective, dressed as a janitor, on duty to protect his mother's home, and her when she came back later.

He pulled away from the curb with a heavy heart, thinking of those he loved and had loved and could have loved, leaving them all behind, as he headed north for the drive to England.

He was in London by the end of the day and gained an hour with the time difference from Paris. He went to his small flat, which he hadn't used in months, and called the agency to let them know he was back, had left his temporary job, and was ready to take a job in England. They said they would get back to him and would check their books. Until then, they hadn't put much energy into it, since they knew he had a temporary job in Paris, and he had been picky about what he would interview for. Joachim said that now he was willing to look more broadly. He bought fish and chips and ate in his room that night.

When he called his mother, she sounded sad and scolded him for his uninvited housekeeping and wanted to know what he had done with her latest art magazines. He laughed at the question.

"I knew you'd accuse me of hiding something. I put them on your night table." They talked about her day, and his drive to London, and she said she missed him. One of the things he loved about her was how normal their exchanges were. It had always been very simple, and he never doubted for an instant how much she loved him. It had fed him in the darkest times of his life. It was a shame that Javier hadn't been able to derive the same sustenance from her, although she had loved him just as much and always told him so when he was still at home and when he called them in France. But some part of Javier had always blocked her. He preferred to believe himself unloved to justify the choices he made and the dark turns his life had taken as a result. Although they looked identical, it always shocked Joachim, and his mother, how profoundly different they were.

Joachim went to bed early and was woken by the agency calling him in the morning. They had four interviews set up for him. They had taken him at his word, and were putting him forward for their butler positions, although none of them were quite up to the level of what he'd had before. But he expected that.

The interviews had been set up at ninety-minute intervals at the agency in Knightsbridge. If both parties had further interest, a second interview would be set up, in their home. It seemed an efficient way to handle it and wouldn't waste everyone's time if it wasn't a match, or even close.

Joachim showed up at the agency in one of his well-tailored black suits. He had always been vain about his clothes fitting well, and, with his generous salary, had his suits made by a tailor on Savile Row. He wore highly polished sober black leather shoes, a white shirt and a navy and black Hermès tie, and had a haircut before he went to the agency. He looked impeccable.

He liked the first couple more than he'd expected to. They were a young Saudi couple, and had a large house in London that was fully staffed. The wife was quite beautiful, and wasn't veiled, although he suspected she would be in her own country. They had a house in Geneva too, and a home in Riyadh. They only wanted him for the house in London. They had six children and four nannies, and the kind of staff he was used to. The rest of the house staff was from the Philippines, the nannies were British, and a house manager and secretary were both Saudi. The way it was set up, Joachim guessed that he would have less authority and control of the staff than he was used to. The two Saudi men essentially ran the staff and made all the decisions, and Joachim got the distinct feeling that he would be window dressing, and nothing more than a British butler who would look good to their guests at dinner parties. He was used to a job with more substance than that, and a free hand with decisions. They only spent a few months a year in London, and although he liked them, he had the feeling that he would be bored most of the time, except when they were in residence, entertaining. It was made clear to him that the two Saudi men would outrank him, and he would take direction from them.

He genuinely liked the couple, who were warm and very polite to him, but he suspected that the lack of authority he'd have would rankle him. And he guessed that they were more likely to favor their own countrymen than an English butler. It was a good job, and paid well, but he didn't think it was the right one for him. He wanted a position with more variety and broader scope now, after the diverse projects he'd handled for Olivia.

He had enjoyed that more than he'd expected to. He turned the Saudi position down. The agency wasn't surprised.

The second job he interviewed for was with an American couple. The husband was well into his sixties, his wife (his fourth one, the agency had whispered to him before the interview) was twenty-two. Her husband treated her like a teenager and she acted like one. The husband couldn't keep his hands off her during the interview. She was wearing a miniskirt that was so short Joachim made a point of not looking in her direction for fear of what he'd see, but the interview was so amusing that he had to struggle not to laugh at their questions. They had just bought a house in London, were from Texas, and also had a home in Palm Beach, which was already fully staffed. They had been married for six months. They planned to have a cook, two or three maids, and wanted him to double as butler and chauffeur, which he wasn't entirely opposed to, and they asked if he'd mind helping the maids with the heavy cleaning. His three grown children and eight grandchildren would be using the house occasionally, and with an adoring look at his young wife, he said he hoped they'd be having more children soon. The salary they were offering was not what he was used to, and he could easily envision himself in the midst of chaos, with the owner's family showing up with their children, while he drove, cleaned, and played the role of butler to all of them, with nothing very interesting to do. There was nothing very creative involved, there would be no travel or entertaining, and it sounded like there would be way too many people in the parade, especially with the child bride who wanted to know if he had any experience as a trainer, and would he be willing to give massages, which sounded like dangerous ground to him.

The whole setup made him very uneasy. Sitting through the interviews was like speed dating, but it was one way to rule out the ineligible households quickly. He got a good view of the young American wife's legs, seen from the rear, when they left the room, and he had to admit, she had fabulous legs and an incredible figure. The back of her leather miniskirt barely reached her thighs, and he felt panicked just watching her, as her husband patted her bottom on the way out. She gave Joachim a killer smile coyly over her shoulder before she left the room, which he did not return. He could just imagine the awkward situations that might arise if he worked for them, a headache he did not want or need. For an instant, he wished he could have described the interviews to Olivia. He knew she would have seen the humor in them, as he did. But he was straight-faced and candid when he expressed his concerns to the agency representative who checked in with him after each interview. He could understand Joachim's concerns, but reminded him that in today's employment scene, he would have to be flexible. And he thought the last two jobs they had set up interviews for would be more to his liking. The couples were more typically English and were offering more traditional butler's jobs.

For the third interview, a touchingly old, incredibly sweet couple walked in. Joachim had in the notes he'd been given that Lord Hallbrook was ninety-two, and Lady Hallbrook had just turned ninety. They appeared fragile, but seemed to be managing. They looked at each other lovingly throughout the interview. They said they seldom came to London anymore, and lived on their estate in Norfolk. They no longer lived in the main house, but in the dower house, and their son occupied the manor house and had his own staff. They had a cook and a maid, and their butler had recently passed away. They said they didn't need much, and lived a quiet country life, and would be grateful if the butler would drive them as well. What Joachim could see was what the job with the Cheshires would have become if they had lived even longer and relinquished their properties to their children during their lifetimes. With the Hallbrooks, Joachim would have been one of a staff of three, in a tiny country house, for a very elderly couple who might not even live much longer, and he would be out of a job again, with nothing to do. It touched him to see them together, and they admitted that the dower house was quite small, the two women who worked for them were quite old as well, sisters who had worked for them for almost fifty years. It wasn't likely to be a long-term job, given the age of the employers. They were lovely people, exquisitely well-mannered and very distinguished, but Joachim felt claustrophobic just thinking about it. The job with the Cheshires had been more interesting because he had a large staff and two big houses to run. Lord and Lady Hallbrook were adorable, but it was another strikeout for Joachim. He was beginning to lose hope that the fourth position would be any better.

The man who marched into the room ten minutes later was like a gust of wind, full of energy. He was slightly younger than Joachim and full of good humor. Halsey Mount-Williams was almost a caricature of the British aristocracy. He commented that he'd had three wives already, one worse than the other, and all dreadfully greedy. One of them, a Russian girl, had stolen some of the silver. He made a joke of it. He divided his time between his club in London and his family estate in Sussex, having lost his London house to his first wife. He admitted that some of it was in quite bad shape, but they were managing to hold it together with spit and baling wire, and he and his sister had come up with a clever plan to offer paying tours of the Sussex house, so they kept that part of the house and grounds in quite good order. The rest really didn't matter. He said they kept up the front gardens for the same reason, but the park and back gardens were sadly overgrown. He added that they made quite good money with the tours, and the house was listed in all the guidebooks of England. He said that he put all his money into the stables and the Thoroughbreds he bred. He had a fairly large staff in the stables, and some excellent horseflesh according to him, people to run the tours, and they kept two maids, a cook, and a butler. "Rather a poor man's Downton Abbey," he said jovially, which reminded Joachim of Olivia's comments about Carson the butler. He couldn't see himself in that role, but it sounded as though the job had potential. He could perhaps refurbish the house a little, and get things back in good order, and oversee the gardeners. He was familiar with the name of the estate, but had never seen it, Pembroke Manor.

"I spend most of my time in the stables, with the horses," the employer readily admitted. "The house would be your job, and making sure the tours go smoothly, that none of them wind up in my bedroom by mistake, and making sure that my current girlfriend, a very sweet Czech girl, doesn't sell what's left of the silver. Both of my parents are dead, thank God, so there's none of that to worry about. And my sister hates the place. She lives in Italy, married to an Italian, and only shows up to make sure she gets her share of the money from the tours." It sounded like chaos to Joachim, but a kind of chaos he understood, of British aristocrats who had run out of money, were trying to find resourceful ways to hang on to their estates and still run them, and keep the place looking decent. He knew of several homes that had turned into tourist attractions and managed to survive that way. He wasn't opposed to it, and he thought it might be fun to be involved in it. And it was obvious that the only thing the owner cared about were his horses, and possibly his girl-friends. But Joachim thought that the many hats he was now able to wear, especially after working on the chateau, might be useful to this employer. It wasn't a formal, elegant job like he'd had with the Cheshires, but more like working for one of their profligate sons, if they'd had one, which they didn't. The Cheshire heirs were all quite nice and well be-haved, even if they didn't want to live as grandly as their parents. Joachim had the distinct impression that this man had run through whatever he'd in-herited, or was working on it, and shoring up the estate wherever possible.

Of all the jobs he'd just interviewed for, the last one seemed the most interesting, and possibly even amusing. At least it would be different. The poten-tial employer seemed like fun. And it was just dif-ferent enough to be intriguing.

"I'd be happy to come to Sussex, sir, to have a look, if that would be all right with you."

"Fine, whenever you like. Very decent but-ler's quarters. My parents were always very good to the staff. You'd have your own cottage on the grounds." He quoted a salary, which was less than the Cheshires had paid, but more than the Texans had offered, and the job seemed like it was worth a look. "I'm master of the local hunt, so we do hunt breakfasts in the season. Something for the tourists to look at. We serve them breakfast if they like too, at quite a jolly price." He winked at Joachim, who laughed. They seemed to be commercializing everything they could, without embarrassment.

They agreed that Joachim would come for a visit before the end of the week and shook hands on it. Halsey Mount-Williams left, and Joachim told the agency he was interested in the position, but still willing to interview for others. He thought the job in Sussex would give him the most latitude to run things as he wanted, with a fairly relaxed employer, and it was also well enough out of sight not to draw attention from Javier's cohorts, if any of them showed up in England.

Joachim told his mother about it that night, and she said it sounded like a bit of a mess to her, and very English.

"It probably is a mess. I think that's what I like about it. It'll give me something to do. I would have been bored with the others I saw, and the Texan child bride would probably have raped me, which might not have been an unpleasant experience, but then her husband would have killed me."

His mother laughed. "Aren't there any proper jobs left, with respectable employers in decent houses?"

"Apparently not. I suppose there are some, but no one ever leaves those jobs until their employers die or they do."

"Well, go to see the one in Sussex. He sounds like a black sheep to me."

"Probably. And he's horse mad. He sounds like he spends all his money on his horses. But he doesn't look like a bad guy." She was happy that he had found something, but still sad that he had left Paris.

Joachim went to see about the job at Pembroke Manor in Sussex two days later, and it was even more disorganized than he had imagined. The front of the house was in relatively good order. Two very attractive young women were running the tours, and they had set up several bedrooms to look the way they must have originally, along with a drawing room, and a dining room with a formally set table, which was quite dusty. They had managed to keep an aura of grandeur and dignity at the front of the house, with some very handsome family paintings, and heirlooms. The back of the house where Mount-Williams lived was a mess and didn't look as though it had been cleaned in a decade. The first order of business if Joachim took the job would be to clean it up. You could see that a bachelor lived there. The furniture was threadbare and the once-beautiful curtains in shreds from age and sunlight.

The gardens were in total disarray. Even those the tourists saw needed attention. The entire aura of the place was of decaying aristocracy and the thin remains of days of grandeur. Everything around the place was in need of cleaning and repair, and in some cases replacement. It wasn't impossible to do, if the owner was willing to spend the money. And Joachim was willing to put the time and energy into making it shine again.

The stables were far better tended and in better shape, and the horses were magnificent. The park was almost completely overgrown. The butler's cottage was very comfortable, under an inch of dust that made Joachim cough when he visited it.

The main house was quite large, though not enormous. There was a very old maid and her granddaughter from the village. Two very lazy gardeners, who were lounging about doing nothing, and that would have to change. And the cook was a jolly heavyset woman who said she had been there for thirty years, and Joachim could smell alcohol on her breath when he approached her. The three women's uniforms were frayed and dirty, and they needed a good polishing too. The challenge appealed to him, after the work he had done on the chateau with Olivia. This was a much smaller scale venture, with potentially good results, but the chateau had prepared him for it. He wished he could talk to Olivia about it, but they hadn't parted well, and he didn't

feel comfortable calling or writing to her. He realized now that his mother was right, and it was a
mistake to leave people badly. As far as he knew, he
had burned his bridges with her, and he wondered
how she was doing with the chateau. He hoped
things were going as smoothly as possible and she
had found someone to help her.

He liked being back in the English countryside,
though. It was familiar to him after all his years in
England. The estate in Sussex had never been as
beautiful and dignified as the Cheshire homes, nor
as well kept, but he thought he could make something of it and restore some of its original dignity.

"What do you think?" Halsey Mount-Williams
asked him after Joachim had walked around the
houses and property for two hours. He had left
him alone until then, and he had been impressed
by Joachim's credentials. They were flawless, unlike
his own.

"I think there's great potential here, sir," Joachim
said cheerfully.

"We don't want to spend too much money maintaining it, mind," Mount-Williams reminded him,
"except what the tourists see."

"I'm quite resourceful and can do a lot of it myself. A bit of paint, a hammer and nails, a good
scrub and you might even be able to charge more
for the tours." His future employer clearly liked that
idea. "And your horses are magnificent." Mount-
Williams beamed at that.

"Beauties, aren't they? We have a breeding program and have had some very promising results with our racehorses. No huge successes so far, but we're getting there."

"I'm sure you will," Joachim said quietly.

"So do you want the job?" He hoped he would. He couldn't manage the place himself and didn't want to.

"Very much, sir."

"Excellent! When can you start?"

"Tomorrow," Joachim said with a smile. All he had to do was notify the agency, lock up his flat, and drive back to Sussex. "May I stay in a bedroom in the main house for a night while I get the butler's cottage in order?" he inquired politely.

"Take any one you like, except mine." He laughed heartily, and went back to the stables a moment later. Joachim thought he'd be an easy man to work for and wouldn't interfere. On his way back to London, he thought about what he wanted to do, and the next day he drove back to Pembroke Manor, his new home. There would be lots to do, to keep him busy. He was looking forward to it. He had a job and could turn his mind to that instead of his recent losses, his dead brother, and the job he had given up to come here. But at least his mother and Olivia would be safe now, with him away. And cleaning up the house and property would be a challenge. It wasn't as grand as the chateau, but it was enough for him. He was relieved to be employed again, and as a proper butler. He'd never been a butler at a tourist attraction before, which seemed a little undignified. But why not? The key to life was being flexible and taking on new challenges. It was going to be an adventure.

Chapter 16

Anatole, the assistant Olivia had hired, was a lovely, gentle person. He was polite to everyone on the phone and was sweet to Fatima. He was kind and helpful and showed up at work every day with some delicious pastry he had made earlier that morning, or croissants, and whenever she was at home at lunchtime, he made Olivia a delicious lunch. He kept her desk and his own impeccable, but he was terrified of the workmen, who bullied him and followed none of his instructions at the chateau. He was useless to her there.

What it took in the end was Olivia getting as tough as the workmen were, threatening to fire them in her basic French, checking their bills diligently and calling them on it when they cheated her, and occasionally replacing them. She was determined to complete the chateau on schedule for the employer. The checks from him were continuing to come in regularly, but he called her less often and she didn't want to disappoint him. She wanted the chateau to be a showplace for him, and an accomplishment she could be proud of, so she could do another one if she wanted to. Joachim leaving her had almost made the task impossible, but she refused to be defeated by it, and she did his job and her own after he left.

Anatole was virtually useless as an assistant. She was basically paying him to bring her croissants for breakfast, and make her lunch, which she didn't have time to eat. She needed to be at the chateau every day now, getting each aspect of the work completed. The floors were perfectly polished, all the bulletproof windows were in, and replaced where necessary, most of the carpentry had been done, the plumbing was still in progress, the electricity seemed to be solid now. The technology was being handled by a subcontractor. The painting was almost finished, and she was storing the furniture and art she bought, rugs, and electrical fixtures in a warehouse set up for storage. It was coming together, and she was spending every waking hour on it.

It was far more stressful than the project had been when she had Joachim to rely on. But she no longer did, so she made the best of it, determined not to be daunted. She tried to give Anatole a little more backbone, but it was hopeless. He hated going to the chateau. All he cared about was cooking, and all he could think about were the two weddings he was going to do. He spent so much time on it, that when he left a week early to prepare the first one, Olivia gave him a month's salary and let him go. He looked relieved when she told him. He said he didn't know how she dealt with the workmen, they were so rude, and many of them were dishonest. It had grown familiar to her, and she didn't waste time being gentle with them anymore. She met them on their own turf, and was as tough as they were, and then they did what she wanted. It had taught her a lot about human nature and how strong you had to be sometimes, but she was proud of what she was accomplishing. And she didn't bother trying to find another assistant. It was too late now and the project was almost finished. They were coming in on schedule. She wanted the owner of the chateau to be thrilled with it, and was continuing to give him reports, although he hadn't responded to her last three emails. He was probably busy. He was continuing to feed the account she paid the expenses from. Her bookkeeping was meticulous too.

Joachim's victories in Sussex were more human scale than Olivia's. In his first weeks there, he had managed to clean up the part of the house included on the tour. He got the two tour guides to help him, and the silver and antique furniture gleamed, with some help from the maids. Joachim had them put fresh flowers on the tables every day. He had done some minor repairs, improved the lighting, pulled back the curtains and let more sunlight in, moved some of the furniture, and rehung some paintings. It was housekeeper's work, but he didn't mind doing it, and the results were quite good.

And then he had turned his attention to the part of the manor that his employer lived in. Some of it was beyond redemption. He put what was too dam-aged to use in one of the outbuildings and moved things around to compensate for it. He had the maids wax all the furniture and the floors, turned some rugs around, and switched the curtains so the frayed edges didn't show. By the time he finished, the place had a distinct charm and polished look, rather than the threadbare, filthy appearance when he'd arrived. He put the gardeners to work night and day, and brought three more in to help them, first in front and then all around the property. By the time Joachim had been there a month, it looked like a different home, and Halsey Mount-Williams noticed it and complimented him.

"You've got a magician's touch. I hardly recognize the place. I think you're right, and we should raise the tour prices." Joachim didn't think they were quite there yet, but the place was looking better than when he'd arrived. And he had spent two days cleaning and repainting his own quarters and they were quite pleasant now. He was very satisfied with the way it all looked. And Joachim had borrowed a horse from the stables a few times to ride around the property. He liked the area and his life there. His mother was pleased for him. She missed him more than she admitted to him. He could hear it in her voice. Her only real pleasure was her work now, which was still rewarding, but with one son dead and the other living far away again, there was a sadness to her life that she couldn't escape. She had nothing to hope for except the joy she gave others by returning their paintings to them.

Joachim decided to surprise her when he had a weekend off. Mount-Williams was going to a horse auction with friends and told him he was free to go.

He drove to Paris on Friday morning, was comforted to see the same police guard in plainclothes still there, and rang the doorbell when she came home from work. She screamed with delight when she saw him and threw her arms around his neck.

"What are you doing here?"

"I came to spend the weekend with you. Get your coat, I'm taking you out to dinner." She was shaking when he helped her put it on, and he took her to a bistro he knew she liked in the neighborhood, and then they walked home arm in arm, and he told her about his job in Sussex. "It's a mess, but it's rewarding putting it to rights again. I have to be resourceful. I think the owner is mostly out of money, and he only spends what he has on his horses, or women. He gambles. He makes a little money from the tours of the house to support the place. It's not a job I'd have wanted ten years ago, but it's fine for now. I can do whatever I want, as long as it doesn't cost him any money." She looked at him seriously then.

"He might lose the house one day," she warned him.

"I don't care. It's fun for now, and it's a decent wage. He's not a bad man. He's just irresponsible."

She thought about something else then and looked at him. "Did you ever put it right with Olivia?" She hadn't wanted to ask him before on the phone. He shook his head as they walked home after dinner.

"It was too late. I did it badly when I left. What can I say now? We've both moved on. I'm sure she has a new assistant, and she's busy too."

"It would be nice for her to know you're not as callous as you must have sounded when you left."

"I was upset about Javier."

"That's no excuse. 'I'm sorry' goes a long way, even if you've both moved on. Or you could drop her a note." It was a boundary he didn't want to cross, but his mother's words haunted him that night. He stood looking out the window in the morning, while his mother was still asleep, and with a sigh, he picked up the phone and called her. Maybe his mother was right. She often was. And the drama over Javier had begun to fade a little. He had been dead to them before, and now he was again.

Olivia saw Joachim's name appear on her cell-phone and was surprised. She was at her desk, going

over her weekly accounts for Petrov, and answered
her phone, wondering why Joachim was calling her.
She had thought of him often in the last month,
angrily at times, but as he had said, it was just a
job, she had no reason to contact him. Their time
was past. She had figured out for herself how to
manage at the chateau alone. It was hard, but she'd
learned a lot in the process.

He heard her voice and felt a pang of guilt again,
like a knife in his stomach, and he was sorry he
had called her. It was going to be uncomfortable
for both of them, and there was no purpose to it,
except to apologize.

"How are you, Olivia?" It seemed like a good
place to start. He couldn't think of any other.

"I'm fine. And you?" She was always polite, even
when she was angry. He couldn't tell if she still was.
Her tone was neutral, and she was keeping him at
a safe distance.

"I'm fine too." It was as awkward as he had feared.

"Where are you?" she asked him.

"I'm in Paris, visiting my mother for the weekend."

"Are you working?" She was curious about him.

"I took a job in Sussex. The house is a combination of **Downton Abbey** and 'The Fall of the House
of Usher,' mostly the latter. They charge money for
tours, and the place is falling apart. Mostly, I've
been scrubbing floors, waxing furniture, and polishing silver." She laughed at the way he described
it. "What about you? Did you find an assistant?"

He cringed when he asked her, fearing the response, if she was doing it all herself.

"I did. He was a chef in wolf's clothing. Or actually a very sweet mouse. I fired him. He made delicious croissants and was terrified of the workmen. He wants to be a chef when he grows up. It's easier alone now. I wind myself up to be a bitch every day, and it actually works very well. We're almost finished."

"I'm sorry," he said, and genuinely meant it, and it soothed her heart, although she wouldn't admit it to him.

"Being a bitch is actually a very useful skill. It works incredibly well," she said with laughter in her voice. She sounded pleased to hear from him, and she was being nice about it, which made him feel even guiltier.

"I find that hard to believe. You're never a bitch, even when you should be."

"I'll be better at it now," she said, and he smiled. "In two languages. My French has improved immensely."

"I owe you an apology. I'm sorry about the things I said when I left. I was upset about my brother, and what I said wasn't true. It was never just a job, I cared about it, and about you. I felt terrible about leaving, and we were friends. I just didn't know how to leave, and I was worried about you and my mother."

"Thank you," she said softly. "It's nice to hear. I thought you were right about it just being a job when I didn't hear from you."

"I didn't know what to say, and I was sure you were angry at me, and you had a right to be. I didn't know how to clean it up."

"It's okay. I'm doing fine. I think we'll even come in on time if I keep threatening them."

"That's a miracle. I don't think even I could have done that. Would you ever do it again?"

"I'm not sure. I think I'd like to. Maybe a smaller home, and less time pressure. I'm trying to figure out if I want to extend my lease and stay. I love it here."

"I hope you do extend. Maybe we could have coffee sometime," he suggested cautiously, not sure what she'd say.

"Sure. I'll send you pictures of the chateau when we finish. It's going to be pretty spectacular. I hope Petrov loves it."

"He will. I'm glad you're all right, and that you don't hate me."

"Actually, I curse you a lot when something goes wrong I don't know how to do, and then I figure it out." He laughed. "You taught me a lot," she said in a serious tone. "About being brave, and going on no matter what, and having the courage to do what you believe in. I was brought up by cowards, courage has never been my strong suit, until I came here."

"That's not true. You're braver than you think, braver than I am at times. Actually, my mother is the bravest woman I know."

"So I gather. I'm glad you called."

He had opened a door, he didn't know if he would ever walk through it again, but it was nice to know he could. He realized that that was what his mother meant when she told him to leave nicely.

"So am I. Take good care of yourself and send me those photos of the chateau when it's finished."

"Good luck with the House of Usher," she said, and he laughed. They both hung up feeling better, and surprised by how easy the call was.

He told his mother about it when she got up and he made her breakfast. She listened quietly, and then looked pensive for a minute.

"You did the right thing. And she sounds very gracious. She didn't have to answer your call." And then she looked hard at Joachim. "I'd like to meet her." She sounded matter of fact about it.

"Maybe you will sometime," he said vaguely. He didn't feel ready to see Olivia again. The call had been enough, probably for her too. It had been a big step for him.

"I mean now," Liese said with a determined expression. " 'Sometime' is fine at your age. Not at mine."

"Don't be so dramatic," he scolded her.

"Don't be such a coward. She sounds like a nice woman. I want to meet her. For a cup of tea."

"Why?"

"Why not? It's always interesting to meet new people. I have questions in my mind about her. I want to see why you like her."

"She was a good employer and she paid me well."

"Nonsense. She was more than that. Please invite her to tea," she said, sitting up straight, and he could tell that she wasn't going to give up until he agreed. He felt foolish calling her again, but he did. It was easier than arguing with his mother.

Olivia answered his call again. "What's up?" She sounded busy and he was embarrassed to bother her.

"My mother wants to have tea with you," he said bluntly.

"That's why you called?" She thought he was kidding at first.

"Yes. She'll drive me crazy if I don't at least ask."

"Actually, I'd like to meet her . . . Sure . . . Why not? . . . When?"

"Today apparently," he said with a grin. "Name your time. Our schedule is free."

"My place?"

"That's too much trouble for you, and you don't have a butler anymore," he reminded her and she laughed. "Why don't you come here at four o'clock? Jeans are fine. Don't get dressed up."

"Perfect, and tell her thank you." He did, and his mother smiled from ear to ear.

"What are you scheming about?" he asked her, suspicious.

"I am not scheming. I want to meet your friend. I always did when you were young."

"I know. I hated it. I felt like you were checking up on me."

"I was. I still am." She laughed, and he shook his head, but he was happy to be able to see Olivia again, and grateful to his mother, although he didn't admit it to her.

Olivia arrived promptly at four, with a small bouquet of white roses and a box of chocolate éclairs, which she knew he liked and hoped his mother did too. Joachim thought she looked beautiful. Thinner, but healthy and energized and her eyes were bright. He thanked her for the éclairs, and walked her into the living room, where his mother was sitting on the couch. She smiled and stood up when Olivia walked into the room, and Olivia greeted her warmly, and sat down next to her. The two women never stopped talking for the whole hour Olivia was there. Liese told her about the Monet she had found, and how the process worked, and Olivia was fascinated. She told her stories about Joachim as a boy too, and some of the sweet things he did, and a mischievous story or two.

"This is embarrassing, Mother," he reminded her. "I worked for Olivia, as a grown-up. She didn't adopt me."

"No, but you two are friends, I think. That includes

how naughty you were as children, and how sweet.
I'm sure Olivia got up to mischief too."

"Never, I was perfect. Except when I borrowed
my mother's favorite sweater and loaned it to a
friend and forgot to get it back, or when I stole her
new high heels and broke one . . . and locked myself in the bathroom at five and the fire department
came and had to remove the door. Stuff like that."
She laughed, and got up to leave, and thanked Liese
for the visit. "It was a great honor to meet you,
Mrs. von Hartmann. I've been a great admirer of
yours from a distance ever since I met Joachim."

"I admire you too. Thank you for being a friend
to him, as well as his employer. We all need our
friends." Olivia nodded, touched, and a look passed
between the two women that only they understood.
"Thank you," Liese said again, they kissed on both
cheeks, and Olivia left. She thanked Joachim again
at the door, and they didn't kiss, but a warm look
passed between them. And Liese was eating one of
the éclairs when he came back into the room. She
looked up at him with a grin. "I don't know if you're
in love with her," she said, licking the chocolate
off her fingers delicately, "but I am. What a lovely
woman she is. And she is your friend, whether you
know it or not." He nodded, not sure what to say.

He sent Olivia a text an hour later. "Thank you for
making my mother so happy." And she responded
immediately.

"I'm in love with her. You're a lucky man."

"I know," was his response, and he wondered when he would see Olivia again. Probably not for a while, but the air had been cleared, and he was happy the two women had met.

Olivia thought about Joachim and his mother that night. He was a complicated man, with an unusual background. A war criminal grandfather, a drug lord identical twin brother, a father he never knew, an extraordinary mother, and all of it had made him who he was. Her history was much simpler. A father pretending not to be, a mother who had given up her life for a married man. Her mother had taught her everything she didn't want to be, including being dependent on a selfish, dishonest man. They had both been weak, selfish people. Joachim had terrible people in his history, and also a mother who was a shining example of everything one should be. She had been the greatest influence on him of all.

Chapter 17

Just as Olivia had hoped, the chateau was finished right on time, in less than the eight months she'd allowed for. She had done it by sheer grit, determination, and hard work. She had the whole place cleaned, the gardens were as beautiful as Nikolai Petrov had hoped. She completed the interior installation in three days of nonstop work, curtains, paintings, furniture. It was a showplace beyond the owner's wildest dreams, and hers. She took photographs of it for Nikolai and herself and emailed a set to Joachim too. He texted her that he was stunned at how beautiful it was and what she had done since he'd left.

She waited for a response from Nikolai Petrov and got none. She emailed him again, and still no response. He had transferred all the money she needed for final payments, and paid her fee, but there was no letter, no email, no text, no call. It didn't make sense to her and she called Audrey Wellington in New York to ask her to check with her original contact if everything was all right. Audrey sounded shocked to hear from her.

"You haven't heard?"

"Heard what? Did someone kill him?" It was the only thing she could think of to explain his silence, now that he was the owner of such an exquisite property and home. It almost did look like Versailles and every inch of it gleamed. Olivia had been waiting for him to arrive so she could show it to him, and how all the technology worked. Even that had been installed on time. Even the pool was complete. It really was a miracle. She'd never worked so hard on anything in her life. She'd been too busy to read the papers and see it.

"He was convicted of money laundering in France. All of his property has been seized. I think he had three or four houses in the South of France, and some apartment buildings in Paris. The government is taking them all. Including the one you just finished, I'm sure."

"That's it? And then what?" Olivia was stunned. She had worked like a slave to finish it for him, and now the government was taking it and she hadn't heard a word from him.

"They'll sell it at auction, probably for much less than it's worth, a fraction of it. It will be a fabulous deal for someone. Government seizures always are."

"How does that happen? Will someone notify

me? Who do I give the keys to? I've been writing to him for ten days and he hasn't answered."

"He may be in jail. And don't worry. When they get around to it, someone from the Treasury will show up, and take whatever they need. Did you get paid?"

"Every penny. All the suppliers have been paid, and I got my entire fee three weeks ago. I thought it a little odd that he paid me before I finished."

"Maybe somewhere under the crook, he's a decent guy. Honor among thieves. I think he was convicted two weeks ago. I've been afraid to call you. I was sure you'd be furious with me if you got burned. I honestly didn't know he was a crook when I gave you the job. I thought I was doing you a favor."

"You did. I just can't believe this." She was shocked.

"It happens with the Russians sometimes. He owes the tax people millions. He might have paid eventually, but with money laundering charges and a conviction, they won't give him the properties back. I think he was making illegal arms deals, selling missiles. It was big league stuff."

"How sad, I don't even know who'll wind up with this beautiful house." But she hadn't met Nikolai either. He was just a voice on the phone and wire transfers to the bank.

"I've been wanting to call you. You may want to kill me after this, but I have another project for you. Not as massive as this one. An American, not a Russian. One of my regular clients just bought a very pretty small chateau, more like a manor house, he says it's a little jewel, and he wants someone to do it for him. He's a totally honest guy. A Texan. It's completely on the up-and-up. Can I give him your name? And are you staying in France for a while?"

"I am," she said, making the decision on the spot. She knew now that this was what she wanted to do, refurbishing houses in France, preferably for American clients. She was going to renew her apartment lease for another year, or two.

"He's very attractive by the way, and single. This might be a bigger deal for you than just a decorating project," she said pointedly, and Olivia laughed. Audrey had always thought Olivia was very attractive and was surprised she was unattached.

"Do you throw in the matchmaking services for free?" Olivia teased her, and they both laughed.

"Definitely." Normally, Olivia would have balked, but it was very appealing. She'd been thinking lately, now that the chateau was finished she had to make a real effort to get out and meet people, and she hadn't had a real date in too long, not since New York. She wanted to meet some men. She wasn't shopping for a husband, but a dinner date would be nice. She didn't want to sit at home alone forever. She had come to Paris to live life, and she was. A man could be part of that. "I'll give him your number. He can talk to you about the house, and take you out to dinner," Audrey said, pleased. "I think he's going to Paris soon. His name is Guy Fellowes, so you know who he is when he calls. And, Olivia . . . I'm really sorry about the Russian." She genuinely meant it. But Olivia wasn't sorry she'd done the job. It had been a labor of love and she'd learned a lot. And she'd made a lot of money on it.

"You couldn't know," Olivia reassured her, but she was still shocked about Nikolai Petrov when she hung up, and pleased that she had the prospect of another job from Audrey, for an honest client this time. She felt sorry for Nikolai Petrov. He had sounded like a nice man, and he had been fair with her, whatever else he'd done. She was sorry he would never see the lovely chateau. She was grateful he had paid her in full before his conviction by the French courts.

She sent Audrey the photos of the chateau after they talked and Audrey emailed her and said it looked spectacular.

Guy Fellowes called her that night. He had a very pleasant Texan accent. He told her about the small chateau he had bought, and what he hoped to do with it. It was in the south, close to Provence. It would be more of a commute for her, but she said she could manage it. He was coming to Paris in three days and staying at the Ritz. He invited her to meet him for a drink so they could discuss the project, and she said she'd be delighted to. She had no idea if he'd turn out to be someone she wanted to go out with, but she liked the sound of the house he had bought and what he wanted to do to it.

After the chateau, everything would be easy for her. She promised to send him photographs of it, to give him an idea of the scope of what she was capable of.

After she hung up, she called Joachim, to tell him what had happened to Nikolai Petrov and that the chateau was going to be seized by the government. She expected him to be as shocked as she was. He sounded distracted when he answered, and there was a lot of noise in the background. She told him what had happened, and he didn't sound surprised.

"Things have been crazy here too. It turns out that my delightful employer owes over a million pounds in back taxes. He's a heavy gambler. He tried to burn the barn down last night, for the insurance money. They've arrested him for it. The house is mortgaged to the hilt, so he tried to set fire to the barn. He had just taken out a huge insurance policy. All the horses are safe, but they arrested him for tax evasion, insurance fraud, and animal cruelty. He saw to it that we got the horses out quickly, into trailers and off the property. It was all very obvious. It was a scheme of massive proportions. He was desperate to do something that brazen. I'm afraid it's going to go badly for him. His girlfriend reported him. He told her he was going to do it, and he's been cheating on her, so she called the police. The firefighters were here all night, the animal protection people came for the horses. And the police took him away about an hour ago. Things are a little busy right now. I'm not staying obviously. But

I want to stick around till somebody takes charge here. His sister and her husband are coming from Italy. I swear, the world is full of criminals. Being a butler isn't what it used to be." He sounded shocked himself. "I'm sorry about the chateau. Did he stiff you for what he owed you?" It seemed inevitable and he was sorry for her. He wasn't going to be paid by Mount-Williams, but he was relieved that no one had gotten hurt.

"No, he paid me in full three weeks ago, right before he got convicted. And I just got another job from Audrey Wellington. A Texan who bought a small chateau near Provence. I'm meeting with him this week." Joachim was happy that things were turning out well for her. She deserved it. She worked so hard.

"I'm glad for you. I'll send you a text and let you know where I am. I'm going to turn the whole mess over to Mount-Williams's sister when she arrives. He did some serious damage to the barn, but we got all the horses out, with no casualties. The world is a crazy place."

She didn't hear from him again after that. Her meeting with Guy Fellowes went well. He was as handsome and charming as Audrey had said. He hired her to do the chateau after their meeting at the Ritz, and he took her to dinner at Le Voltaire to celebrate. She sent flowers to Audrey to thank her.

Olivia was sitting at her desk a week later when she got a call from the Treasury, wanting the keys and anything else she had relating to the chateau. Two men came by shortly after to collect what she had. She had all the keys carefully marked in a lockbox and some papers in a manila envelope. She had all the paperwork related to the renovation for whoever would eventually buy it at auction. The man who picked it all up was very formal, and he brought a huissier with him, a legal witness to testify in court that they had collected the keys and whatever documents she had. It was a strange end to the story after eight months of hard work on her first big decorating project.

Joachim called her the next day and sounded upset. She hadn't heard from him since his employer got arrested almost two weeks before.

"Where are you?" she asked him. "Are you still in Sussex, or back in London?" He was unemployed again, and would have to start the job search all over.

"I'm in Paris," he said quietly, and she suddenly got a bad feeling about it. There was something in his voice.

"Is everything all right?" There was a long silence at the other end.

"It's my mother. I talked to her last night." He sounded dazed. "She was so happy. She turned the Monet over to the family yesterday. She's been working on it for over a year. She finally found a distant cousin, and they needed the money desperately.

They have a special needs child. She was fine when I talked to her. But she didn't answer her phone this morning. I called the police, and the guardian let them in. She had died peacefully in her sleep. I think she must have sensed something. I just got here. The apartment is perfectly neat, and it usually wasn't. Everything is in order, her papers, her clothes, her desk. She looked so peaceful, and so happy. She just went, quietly." Tears slid down Olivia's cheeks as she listened to him. "I'm glad you met her." His voice broke as he said it.

"So am I," Olivia said, crying openly. They both were.

"She loved you. She thought you were terrific," he said.

"What can I do to help?" she offered. She didn't want to cross any lines. She knew how private he was, but he sounded lost, which wasn't like him. And he needed a friend now, not an employer.

"I'll take care of it. I need to get everything organized. She's at the funeral home now," he said, pulling himself together.

"Can I do any of it for you?" she offered again.

"No. I'll let you know what I'm doing. Maybe we can have lunch afterward."

"If there's a service, I'd like to go." She could hear that he was crying when he answered her.

"I'm not sure. She had kind of her own arrangement with God. I don't want to do anything she wouldn't have wanted. I suppose I'll bury her next to Javier. She'd like that. Francois was buried with his own family in Brittany, so I can't put her with him. I still can't believe she's gone." Neither could Olivia. She had seemed so vital and alive only weeks before.

"Maybe she felt she had done everything she was here to do," Olivia said gently. But Joachim still needed her. They loved each other.

"Maybe so," he said, and they hung up a few minutes later. He texted her that night that the service was going to be in a small church near his mother's apartment, and then she would be buried next to Javier. He said that her colleagues from work were going to come, and a few of her remaining friends. He said he thought his mother would like it if Olivia was there. He was especially glad now that Olivia had met her.

She wrote back that she would like to come, if it wasn't an intrusion. He didn't answer for a long time, while he wrestled with the response and didn't know what to say. He finally typed it out slowly half an hour later, weighing every word. Words were dangerous, they could commit you, and attach you to people, or hurt them. He looked at the message he had written, was satisfied with it, and finally pushed the send button. He knew his mother would have approved of what he'd written.

"I need you there with me. Please come." He had never felt so naked in his life or so scared after he wrote it to her, and she responded immediately.

"I'll be there. I'm here if you need me. Call anytime."

He didn't write to her again. She saw him as soon as she walked into the small church, holding a small white bouquet. He was wearing one of his dark suits, impeccably groomed, and his eyes met Olivia's as she walked down the aisle toward him, and slipped into a pew, halfway down the church aisle, not too close to the front, since she didn't know his mother well, and wanted to respect Joachim's need for space and boundaries.

He came to find her a few minutes later. "Will you sit with me?" he asked in a whisper. She stood up and followed him to the front pew. The casket was in front of the altar. He hadn't had her cremated. It was a simple, unpretentious white wood casket, and seemed right for Liese.

There were about thirty people in the church, and Joachim didn't know many of them. He whispered to Olivia before the service started. "My mother and I came so far together. The years in Buenos Aires, and then we came here . . . Francois . . . She was so brave. She always moved forward. She never looked back. No matter what happened, she always kept going." Without thinking, he had laced his fingers into Olivia's. "I've never been as brave as she was."

"Yes, you have. You just don't realize it," she whispered. Olivia could feel Liese there with them, and she could feel her love for her son, and so could he.

The service was very brief. He shook hands afterward with the people who had come, whether he knew them or not. They each had something nice to say about his mother, and how extraordinary she was. He remembered how she had insisted on meeting Olivia. He wondered if she had sensed what was coming even then, and wanted to see Olivia before she left. She had always been intuitive, as well as wise.

They drove behind the hearse to the cemetery in Joachim's station wagon, and some of the others followed. The priest read from the Bible at the cemetery, and said a few more words, and Olivia left the little bouquet of white flowers she had brought, and then they left Liese there next to Javier. Joachim's whole history lay in the ground there now, his twin brother and his mother. He had loved them more than anyone on earth. He had never needed anyone else because of them, and Olivia could sense that.

He didn't speak on the way back to the city, and then he turned to her. "Do you want to take a walk? I need some air." She nodded, and they stopped at the Bois de Boulogne, parked the car, and started walking. She could feel him become more peaceful as they walked, and they finally sat down on a bench side by side. He was quiet and calm in the peaceful setting. He took a long breath of air.

"I'd like to work with you on the chateau in Provence, if you need an assistant," he said, and she smiled.

"No more butler?"

"That too, if you want." He smiled and sat quietly staring into the distance, thinking. Olivia waited for what he would say next. "My mother said I was in love with you. She was right, as usual. She accused me of being a coward. And she was right about that too. I was afraid to say it, or even to feel it." He was crossing the line between them to a place where he'd never been. He looked her in the eye then. "I've never told a woman I loved her. I'm not sure I've ever loved anyone, except the two of them. I was too afraid to care that much. I didn't want to get hurt and lose someone I love. And now I've lost both of them."

"Me too," she whispered. "I didn't want to be a prisoner like my mother. I didn't want to let any man own me or destroy me." She knew Joachim's history, the good and the bad of it, the terrible grandfather and brother, weak father, and the powerful, brave, loving mother, a woman of integrity and courage. He was like her, not like the others. Olivia knew she was nothing like her weak, selfish mother, or the man who didn't have the courage to be her father or even tell her that he was. Together, she and Joachim were so much better than the people who had hurt them. She wasn't afraid now as she sat next to him, holding hands. They were on the brink of courage, willing to be there for each other, already attached in all the ways that mattered to both of them. It had happened effortlessly while they weren't looking. "I love you, Joachim." She was the first to say the words, and cross the line, to show him that she could. The sky didn't fall in when she said it, and she smiled.

"I love you too," he said, and discovered that the words he had always been so afraid of weren't frightening when he said them to her.

They had found what they needed and the courage to accept it. Maybe a final gift from Liese to both of them. He kissed Olivia then, and they both wondered what they had been so afraid of for so long. They had run away from it all their lives. She wasn't afraid anymore, and neither was he.

They sat on the bench, thinking of his mother, aware of the gift she'd given them. He kissed her, and then they drove back to Olivia's apartment. As they walked in, he remembered his mother eating the chocolate éclairs Olivia had brought her. "She wanted to see you that day," Joachim said. "I think she knew she was going soon." Olivia nodded and believed it too.

They went into her bedroom, and as though it was always meant to be, they made love for the first time. Everything about it felt right, and they lay in each other's arms afterward, holding each other and feeling peaceful. He pulled her close to him. She had come to Paris to live life, and to find him. Destiny had a hand in it. And everything that came before had been preparing them. They had found what they needed at the right time. Liese's wishes for her son had finally come true. He had found a woman as brave and honorable as she was. And the future would unfold as it was meant to, as they faced it together. They had so much to look forward to.

About the Author

DANIELLE STEEL has been hailed as one of the world's bestselling authors, with almost a billion copies of her novels sold. Her many international bestsellers include **Complications, Nine Lives, Finding Ashley, The Affair, Neighbors, All That Glitters, Royal, Daddy's Girls, The Wedding Dress,** and other highly acclaimed novels. She is also the author of **His Bright Light,** the story of her son Nick Traina's life and death; **A Gift of Hope,** a memoir of her work with the homeless; **Expect a Miracle,** a book of her favorite quotations for inspiration and comfort; **Pure Joy,** about the dogs she and her family have loved; and the children's books **Pretty Minnie in Paris** and **Pretty Minnie in Hollywood.**

daniellesteel.com
Facebook.com/DanielleSteelOfficial
Twitter: @daniellesteel
Instagram: @officialdaniellesteel

LIKE WHAT YOU'VE READ?

Try these titles by Danielle Steel,
also available in large print:

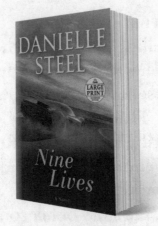

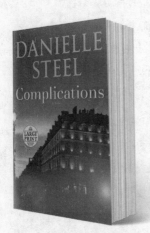

Nine Lives
ISBN 978-0-593-41473-6

Complications
ISBN 978-0-593-41474-3

Finding Ashley
ISBN 978-0-593-39555-4

For more information on large print titles, visit
www.penguinrandomhouse.com/large-print-format-books